HYSTERIA

MICHAELA WRIGHT

DEDICATION

For Scott.

The Scotsman whose banter helped me get my literary
Scots on.

ACKNOWLEDGMENTS

A thank you to the city of Edinburgh, a place that feels more like home than any other I've found. Also, my gratitude to historians of the city for their universal love of murder and mayhem.

And finally, thank you Edinburgh for the deep fried Mars bar. You changed me.
Mostly by going directly to my muffin top, but it was a delicious journey, I assure you.

CHAPTER ONE

"Ah love, you look as lost as a lamb in here."

Liv turned toward the voice, finding a ruddy cheeked matron standing by the door of the pub. Liv glanced around the establishment, her stomach in knots. It wasn't her first time in such a place, but the only pub she'd seen in Inverness seldom catered to more than three older men at a time. This pub - The White Dog was busy, filled with lads and lasses of all ages, and it was only half past noon.

Liv curtsied to the older woman, sheepishly searching for words as flecks of rain spattered from the brim of her hat.

The matron laughed at her gesture. "You lost then?" She asked. This woman wasn't from Scotland, or if she was, she'd successfully managed to lose her accent, sounding more like an Englishwoman than a creature born of Edinburgh.

Liv nodded. "I'm trying to find -"

"Och, will ya look here! Come on, love. Have a seat. This round's on me."

Liv felt a presence at her shoulder and turned to find a man smiling at her, his arm outstretched in invitation. The man's brogue was strange somehow, and he was very tall, but he had a round, boyish face framed by long sideburns. He beamed at her, waiting to lead her toward the bar.

"No, thank ye, sir. I'm already later than I'd like."

"Where ya from then, love?" He asked, ignoring her protests as he wrapped an arm around her shoulders and led her across the pub. It wasn't packed by any means, but there were several faces along the bar, including a somewhat displeased fellow behind it, dressed in white shirt and black suspenders, a dark bushy pair of mutton chops almost completely obscuring his neck from view. "Pour this lass a pint, will ya, Martin?"

Liv shook her head again. "I'm sorry, sir. I don't mean to be rude, but I'm tryin to find -"

The pint appeared on the bar and her newfound companion slid it in front of her. Liv felt the corners of her mouth pulling down, but fought to smile at the man anyway.

"Name's Will. And you are?" He asked, raising his glass to her.

"Liv."

"Live? Well, ain't that a grand name. Is it short for sometin?"

She shook her head. "Are ye Irish?"

Will beamed at her. "That I am, lass. That I am. Ulster born and raised."

Liv politely sipped at her beer, cringing at the sour taste of it as she rustled in her pocket for the tiny shred of newspaper that she carried. Liv leaned across the bar toward the barman, holding the paper out before her. "Pardon, sir, but might ye know where I should find this address?"

The barman glanced at the paper as William reached for her wrist, tugging her hand toward him. Something about the action, the unwelcome touch unsettled her and she jerked her arm from his grasp with enough force to startle the ladies beside her and knock her beer askew. The barman caught it before it could splash down his shirt front. Liv surged toward him, stumbling over her words in apology.

"Hey now, you're alright, lass. You're alright," Will said, displaying his palms in apology. "Just tryin ta help, is all."

Liv swallowed and turned back toward the barman. He shot Will a glance, then gave Liv an eyebrow raise. Will was what her mother would call 'day drunk' – and by his expression, not an unfamiliar sight to Martin the barman.

Martin settled her drink aside and leaned toward her. "Where ye tryin to get then, lass?"

Liv glanced at her newspaper clipping, trying to make sense of what was now smudged print. "Surgeon's Square? 14 Glover Place in Surgeon's Square?"

The two women beside her burst into excited chatter. "Ye lookin for Dr. Lennox, then? Good girl."

They leaned into one another, the darker haired one giving her friend's arm a good squeeze.

"Do ye know where I mean?" Liv asked, turning to face the two women. Despite their demeanor and their somewhat shabby dress, to Liv they were as glorious as queens if they could help her find her way. She'd traveled three days, not seen a proper bed in longer still, and all the while, still wasn't even sure the position would be available when she arrived.

"Oh aye. We know the doctor quite well!"

Again they burst into giggles. Clearly being day drunk was a common occurrence in the Canongate pubs of Edinburgh, Liv thought. Not far removed from Inverness.

Liv touched the dark haired woman's shoulder, praying the touch wouldn't draw ire from the city girl. "Chance ye could draw me a map, or -?"

"Oh, we'll do ye one better, love. We'll take ye."

"Oh, bless! Really? Thank ye so much! Is it nearby?"

Liv fondled the worn piece of paper before tucking it back into her pocket. She was so excited by the prospect of getting to her destination – of maybe having a destination – that she took up her pint of beer and swigged gratefully.

"Atta girl," Will said beside her. "So heading up through Cowgate, then? Safe travels, dearie."

The two women snatched up Liv's arm and turned her for the door, Will happily claiming her half pint of beer. The three of them ducked out into the rain, Liv's hat shielding her face as the two women held their bags or a folded newspaper over their own.

"What's your name then, girl? I'm Mary. This here's Janet."

Janet was a bit taller than Mary, and her hair a lighter brown. She smiled at Liv, betraying a missing tooth at the corner of her mouth, but an otherwise warm smile.

"Ye may call me Liv."

Mary tucked an arm around Liv's waist and led her up the hill, the rain sheering down into their faces. "Well Liv. What brings ye to our dear Dr. Lennox?"

Liv thoughtlessly patted her hand against her pocket, remembering the words on her tiny newspaper advertisement – *WANTED Scullery Maid, Surgeon's Square, 14 Glover Place. Household Experience Preferred.* It said nothing of a Dr. Lennox.

"I'm hopin for employment there?"

It was almost a question. She wasn't truly sure what brought her to Mary and Janet's 'dear Dr. Lennox,' save for chance. If she were honest with her newfound friends, the truth was that any place would be better than Inverness.

"Oh, ye workin for him, then? We thought ye were one of his patients. Had half a mind to be jealous!"

The women laughed again as they ducked around a corner. The buildings were taller here, their bricked facades growing more austere and pristine. Canongate didn't boast such friendly doorways and windows, and it smelled fouler than any unkempt pigsty she'd ever tended. As they passed the high buildings, Liv caught sight of a few young men clamoring across the cobblestones, satchels over their shoulders just teeming with books. They surged into a nearby doorway, disappearing out of the rain into one of the buildings.

"What is this place?" She asked.

Mary turned to her and winked. "That's a part of the Medical College, there. Here we are. Come along, now."

Mary tugged at Liv's sleeve, pulling her down a small side street. There were flower boxes under the windows along the left side, a friendly sight compared to the dreary windows of the college and the Canongate houses. Along the gray stone walls, a short staircase led up to a black door. Mary and Janet bustled up the stairs, setting their sleeves and curling their hair around their fingers as though making final adjustments for a ball. Liv stood just a step or two below them, her stomach in maddening knots.

"Afternoon, girls. Come on in. Is the Doctor expecting ye, then?"

The woman in the doorway stood aside as Mary and Janet entered, scampering like schoolgirls down a hallway and out of sight. Liv moved up the stairs slowly, waiting for the older woman to meet her gaze. The woman was wide around the bust and hips, but her waist cinched in beneath her black dress. Her gray hair was up and perfectly pinned away from her face, plaited just above her left ear. Liv stood outside the door, staring at the side of the woman's face. When the woman finally glanced down at her, it was with a look a complete exasperation.

"Well, what on earth ye waitin for? The rain's pourin in, lass!"

Liv moved forward, stepping into the dry warmth of the hall, listening for her new companions in the distance.

"I'm sorry. I'm lookin for -"

"Yes, yes! I know bloody well who your lookin for. Down the hall. Follow your idiot friends, there."

With that the woman disappeared into a nearby doorway, the smell of the day's supper drifting out into the hallway as she slammed the door behind her. Despite her nerves, Liv's stomach growled at the smell of lamb stew. She hadn't eaten in two days.

Liv followed the sounds of Mary and Janet, coming to a small parlor, the walls yellow with a satin finish wallpaper. The room boasted three more doors, two closed and the other leading deeper into the house.

"Oh, ye havin a go at Dr. Lennox then after all? Ye liar!"

Janet nudged Mary, sliding down the settee to make room for Liv to sit down. Liv joined the two women, resting her fidgeting hands in her lap.

"Tell ye what, I scrubbed downstairs like ye wouldn't believe this mornin!"

Janet bent over in laughter, swatting at Mary. "Ye don't scrub downstairs every day, then?"

"Who does? Most lads're lucky if I even think of it. They ain't payin me to wash, they's payin me to spread."

"Och! Mary, you're a disgrace!"

The two women laughed as Liv's eyes went wide, but she didn't speak.

"So, tell us, Livvy. You've never been to visit our Doctor Lennox before, then?"

Liv shook her head. "No, I really am here for a job."

Mary scowled at her as the sound of footsteps traveling up stairs drew their attention to the nearby door.

Mary giggled, curling her hair as they watched the door. "I'm goin first, ye scoundrels."

The door opened and a tall figure appeared, stepping out into the parlor. Liv stared up at the man, startled by his sheer size. He was tall and broad-shouldered, a mass of red hair atop his head that grew free and tussled, not a stitch of pomade to hold it. The mass of red traveled down his jaw line in clean mutton chops, ending in a frame around his chin. He wore black trousers and a black vest coat, his white shirt sleeves rolled up past his elbows. He shot her a glance or two as he let the door close behind him, then he brushed his hands against his trousers. He held his hand out to Mary first, then Janet, giving each woman a warm greeting.

"And who's your friend, then?" He asked, holding Liv's gaze for a moment.

Liv rose from her seat to meet him, but Mary lunged forward. "That's Livvy. She's come along from The White Dog. Though I've told them both that I'll be goin first today."

Dr. Lennox stared at Liv a moment. "Are ye here to see me, as well?"

She swallowed and nodded, but Mary answered for her. "Of course she is, but she'll wait her bloody turn, won't she?"

Mary shot Liv a playful glare as she made her way to the door. She was gone into the deeper reaches of his office before he could say another word.

He gave Liv and Janet a quick nod, his eyes settling on Liv again for a moment. "I'm sure to be quick. Thank you again, Janet. And Livvy?"

Liv nodded, mumbling along with Janet as she graciously waved the doctor away.

"But of course. Least we could do," Janet said, then sputtered laughing as the doctor disappeared into his office.

"I'm tellin ye, if ye can, get him to see ye as his patient first. Before ye tell 'im about the job, aye?"

Liv turned to Janet. "Why? I'm no feelin sick."

Janet laughed. "Ah, he's no that kind of doctor."

Mary could be heard laughing beyond the office door, though her voice sounded distant, almost echoing from across some chasm.

"Then what kind of doctor is he?"

She was beginning to feel more nervous, something

she'd have never thought possible. Yet, Doctor Lennox was an imposing figure. He was foreboding in size, yes, but more so in something intangible. The way he looked at her – soft eyes in a piercing blue. To see such a soft expression on such an imposing man unsettled her somehow.

Janet was on her feet a moment later, pressing her ear to the door of the office, listening. "Well, he's a surgeon, ain't he? But he's a magician as well."

"How so?"

"Expert on the female anatomy, for one. Och! Will ye listen to that!"

Janet went to say something further, but a strange cry startled both their attentions to the door. Liv's brow furrowed, but Janet just laughed as the cry returned. It sounded as though Mary was weeping, or in pain.

"Oh Christ, she's no bein half as loud as we promised!" Janet whispered, hissing through laughter. Finally, she lunged back to the settee and settled beside Liv, taking her hand as though to soothe a mourner at a funeral. "Now, promise me you'll have him perform his procedure on ye, at least once. Christ, if I knew the bastard were lookin for a maid, I've half the mind to steal the position from ye! Shame I've never worked in such a household. Imagine getting that man's hands on ye every day."

"What?" Liv's eyes went wide and she glanced toward the door as if the impressive figure had reappeared, a glower in place of that formerly soft expression.

"Look. Mary and I come in here once a week. He pays us each a couple shillings and does these -" Janet searched Liv's face, as though she pitied her. "He has this procedure he's workin on, ye see? It's for the ladies with troubles. Helps with the troubles of the mind. Settles 'em down, he says. He's been practicing on us for a few months now, perfecting his approach, ye see? And boy does it bloody work!"

"What is it that he does?" Liv asked.

"Well, soothes your troubles, don't it?"

"But how so?"

Janet swatted at Liv's arm. "Oh, I can't tell ye. Ye have to experience it yourself! I wouldn't dream take that from ye."

The cries suddenly tripled in volume, the sounds coming in a strange rhythm as each one piqued higher and higher. Finally, the cries bled together and Mary was screaming beyond the office door. Liv clutched the arm of the settee, fighting the urge to run back down that narrow hallway and out into the strange city of Edinburgh.

Janet just chuckled beside her. "Oh, I can be louder than that, Mare. Given half the chance!"

Janet leaned toward Liv, speaking in hushed tones as Mary's screams quieted down. "Ye tell him ye ain't feelin well. Say you've got troubles playin on your mind. Say whatever!" There was a noise beyond the office down and they both sat quiet together, waiting. A few moments later, footsteps could be heard ascending a staircase beyond the door. When it opened, Mary appeared, making a show of being breathless as she swooned into the room.

Janet lunged from her seat. "Ye bitch! How was it?"

"Oh, go and see for yourself. Man is a master at what he does, I tell ye!"

Janet was gone through the doorway in a flash, leaving Liv with Mary, her dark hair now tussled about her head.

"Are ye alright, Mary?" Liv asked when the woman slumped down onto the settee beside her.

Mary leaned back in her seat. Despite the familiar demeanor of her company, Liv still sat upright, her hat still tied to her head.

"Oh, I've rarely been better, dearie," she said and sighed. She brushed a hand over her hair, patting it down as a woman's voice wailed from within the doctor's office. "Oh, that bitch. He'll know your fakin,' ye trollop!" Mary yelled toward the closed office door. In the distance, the stern maid in the black dress could be heard hollering something back from the kitchen.

Mary laughed and swatted at Liv's arm again. Liv's arms were beginning to get sore from their company and constant swatting. Mary sat there beside her, laughing as Janet continued to wail. Liv turned toward the office door, her heart racing as she listened. This sound reminded her of keening women at a funeral.

What on earth was he doing to them in there?

"Don't worry. She never takes long," Mary said, pulling a snuff box from within her small hand bag.

The wailing rose and fell, then rose again, punctuated by sudden high pitched shrieks. Then it crescendoed in a long warbling sound, finally going silent a moment before Janet's voice could be heard calling up to them. "How'd ye like that one, Mare?"

"Nobody'll believe ye!" Mary called back, jumping up to press her cheek to the door. Then the dark haired woman turned around and smiled at Liv. "Too bad it ain't your turn. God, if anything were to get that stick out your arse, it'd be Doctor Lennox."

Mary hovered by the door as they waited, finally

snatching up her bag as the sound of footsteps betrayed Janet and the doctor's return. Liv straightened in her seat, praying to look as presentable and professional as three days' travel in carriages and on foot could look.

The doctor slipped through the room and into the house, then returned a moment later with a few coins for each of the girls. "Thank you again, ladies. You do me a great service."

Janet gave the doctor a flirtatious swat on the shoulder. "Oh believe me, you've got that backwards, love. Alright, Livvy. Your turn!"

With that Janet and Mary stumbled toward the hallway as though remembering they'd been drinking, laughing boisterously all the way down the hall.

The doctor made his way back toward his office door and stood a moment, patting his hands against his pockets. "They left ye, then?"

Liv swallowed. "Aye. I've only just met them, really."

He nodded, appraisingly. "And they brought ye with them? Clever lasses. Well, then. D'ye mind if I ask ye a few quick medical questions before we get underway?"

"No, I don't mind."

"Good then," he said, leaning into the door of his office, averting his eyes from her face. "Well, alright. Are ye a virgin?"

Liv's mouth fell open as she stared at him.

He chuckled, softly. "It's a common question before an appointment of this sort."

She swallowed. "Oh. Aye. I mean, I am. Yes."

He nodded. "Alright, then, when did ye last have your courses?"

"My what?"

He gestured in her direction, glancing toward her skirts. "Your courses? Your monthly?"

Liv turned her eyes to the floor. She didn't discuss this sort of thing with even her mother, let alone a man. Still, he was a doctor. Wasn't he?

"Two weeks, I think?"

He smiled. "Ye think?"

She nodded. "Aye. Two weeks."

"Well then, that will put ye mid-cycle. Now, ye sure ye want to volunteer for this? Your friends there have had a bit more experience than -"

"She said she'd never worked in such a household before!" Liv blurted, touching her hands to her lips just after the words slipped.

Dr. Lennox stopped and looked at her. "In such a household. How d'ye mean?"

Liv fidgeted with her coat, trying to reach into her pocket, but finding it tucked up under her on the settee. She finally stood up just as the doctor held the door to his office wide open for her. Liv could see into the recesses beyond, a dark staircase leading down into the unknown. She pulled the piece of paper from her pocket and handed it to the tall man before her. He raised a brow, taking the worn piece of newspaper to inspect it.

His face split in an embarrassed smile. "Ah, good grief. I'm so sorry, lass. I thought ye were here to volunteer for – never mind. How long have ye had this, then?"

"How long?"

"Aye. Placed this advert well over six months past."

"Oh no," she said, and the frown overtook her face. "I - Just a week or so. I came as soon as I saw the advertisement."

The doctor flipped the piece of paper over in his hand, giving a half laugh. "Ye come from a ways, did ye?"

"Inverness."

"Inverness?" He exclaimed. "How'd ye come upon my advertisement all the way in Inverness?"

Liv took a deep breath. "My auntie came to visit us – my mum and I. She brought the paper with her."

"Did she now? Must enjoy keeping old papers lyin about, then."

Doctor Lennox quietly shut the door behind him and gestured for Liv to take her seat again on the settee. Liv felt her heart sinking with the fervor of a brick thrown into a loch. He sat down beside her, turning his body to face her as he glanced down at the tiny advertisement she'd carried for three days of travel.

"Have ye experience keeping a household?"

Liv nodded, vehemently. "I do. I've kept my family home for many years, and I'm quite clean, and I keep to myself -"

"That's fine, that's fine," he said, chuckling. "How old are ye? Seventeen?"

Liv's eyebrows shot up. "I'm twenty four."

He smirked. "Aye, I see that now. It's no much, now. Position pays six pound a year."

"That'll be fine," Liv said, and she honestly felt her heart leap at the thought of having her own wages. Six whole pounds, she thought. She could buy a new dress with that.

Doctor Lennox glanced down at the advert again. "Don't imagine you've any medical knowledge, then, aye?"

"I haven't."

He took a deep breath and rose from the settee. "Well, this seems rather serendipitous. The young lady who answered the original advert has gone for some time now. Hadn't the mind to post another advert as of yet."

"No?" Liv asked, and her voice squeaked just slightly. She prayed he hadn't heard it.

He shook his head. "No. Come along then, I'll let Fionnula show ye the rest of the house, but let me show ye downstairs, and ye can decide if ye'd still like the position."

She swallowed, staring down the dark stairs as Doctor Lennox opened his office door. "Is the position still available?"

He stopped in the doorway, scratching at the curls of red that collected like brambles at the crook of his jaw. "Aye, I suppose it must be if you've come all this way. Just come along here, and let me show ye some of your responsibilities. Ye might no want the position once ye have a look around. The last lass certainly didn't."

Liv furrowed her brow, but followed him. "Oh, I'm – I'm sure I will."

Dr. Lennox ducked through the office door and disappeared down a flight of stone steps. Liv followed him, her stomach twisting as she stepped down the first stair. The space was immense - startlingly so. The steps wound around the outer wall of a massive, round room that stood two stories high. Just a few steps down, there was a landing filled with seats; a viewing platform that framed the outer wall, giving an open view of the floor below. In the center of the lower floor was a metal table surrounded by other tables and counters, all of them covered in strange tools. Dr. Lennox bounded down the second staircase to the floor below. Liv made her way down with trepidation. The room smelled strange, like alcohol and something more – something human. Sweat, perhaps?

Her boots hit the stone floor of the examination room, and she stopped, watching Dr. Lennox move about the room with a strange comfort.

"What is this place?"

Dr. Lennox moved a metal object from one table to another, then patted his hands on his trousers. "Well, this building was once part of the Medical College. This room is an operating theatre."

Liv cringed, moving away from the metal table at the center of the space. "D'ye operate on people down here?"

Dr. Lennox shook his head. "If it calls for it, aye. Sometimes. There are bigger theatres of its kind still within the College. One of my mentors holds dissections that draw nearly five hundred students at a time. It's quite enormous in comparison."

Liv swallowed. "Dissection? D'ye mean of people?"

He glanced at her, trudging his hands deep into his pockets. "Aye, dissections. We've some of the best anatomists in the world here in Edinburgh."

"D'ye do dissections here?"

"No, no anymore. Couldn't stand living with the smell."

Liv turned for the stairs, fighting to move faster than her belly. She failed, and curled over on the steps as her throat constricted. Luckily, her belly had nothing in it to toss up.

"Och, my apologies, dear. I'm so accustomed to

other doctors, I forget who I'm speaking to at times."

She felt his hands at her shoulders and her back, the size of him hinted by the massive shadow he cast over the steps beneath her feet. She straightened there, fighting to regain her dignity.

"Ye alright, then? Let me know if ye need to be sick."

Liv shook her head. "No, no. I'm fine. It's passed."

She turned to find him standing on the step below her, but still she had to look up to meet his gaze. He smiled down at her, holding his hand out. "Will ye come down again? I've a few chores that I'll need ye to perform down here if ye work for me. Might sway your decision."

Liv took his hand and descended the last few stairs again, coming to stand by the metal table.

"Though much of my practice is general medicine, my specialties sometimes result in a bit of a mess down here."

Liv braced, determined not to cringe again, no matter what he said. She thought of the two women screaming beyond the door. She didn't see a mess now. What could he have possibly been doing to them?

"I need the floor swept every other day. I need hot water brought down for sterilizing and washing my hands when I see patients. I will sometimes need the floor mopped if ever I do need to perform surgery down here. Fionnula is accustomed to such work, but I'm sure she'd appreciate the second pair of hands."

He kicked a foot over a grate in the floor. "There is a drain built in here for blood and the like."

Liv doubled over, but didn't gag.

Damn it, lass. Settle down! She thought.

"I know this is a lot to take in, but it is ideally a part of the position. If it isn't something ye feel ye want to –"

"No, no. I said I'm fine. I'll be fine. Whatever ye need, I will do."

Dr. Lennox stood against one of the counters, his hands in his pockets. He had an easy air about him, an almost lazy comfort that made him feel familiar and safe.

He searched her face a moment, then nodded. "What did ye say your name was again?"

"Liv. Or Livvy," she offered, remembering Mary and Janet's teasing as they left the house.

"Liv, aye? Is that short for Olivia?"

Liv shook her head. "No, no Olivia."

He smiled at her, waiting.

Despite her abject hatred of hearing her full name spoken, she couldn't keep it to herself as those blue eyes smiled down at her.

"It's Deliverance. My name is Deliverance Baird."

His eyes went wide and his brows shot up. "Deliverance? Really? That's a powerful name if ever I heard one. Protestant parents, I take it?"

He grinned, but she shook her head. "Mother is a protestant, but Father was a papist. He chose my name."

Dr. Lennox stepped forward, holding out his hand to her. "Well, Deliverance – d'ye mind if I call ye that?"

She shook her head. Oddly, she didn't.

"Well, Deliverance, it's a delight to meet ye. I'm Dr. Findlay Lennox. Since you'll let me call ye Deliverance, ye may call me Findlay. Sound fair?"

Liv fought to keep a professional demeanor with his

powerful presence, but she found herself smiling back at him. She nodded. "Aye, fair enough."

The door to the house above burst open as a figure appeared in the doorway. "Those harlots left the bloody door wide op – Oh! My apologies. I didn't realize ye had someone still. I'll be goin, then."

Findlay rushed up the stairs toward his housekeeper. "No, no. Fionn! It's fine. I've need of ye, anyway."

The older woman returned to the doorway above, eyeing the two of them below. "What's that, now?"

Findlay held a hand out towards Liv, as though gesturing over the landscape to show the way north. "This is Deliverance – ehm, Liv. She's come to inquire about the maid's position."

"Is it now? How'd she hear about that, then?"

"Fate, I'd say," Findlay said, smiling.

The older woman glowered down at her employer with a stern air that betrayed a more maternal relationship than a business one. "Oh, what rubbish? Never mind, doesn't matter. Is she hired, then?"

Findlay nodded. "She is. I've shown her around the theater, if ye might show her about the house, I'd be most appreciative."

The woman glared at her a moment, then snorted softly. "Fine, then. Come on up to the kitchen when you're ready. Ye can leave your things in the hallway for now, s'pose."

Liv fidgeted a moment, glancing down at her hands.

"D'ye no have anything with ye, Deliverance?" Findlay asked, coming down the steps toward her.

Liv shook her head. Her departure from Inverness hadn't allowed for much in the way of packing or planning.

"That's fine. It's customary for the employer to provide your meals and attire. I'll have Fionnula fetch your uniforms in the mornin. Will ye, love?"

He called these last words up the stairs, smirking as Fionnula grumbled her displeasure to herself.

"I'll be in the bloody kitchen," Fionnula said, disappearing from view.

Liv swallowed, watching the empty doorway above. This woman would be her direct superior, and the person she took her orders from. If this interaction was any warning, Fionnula didn't promise to be a cheerful manager, by any means.

The two of them stood in silence a moment, Findlay watching her face. When he finally spoke, he did so as he turned toward the upstairs, bounding ahead of her three steps at a time. Liv watched him in awe a moment. He had the legs of a giraffe, she thought.

"Come on, then. S'pose I'll have to give ye the tour. Show ye to your quarters at the very least."

Liv followed the impressive figure up the stairs, careful not to draw too close to him. Liv wasn't a short girl, by any means, but this man stood at least a foot taller, and his broad shoulders made it feel as though he loomed above you in all directions when he was close. She slipped past him into the parlor, watching him shut the door to his office theater before slipping through the parlor into the main house.

Liv was pleasantly surprised to find that Dr. Findlay Lennox's house was lived in. The parlor gave way to a reception room and a study, both equally boasting shelves heavy with books. There was a green leather chair in the study, a small table beside it with a pile of books. The top one lay open, its spine bending from the weight.

They slipped up a back staircase, Findlay gesturing to each door, whether open or not, 'this is my room. This is the washroom. These are the guest quarters.' She didn't see more than a glance inside each room as he ushered her up a second flight of stairs, these narrower than the first.

"It's a bit cool up here at the moment, but we haven't had anyone in these rooms for weeks, so - we'll be sure to have the fires lit tonight, aye?"

Liv nodded as she reached the top step. The landing on this floor was small, offering only three doors. Findlay gestured toward two of the doors, an attic and a small washroom. Then, he stepped up to the third door and opened it, stepping aside to allow her in.

Liv stepped into the small space and swallowed hard. There was a small bed against the wall, a table with oil lamp and a chest of drawers, as well as a large window, three panes wide, casting the gray colors of the day across the hardwood floor. Liv pursed her lips, trying to find words to speak as she took in the sight of her quiet attic bedroom.

"Are ye alright, lass? I know it isn't the most palatial of quarters, but -"

"No, no! It's grand."

The words shook in her throat as she spoke, but she hoped the doctor hadn't heard. There was a flood of emotion coming up; a raucous wailing that she'd been fighting for days now, traversing from highland town to highland town, praying to come to a place where she might settle in, far from home. This room, with its tiny table and white linened bed, was the most breathtaking and welcome sight she'd ever laid eyes on.

"Well, I'm sure you'll make it your own in time, aye?"

Liv turned to meet the doctor's gaze, but instantly regretted it. His expression shifted when he laid eyes upon her face. Despite her best efforts to hide her emotional state, he'd seen it as plainly as though she'd torn at her hair and collapsed to the floor in a wailing fit.

"I imagine you'll want to get settled? I'll leave ye to it, then? I'm sure Fionnula will holler for ye soon enough," he said, heading for the door. Then he stopped in the doorway, grabbing the doorjamb as he leaned back into the room to whisper. "And she *will* holler. Doesn't like climbin all those steps."

He shot her a mischievous grin, then ducked out of the room, pulling the bedroom door shut as he went. Liv stood there in the small room, the open wooden beams overhead betraying any number of little spiders and critters to share the space with her. Yet, despite the dust and gray light of the rainy day outside, the walls were as good as gilded in gold to her. She had a roof over her head. There were four walls around her. There was a bed and a pillow, and a light to read by, and above all, there was no Amelia Baird.

Liv slumped down onto the dusty hardwood floor and wept grateful tears.

CHAPTER TWO

"Deliverance! Get down here, child!"

Fionnula teemed in the kitchen that night, fighting with habit to instruct Liv of her duties – scrub kitchen floors, counters, stove, pots and pans; light the evening fires around the house, clear chamber pots in the morning. Liv had done the latter early, struggling to find the gall to enter the doctor's chambers, even with him down in his office at work. Still, she found the pots all empty. It seemed the doctor was content to empty his own.

Fionnula made quick work of taking Liv's measurements the night before, and appeared early that morning with a bundle wrapped in brown paper; two identical black dresses, similar to Fionnula's. They'd fit perfectly as Liv hustled to meet Fionnula in the kitchens.

Chop those parsnips!

Scrub down the table before ye do that, girl!

Why hasn't the doctor had his tea?

Despite the woman's austere demeanor, when three

o'clock struck, Fionnula pulled a chair up to the kitchen table, demanded Liv sit, and set a big plate of boiled chicken and parsnips with gravy before her. Liv took a single bite and had to stifle a moan. Fionnula's stern exterior cracked for a split second as she took her seat across the table, covering the smile with a curt nod before digging into her own meal.

Liv hadn't seen Dr. Lennox for more than a minute since the previous afternoon, delivering his tea to his study and knocking on the office door to let him know it awaited. When she returned an hour later, the plate remained there, untouched and cold.

The front doorbell clanged in the kitchen several times during the day, all met with an inconvenienced huff as Fionnula untied her apron and stormed out into the hallway to greet the visitors. Most were colleagues, only a couple were patients. Liv listened intently to each voice, but heard very little.

By mid-evening, Liv was shooed off to check the fires for the evening, and collect the doctor's untouched tea. Liv slipped into his quiet study, the sound of the nearby grandfather clock ticking away as its face watched her work. The study was a state of mild disarray; books left to collect dust, still open to the last page he'd read, tea cups still tucked away on book shelves, hidden to passersby, their long cold and in one case moldy contents left stewing in secret. Liv's kitchen duties were all but complete, and despite not seeing the doctor that day, she felt overwhelmed with gratitude. Even the crying baby that kept her up the night before felt like a welcome reprieve from the far darker things that would keep her awake at home. Though she'd gotten little sleep, she was too content to let it slow her.

Liv collected the teacups from the shelves, surprised Fionnula hadn't discovered these hidden treasures – or perhaps noticed the missing cups from the china cabinet. Then, Liv gathered up each book, its leather bound covers boasting everything from *The Human Anatomy* and *Confessions of an English Opium Eater,* to *Frankenstein* and *The Three Perils of Woman.* She found the long satin ribbon attached to each book's spine and slipped it into the pages of the books, closing them softly before lining them up along an empty shelf at the corner of the room. The tables now clear, Liv hoisted up her teeming tray, careful not to spill the unfortunate contents of the teacups, and headed back toward the kitchen.

She made it through the office parlor before the high pitched sound caught her attention. She stopped, staring at the satin yellow wallpaper as she waited for the sound to return. It did, with vengeance.

Fionnula burst open the kitchen door just as Liv approached, slamming the tray up into Liv's chest. Teacups filled with putrid liquid poured down the front of her new dress, staining her pristine apron. An instant later, the sound of china shattering on the hardwood floor turned Liv's stomach.

"Ah, love. You're alright, aren't ye?"

With that Fionnula straightened Liv's shoulders and bounded past her toward the front door. The high pitched sound peaked again and the doctor's office door opened behind her, soon coupled by hurried footsteps.

"Deliverance, are ye alright?"

She frowned, keeping her eyes down as she knelt before the shattered pieces of china, collecting them back onto her tray. She nodded. "Yes, sir."

"Careful there, dear," he said, and suddenly his arms were at her shoulders, hoisting her onto her feet.

The front door opened just as the doorbell rang, and the high pitched sound shattered the quiet of the house. It was unmistakable now – it was the sound of a woman screaming.

"Is he in?" A male voice asked, his tone erratic and urgent.

"Aye! Course he is! Get her in here. You'll have the whole of Cowgate coming down to gawk."

The screaming grew louder, coupled by loud bangs and growls as Dr. Lennox leaned against Liv, pressing her into the kitchen door and out of the hallway. Just as she stepped into the hot kitchen, three figures appeared; two men in strange uniforms holding onto a disheveled woman, her shift so dingy it was practically brown in several places. She had long, black hair, and her teeth were blackened and filthy. Liv could see them, as the woman gnashed her teeth into the air as she was carried past. Despite standing away from the three figures, a strong stench wafted into the kitchen from the hallway. The woman smelled as poorly as she looked.

A man in a black suit appeared just outside the kitchen door, leaning into Findlay. "We've tried everything we can. She can't be left alone at this point. Do ye think it might help?"

Findlay tapped the back of his hands to the man's lapel and nodded. "Get her downstairs and strap her in. I'll be right there."

The man disappeared down the hallway, followed quickly by Fionnula, but Findlay turned into the kitchen. "I need ye to bring a basin of hot water and clean rags downstairs. Can ye do that for me?"

Liv looked up into Findlay's face. The urgency that read on everyone else's expression seemed to only play at the corners of his. She swallowed, glancing toward the fireplace. The kettle was still steaming just enough to betray heat.

"Right away," she said.

Findlay began unbuttoning his shirt sleeves as he disappeared out of the kitchen. The woman's screams grew louder in the instant the door was open.

Liv quickly followed through the open door with the kettle in her hands, fighting to keep her eyes on the steps before her, terrified her shaking hands or knees might fail her and she'd tumble down the steps, pouring more than moldy tea down the front of her dress.

Liv reached the stone floor of the operating theater, and allowed herself a single glance at the woman now strapped to the metal table. Her arms were tied at the wrist and a strap was taut across her chest. Still, she struggled against her restraints, biting at the air and screaming, her face slick with brown and black, oily strands of her hair clinging to her skin as she thrashed. Liv passed the table toward Findlay, only to have him direct her to a nearby counter.

"There, Deliverance. Please."

She followed his gesture to a large metal basin and poured the steaming contents of the kettle into it. The water splashed up at her just so, but not enough to spill. She swallowed hard and thanked God. Hopefully she would still have a job once she returned upstairs and cleaned up the shattered mess in the hallway.

Liv turned passed the table again, heading for the stairs. The woman on the table went still suddenly, staring up at Liv's face with a strange smile. Liv felt chilled to the bone. She doubled her pace, rushing past as the woman responded to her movement with a newfound fervor of thrashing.

"D'ye know her name?" Findlay was approaching the table as the two men in strange uniform took the woman's legs and began strapping her ankles down.

One of the uniformed men, the shorter, dark haired one responded. "No name, sir. Came in two day ago. Been like this since."

Findlay nodded. "Alright. Rags, Deliverance?"

Liv stopped at the fifth step, scolding herself. "I'll get them right now!"

"Thank ye!" The doctor called. "Just hand them through the door when ye return, aye?"

With that, Liv bounded up the steps and into the parlor, Fionnula bellowing up after her, "Linen closet! In the hallway!"

Liv moved through the house, her hands shaking, and found the small cabinet tucked into the wall of the hallway. She pulled three, then four clean rags from within, praying that would be enough. As she returned to the office door, Fionnula appeared within, reaching out to Liv for the rags. Inside the operating theater, the woman's growls and screams changed suddenly, turning into an almost startled, high pitched chirp.

Fionnula met Liv's gaze and gave a stern look. "Ye steer clear of this door a while, ye hear?"

Liv nodded. "I will."

"Ye go clean up the mess in the hallway, get yourself sorted. And get another basin of water on the fire, ye ken?"

"Yes, mum."

"Good girl," she said, shutting the office door as the screams shifted yet again to something low and guttural. As Liv bustled down the hallway toward the mess of shattered tea cups, she heard the crazed woman's voice go soft, then silent. She didn't hear another sound until the mess of shattered tea tray was all but a memory.

The basin and kettle were steaming on the fire when the office door opened, the sound of a shuffling crowd moving beyond the walls of the kitchens. There was no screaming to announce the woman's presence, but instead a soft humming sound to betray her passage. Liv pushed the kitchen door open a crack and watched the woman being escorted by the two uniformed men, her head lolling from side to side as they reached the door of the house and disappeared outside. Fionnula appeared, startling her away from the door to search for some random task to cover her curiosity. Fionnula just stared her down a moment, then turned her attention to the fireplace. She tapped the steaming kettle, making a tsking sound, and nodded.

"Doctor's gonnae need a bath run upstairs. I'd have ye go ahead on up and begin filling the bathtub, please. When you're done, join me in the operating theater."

"Yes mum," Liv said, rushing for the fireplace and the cloth to wrap around the kettle's handle. She was marching her way across the parlor a moment later, the kettle swaying just inches from her skirts.

"Must've been a rare chore, that."

Liv reached the study doorway and slowed, listening to the male voices on the upper landing of the operating theater.

"Woman of that sort? I imagine she's not washed in months."

This wasn't Findlay speaking. Though Findlay's speech was cleaner than many other Scots of Edinburgh and the Highlands where she hailed from, he was still undeniably Scottish. This man was trying hard not to be.

"I imagine so," Findlay said.

"Christ, how do you do it, lad? Poor thing practically purring like a cat when you were done with her -"

"I'll send my notes along to the asylum in the mornin, then?" Findlay asked, cutting the man off.

"Yes. Yes, that'll be fine."

The door to the theater opened wide and Liv doubled her pace, knocking the hot kettle against her knee. Though the skirt of her dress shielded her from burn, it didn't shield her from bruise, and she hissed in pain, quietly. Liv was almost at the top of the first staircase before the men's voices went quiet by the front door.

Though the kettle did little to fill the tub in the upstairs washroom, it was scalding enough to be topped off with water from the spigot. Liv ran her hand through the water as it reached ankle height. Once she brought the basin up from the kitchen, his bath would be set.

Liv rose from the edge of the tub and turned for the door, her face crashing into the solid shape of Dr. Findlay Lennox's chest.

"Goh, I'm so sorry! Daft me!" She exclaimed, touching a hand to his chest as though she might wipe her contact from him.

He chuckled, setting a hand on her upper arm.

"You're fine, Deliverance. It was my fault for startling ye. Ye did very well today. I was pleased to see it."

"What?"

He raised his brows and smiled. "Ye didn't panic when they brought in the unfortunate miss. Well done."

She looked down, shaking her head. "Oh, I – I just did as ye asked."

Liv went toward the door, her head bowed as she made a desperate move to escape.

"Deliverance."

She stopped in the doorway. Oh god, she thought. He's letting me go. Why did I bloody drop those bloody teacups?

"Did ye put away my books?"

She stopped, mouth open. "I did. I made sure to mark every page before I set them right. Was that wrong of me?"

He smiled, wiping his hands over and over on the same dingy rag. "No, no bother. Just gave me a start to see it like that. All sorted like that."

Liv turned to face him. "I shouldn't have, I'm sorry."

Findlay smiled, tossing the rag into the corner of the room. "No, please. It was lovely. I'm no used to it, is all."

"I won't do it again, sir – doctor – Dr. Lennox."

"Findlay. And please, if ye don't do it again, it will just go back to the state it was in. I'm no the tidiest fellow, sadly. Rather prefer my patients see it more like a study than a battlefield."

With that he tugged his shirt sleeves down. Next, he pulled at the collar of his shirt, unbuttoning two buttons down his front before Liv realized she was watching the man get undressed for his bath.

"I'll get the last of the water, then."

"Thank ye, Deliverance."

Liv was halfway down the stairs before realizing she'd left the kettle on the floor of the washroom. She rushed back in the open door, bending down for the kettle just as Findlay opened his shirt, baring his chest before he realized she'd returned. Still, even when he met her gaze and smiled, he didn't shirk away like some shamed thing. He simply shrugged the shirt down his broad shoulders and tossing it over a chair.

"Ah, can't rightly boil water without that, can ye?"

He shot her a playful smirk as she recoiled back out the washroom door. Liv barreled down the stairs and back into the kitchen, quickly filling the kettle with fresh water and hanging it over the fire before reaching for the basin handle. She hissed loudly, yanking her bare hand away from the hot metal. She was so frazzled by the doctor that she'd forgotten to wrap the handle in a cloth first.

"What are ye on about, girl? Have ye no sense?"

Liv bowed to Fionnula, instantly. "I'm sorry. I'm so sorry. I didn't mean -"

"Well, don't apologize to me. Your the one that'll have to live with the burn. Just use the cloth next time. You'll no survive the week if ye don't think first."

Liv wrapped the handle of the basin and hoisted the heavy thing off the hook. "I should've thought of it, I'm sorry."

Fionnula crossed the kitchen to the door and held it open for her, waiting for Liv to waddle through with the heavy bucket in her hands. "Come straight down, after, ye ken?"

"Yes, mum."

Fionnula disappeared back into the kitchen as Liv made her way back upstairs. She reached the washroom door, still wide open as she left it.

"Dr. Findlay?" She called, afraid to enter and catch the gentlemen in some further state of undress.

"It's just Findlay, lass, and come on in."

She did as asked, almost dropping the scalding hot bucket onto her toes as she took in the sight of the man. He was standing by the tub clad in only his undergarments – a pair of long johns that barely reached past his knee. Clearly, they didn't make such garments for men of his size. He tugged at the waistband of his long johns, pulling them up over his hips. They were loose still, sagging down to betray a line of ruddy curls that grew from his navel downward. She'd seen the hair at his chest, a subtle patch of dark red curls, but this hair seemed obscene, like it was meant to be covered, like the hair she'd desperately tried to hide from her mother as a girl when it grew between her legs.

"Here, let me help with that," he said, moving closer to her.

She slammed the bucket on the floor, stepping away from him as though his closeness might burn or bite.

He shot her a confused look. Then he glanced down at himself and frowned. "I'm sorry, lass. I didn't think. I'll be sure to keep my trousers on next time, shall I?"

"No, it's fine. You're fine. D'ye need anythin else, then?"

Findlay hoisted the bucket up as though it were filled with feathers and dumped the steamy water into the tub. "No, I'm settled here. Thank ye, dearie."

She turned for the door.

"Deliverance."

Liv stopped and turned to face him, fighting every nerve in her body to not shudder at the sight of this undressed man.

He just smiled. "It's nothing. Just rather fond of that name, it seems. I hope ye don't mind my sayin it as often as I do."

Liv shook her head. "It's no bother."

Findlay dunked his hand in the water, then turned on the spigot to add cool to the tub. "Ye did well, today. I'm grateful to have ye."

Liv gave a strange gesture, almost a curtsy as she moved toward the door. "Thank ye, sir. Ye have a good evenin."

Liv shut the washroom door behind her and made her way down the stairs to the parlor. The door to the operating theater was left wide open. She almost didn't want to go in. The memory of the screaming woman unsettled her; of her glare and the way she thrashed toward her, flashing an eerie smile of rotted teeth. She thought of the other things she could do – go sweep the hallway again to be sure all fragments of china were collected, collect those tiny shards of teacups and attempt to glue them back together, or perhaps go hide all the evidence of her failure by burying the pieces in one of those window boxes filled with flowers outside. Then she thought of the room upstairs, of the figure that would surely now be sitting quietly in a tub of steamy water, naked.

The thought of that man being so close, his skin bared to her – it made her stomach turn in a strange, unfamiliar way. She'd seen men shirtless once or twice, but somehow seeing Findlay Lennox's body hair – the hair that trailed to places she should never see – it made her feel ashamed, and it made her feel curious.

"Will ye come down, then, girl?"

Fionnula hollered from the recesses below. How on earth did she hear me? Liv thought.

Liv made her way down the steps into the examination area below. Fionnula was scrubbing down the metal table with something that smelled harsh and overbearing. She wore a white kerchief tied over her face as she worked, her hands clad in heavy gloves.

"Pour that basin of water into the drain. Then bring down another bucket. Hot preferably, but whatever we have'll do for now."

Liv nodded. "Yes, mum."

She made her way across the room, fighting the sudden swimmy sensation from the fumes of whatever Fionnula used to clean the table. She collected up the basin, its water murky and somewhat smelly now, and walked it over to the drain in the floor. She aimed carefully and dumped it. Then she marched back to the kitchens to procure another round.

The two women worked in near silence, scrubbing the exam table more than once each. Once the basins, table, and floors were washed and washed again, Fionnula sent Liv to bed, ordering her back upstairs to stoke the fire in Findlay's bedroom on her way. The doctor was still in his bath, leaving Liv to move about his bedroom unhindered. She felt invasive being there without his knowledge or permission, but each time Fionnula sent her, Liv did as she was told, overstepping a rule that often earned her a boxed ear

– never go into her mother's room without permission.

Liv did everything she could to avert her eyes from his private things; his wide bed, his nightstand and the medical books resting thereupon, their spines bent and cracked. She threw a few small logs onto the fire and gave it a quick prod with the poker.

The sound of the washroom door opening startled her to her feet so fast, she slammed the top of her head into the mantelpiece and nearly toppled onto the fire.

"Whoa there, love. Are ye alright?"

Liv shook her head, squeezing her eyes shut over and over as she tried to focus on the shapes of the room. Everything seemed white and unfocused.

"Come now. Give us a look."

Liv turned her eyes up to find Findlay standing over her, his eyes on hers with a medical concern, his body still bared from waist up. His hair was wet now, slicked back on his head and darker with water. He took her face in his hands, pressing his thumbs to her cheeks as he gazed into one eye, then the other.

"I'm well enough. I'm well," she said, but didn't protest against his professional concern.

Findlay chuckled. "Aye, I saw that stumble of yers. Quite the bump you've had."

"I'm fine. I'm right as rain."

Findlay pulled her cap free from the top of her head and slid his fingers up into her hair, feeling the surface of her scalp. Her sight pulsated with specks of black, ringed in gold. She swayed toward him as he pulled her head forward and down. Her forehead pressed against his chest a moment, cool and still damp from his bath. She lunged back, trying to pull from his grasp. He moved with her, his fingers running over her scalp, careful not to tug at the pins in her dark red hair.

"Feels well enough, I suppose. I'll keep an eye on ye, though."

Liv stepped away, averting her eyes from the sight of him. He was clad in nothing more than long johns again, but this time they clung to his skin in various places, a symptom of still wet skin. She glanced down, catching view of a shape beneath the damp fabric at his groin. She squeezed her eyes shut, shamed beyond reason at having caught an idea of what this man looked like unclothed, and lunged for his bedroom door.

"If you've any need of the kettle, girl, I've just – Christ! Findlay Joseph Campbell Lennox, what in bloody hell are ye wearin?"

Both Findlay and Liv startled toward the door, finding Fionnula there, growing redder in the face with each passing moment.

"What are ye on about, Fionn?" Findlay asked.

The older woman was across the room, snatching a blanket up from the bed and tossing it into Findlay's face. "Cover yourself, ye twit!'

Findlay glanced down at himself, realizing the state of his clinging long johns, and turned away from the two women to adjust himself. Fionnula lunged forward, grabbing Liv around the shoulders and leading her to the hallway.

"Why don't ye retire for the evenin, Livvy? Think ye might need an early night tonight, d'ye agree?"

Liv swallowed, hustling across the hallway to get as far from Findlay's room as she could. Dear God, what if he saw me looking?

Liv nodded, making her way up the second flight of stairs, her head still pounding from her injury.

Fionnula turned on Findlay in the room below. "What were ye bloody thinkin, lad?"

Findlay could be seen through the open bedroom door, pulling a loose nightshirt over his head. "I didn't think of it! I spent half my life with ye washin my backside; I came in from me bath and she was here. There wasn't anything inappropriate about it!"

Fionnula shut the bedroom door, leaving Liv in the hallway in near darkness, save for the lines of gold that framed Findlay's bedroom door. Liv was at the top landing when Findlay's bedroom door opened again.

"That's a gentle girl you've taken in, ye -"

"I know well enough she is!"

"And a naïve one! She doesn't need to worry about stumbling upon ye prancing around the house in your knickers!"

Findlay growled at his housekeeper. "Ah, sod off! It'll no happen again."

"You're bloody right it won't!" With that, Fionnula shut Findlay's door behind her.

Liv stood silent just outside her bedroom door.

"Deliverance, love?"

Liv took a breath. "Aye, I'm here."

"I came up to let ye know there's a hot kettle on the fire if ye would have a bath before bed."

Liv stood there a moment. She'd expected some form of scolding; a warning against impure curiosity, against ogling a man in his underthings. The softened tone almost unnerved her. Why wasn't this woman threatening her with punishment? Perhaps she was saving it for the following morning. Mother liked to do that as well.

"Thank ye. I think I might just try for sleep, instead."

"If ye wish," she finally said, making her way back down the first flight of steps toward her quarters.

Liv reached her own bed chambers and quickly shut the door behind her. It took all her will not to weep right then and there. Despite the relief and hope she'd felt when first introduced to this quiet room – to the notion of claiming it as her own – her first day hadn't gone well at all. Shattering teacups, moving books she shouldn't touch, ogling his body, knowing nothing of medicine, being a gentle, naïve girl – surely it was only a matter of time before these crimes would add up and he would realize he'd hired the wrong girl. Then she'd be out on her own. Jobless and homeless in Edinburgh?

She'd have to go home.

No, she thought. She'd die in the streets before she'd go home to her mother. She'd either make it in Edinburgh, or she wouldn't, but she would never go home.

Liv slumped down into her bed, pulling the crocheted blanket up over her shoulders. She burrowed into the blankets there, the chill of her attic room creeping in from the drafty window. Still, the extra blankets and quilts made for a cozy nest there in the dark. Liv closed her eyes, grateful at the notion of sleep.

Just as she began to drift, a shrill wail echoed through the walls of the room.

The baby was crying again.

CHAPTER THREE

The following days were far less exciting than the first. No desperate women being dragged by asylum orderlies through the front hallway, no giggling girls from the pubs of Canongate teasing each other from the examination room. And Liv didn't have another incident for several days; no teacups shattered and no ogling of the doctor in his drawers. In fact, she didn't see much of the doctor at all for the rest of the week.

Life could be called peaceful, almost content were it not for one unfortunate detail.

Liv hadn't managed to sleep more than a couple hours a night since her arrival. The neighbors clearly didn't tend to their children, leaving the tiny infant to wail all through the night, its screams carrying through the walls of her attic room as though they were paper thin. She'd manage a few winks here and there, but those moments of reprieve were always shattered by the baby crying anew. Liv had half a mind to march next door and give them a piece of her mind by the fourth night. She was dozing off as she sat by the fire in the kitchen, turning the coals to cook their evening meal. By the fifth day, Fionnula was making comment several times a day, snapping at Liv to wake up as she stood swaying with a kitchen knife in her hand, half asleep as she cut up root vegetables.

"Tear up a piece of rag and stuff it in your ears, girl.

That'll set ye right," Fionnula offered on the fifth night. And it had almost worked, but sadly Liv's mind seemed to have trained itself to expect a desperate wail every time she dozed off, almost waking herself before the baby even had a chance to cry.

It had been a week now, and Liv stirred in her bed, her forehead aching from the want of sleep. She'd just dozed off with her face to the wall, but she was awake now, startled by something despite the muffling effect of the rags tucked into her ears. There was no child crying this time. There was no sound at all.

Liv swallowed, staring at the wood planks of her bedroom wall, reading the knots there as though she spoke their language. There was something thick about the air, something strange and colder now. She exhaled into her hand, watching the cloud of steam dissipate just in front of her face.

She took a breath, willing this distantly familiar sensation to be stilled, and turned over in her bed. The windows were still closed, the only light cast through them that of a crescent moon. Liv glanced at her oil lamp, now cold. Then she saw it, a subtle movement in the dark. Her stomach shot into her throat and she turned toward her bedroom door. It was open. She'd shut it before bed; she knew that well.

Yet, the door was not what drew her eye. It was the figure standing therein.

Liv stared at the figure a moment, squeezing her eyes shut to shake off sleep, then glaring in the dark, trying to make this person out. Liv was frozen, waiting for sense to declare itself as this woman stood in her doorway, watching her. Her face was obscured by the bedroom door, and her figure framed only by a subtle glow from the staircase; the dying glow of Findlay's fireplace, shining through the cracks around his door.

She swallowed, then sat upright in her bed, willing this once forgotten sensation to be stilled. "Fionnula?"

The figure swayed, but didn't move. Liv knew it wasn't Fionnula. This figure was narrow from waist to shoulder, her hair a tangled mess above her head.

Liv squinted in the dark, trying to make out the woman's face. A soft hum suddenly filled the room, distant and almost breathy, like the memory of a sound. Then it shuddered, only to begin again.

The woman was crying.

Liv turned to her bedside table, lifting the cap off her oil lamp. She took up her box of matches and struck one, lighting the lamp before lifting it up over her head to shine upon the sad woman's face.

The woman was gone. The doorway was empty.

"Hullo! Are ye there?" Liv called, but there was no answer. She hopped out of bed, her feet cold against the hardwood floor, and hustled out into the hallway, holding the lamp over the railing to shine it downstairs. The hallway below was as empty as the one above. It was as though the woman had never been there.

Liv turned back to her room, searching for her robe. As she set her lamp back down on the table, she could hear the distant and familiar sound of a baby crying.

Liv pulled on her dressing gown and headed down the stairs, quietly shining the light into each open door. The image of the madwoman from days before struck her almost dumb at one point as she searched

42

the study and the kitchen. She fought to push aside the image of that woman leaping out from a cupboard or a closet, clawing at Liv's throat while growling like some ravenous creature. She made her way back up to the first floor, and despite her trepidation, rapped softly on the doctor's door.

She waited in the hallway, watching the light cast from the fire within. There was no sound, no movement.

Liv rapped again louder this time, and waited. No response.

She didn't dare disturb Fionnula, fearing the reprisal of the stern woman. Liv stood in the quiet hallway, feeling the heaviness of the air, hearing the distant wail of the infant child. She took a deep breath. It had been a dream.

Please God, she thought. Not the dreams again. I'll never sleep in this house if I don't do something.

Liv swayed just outside the doctor's door, thinking of all the nights she'd spent at home, awake and wary, waiting for the sound of footsteps outside her bedroom door. She had to find sleep, by any means necessary. She remembered her father's answer to sleepless nights, and despite her trepidation at the thought, turned for the stairs and headed down into the study.

The small cabinet was tucked between bookshelves. Liv set her lamp down on the table and pulled the cabinet open. Bottles of amber and gold glinted in the lamp light. Liv swallowed, touching a fingertip to the stoppers of each of the four bottles. She knew not what the bottles contained, just that they would make her sleep – the way they'd helped her father sleep.

She tapped the top of the bottle with the most

liquid within.

"The one on the left is the better choice."

Liv shrieked, spinning around so fast, her hip slammed into the cabinet. She had no time to wince as she held her hands out to Findlay, his tall frame standing in the doorway of the study, the operating theater door wide open in the parlor behind him.

"Oh please, Dr. Lennox. I'm so sorry! I didn't mean to be stealin. I just don't know what else to do. I'm so sorry! Please."

Findlay crossed the room, waving his hands before him, gently. He reached past her toward the contents of the cabinet and pulled one of the four bottles out.

"Please don't fire me! I'll never think of it again, I promise. Please."

Findlay pulled the top of the bottle free and took a sniff of its contents. "Aye, this'll be the one."

He ignored her pleas and pulled two tumblers from the cabinet behind her. A moment later, he'd splashed a small amount into each glass and replaced the stopper on the bottle. He handed her the glass with less liquid. "I'd say drink up, but I think you'll find this goes a long way."

Liv held her hands out before her, terrified to accept this offer. He seemed sincere, holding his own glass up to his nose. Would he punish her for taking it? Was this a trick, something Amelia Baird would do to lure her into misbehaving, ignorant to the consequences that would come if she didn't pass the test?

"I'm sorry! Please, Dr. Lennox. I'm so sorry! I just can't sleep. And there was someone there, and I just – if I don't sleep, I don't know -"

"Shh," Findlay said, shushing her softly as he took

her hand and pulled her over to the settee. She was losing control of her emotions. A week of sleepless nights had taken their toll. She could no longer hide her worry from this man. "Deliverance, lass. You're fine. Come sit. Have a drink. Just go slow, is all I ask."

She tried to wave away the offer of drink, but Findlay simply set it on the table beside her. Then he swigged at his own. Her hands were shaking in her lap, waiting for the reprimand; the threat and punishment to come.

"Tell me, how long have ye suffered this melancholy?"

Liv startled at this question, turning to meet Findlay's gaze for the first time since he caught her in his liquor cabinet. "What?"

"Melancholy? This sadness ye seem to carry."

Liv looked down at her hands, watching each fingertip shake. She let herself consider the answer before she spoke. "Always."

Findlay set his drink aside and reached for her hand. "And the sleeplessness? Has that always been, as well?"

She nodded. "It's worse here, now. I'd been hopin it would pass, but it's no passed."

"Is there any history of it in your family? The melancholy."

Liv gave a sad smile, her eyes trained on her own hands, now cradled in his. She nodded. "Aye. My father was always very sad."

"I'm sorry to hear that."

Liv shook her head. "It's fine."

She sat there, fighting to keep her hands still in his. He had a gentle manner about him, serene and calming, but still she couldn't settle her nerves.

"Did your father treat his troubles with whisky, then, as well?"

Liv swallowed, glancing toward her untouched glass. "He did, aye. It was the only thing to help him sleep, he said."

Findlay nodded. "Well, you're welcome to it, if ye like. It's no something ye want to become a habit, mind."

"I know," she said, a bit too urgently than she'd have liked. "I do know that. I just – I don't want to – I just don't want to lose the position. I'll do anythin to stay here."

Findlay squeezed her hands. "I had no intention of letting ye go, Deliverance. You've done a fine job."

She shook her head. "I haven't slept in a week. I'm afraid if it continues -"

She stopped, fighting back her emotion. Still it bled out, pooling at the corners of her eyes until it spilled over, running down each cheek.

The doctor took a deep breath and rose from the settee. He took up her glass from the table and quickly downed it. He set it along with his own empty glass on the table. It hadn't been more than a couple swigs between the two glasses. Given the sheer size of the man, she wondered if he felt it at all.

Findlay came to stand in the parlor doorway, staring toward his office door. He took a deep breath. "I may be able to help ye, if ye'd like."

"Help me? With the what?"

He set his shoulder into the doorjamb, his back to her as he spoke. She watched the light of the lamp dance across his shoulders, reflecting off the satin fabric of the back of his vest.

"With the melancholy. The sleeplessness." He

46

shifted to look at her. "I've been working on a procedure for some time – your friends Mary and Janet have helped me in my efforts to fine tune it."

"A procedure?" She asked, swallowing hard. She thought of Mary and Janet giggling as they ordered her to have it done, then thought of them wailing away in the recesses of the doctors examination room.

"Aye. I've found it to work well in treatment of various feminine troubles. Hysteria is its intended application – women suffering from some form of madness or mania. Yet, in my tests, it's been effective for many other troubles."

Liv straightened in her seat, her stomach churning. "Ye think it might help me sleep?"

The doctor bowed his head, nodding. "Aye, it might well do."

"Does it hurt?"

He chuckled. "No, no a bit."

"Then, aye. I'll have it. Please."

Liv was on her feet, standing in the cold study surrounded by books, several already back on various tables, their spines bent open where they lay. Despite the memory of screaming women, when he promised it wouldn't hurt, she believed him.

"Alright, then," he said. "Come with me, if ye will?"

He gestured for her to follow, and headed into the parlor. Before she could join him, he disappeared down the steps into the operating theater. Liv inhaled sharply, her stomach twisting yet again as she approached the door. She wrapped her robe around her middle as she made her way down the steps.

The operating theater was glowing with gold, several lamps lit along the stone façade of the room.

There were several metal instruments glinting in the light below, including the metal table that stood at the center of the massive room. Liv made her way down the steps to join him on the ground floor, watching him as he shuffled and organized pages upon pages of scribbled notes.

He gestured toward the metal table. "Lie down there for me, please. Feet facing me."

Liv approached the table, working hard to empty her mind as each metal instrument glinted forebodingly. He said it wouldn't hurt, she thought.

It won't hurt. It won't hurt. He won't hurt you.

Liv used a small footstool beside the table and did as she was told. The metal was cold against her shoulders, even through the fabric of her robe and her shift. She flattened her bare calves against the table, hissing softly at the cold.

The table clanked and hummed beneath her as Findlay stood by her ankles, shifting something. A metal arm appeared by the edge of the table, paired by another on the opposite side.

"Slide yourself to the end of the table, please. And feet in the stirrups."

"What?"

He tapped a finger on one of the metal arms. She stared up at it. They looked like ancient torture devices. She didn't dare move, watching the doctor mull around from table to table, collecting notes with the idle disinterest of a man oblivious to her presence.

"If ye could answer me a couple questions; are ye a virgin? Did I ask ye this before?"

Liv nodded as he turned to meet her gaze. He glanced down at her legs, and smiled, moving to the edge of the table. He took her foot in his hands and hoisted her leg up, forcing her to bend her knee as he positioned her ankle into the stirrup. Liv's hands shot down to her shift, pressing it down between her legs to avoid showing any part of herself. He raised a brow at her as he moved around the table, taking hold of her other foot.

"Deliverance?"

"Yes? Ah!" She gasped as he lifted her second leg and placed her into the stirrups. She lay there prone, her legs splayed wide open, clamped into place by metal hands, and Findlay standing between them. She pressed her hands down between her legs, craning her neck and back to maintain her modesty. He pulled a stool up to the table and sat down directly between her legs. Liv closed her eyes tight, unable to look at him anymore.

Dear god, what had she agreed to?

"I recall ye said ye were, aye?"

"Oh, aye. Aye, I am."

He muttered softly to himself, as though making note. "And the last time ye had your courses?"

She swallowed. "Over a fortnight."

He nodded, settling himself in his seat. "Well, we should do well enough then. Now, I'm going to apologize for my hands now. I usually have ye bring me hot water to start, but tonight I don't have such a thing. Might be a bit cold, so I apologize."

"Alright," she said, her voice shaking.

"Right. So what I'm going to do here is I'm going to use my hands to perform what is called 'manual manipulation.'"

She fought to still her nerves and listen, but her teeth had begun to chatter.

"I may penetrate ye, but ye will be in tact when it is

49

comple -"

"Penetrate me?" She asked, and it was shrill.

He set a hand on her belly. "Aye, Deliverance. There's nothing to be afraid of. It won't hurt. It'll actually feel rather good. The more relaxed ye are, the better, though. Shoulda let ye drink your whisky."

"It doesn't hurt?"

"No. I promise. Ye may feel your sex getting hot -" She gasped, holding her breath. "- and I've had some women describe a feeling of wanting to make water. That's alright, both sensations are normal and actually a good sign."

Liv exhaled in a sudden sob. She was terrified and losing her battle with her emotions.

He shushed her, softly. "You're alright, Livvy. We can stop at any time if ye feel uncomfortable or if it troubles ye in any way."

She lay there a moment shaking, her hands still pressed between her legs. She thought to stop him now, to run back to her room and forget this miracle procedure he offered, but each time she thought to do so, her eyes grew heavy with more than tears. She remembered the woman in the doorway of her room, and swallowed hard.

"Alright, let's be done with it," she said, fighting to maintain a stern tone despite her abject terror. She looked up at the high ceilings overhead, imagining the viewing seats filled with men in suits; students learning to become doctors all leaning over to see her, her legs splayed for the world to see.

Findlay rose to his feet, coming to stand between her splayed legs. He pulled at the fabric of her shift, but she kept her hands planted there, unable to willingly let him lift her skirts.

He chuckled softly. "Now, I'm going to touch my hand to your thigh now. Let ye get accustomed to the temperature. I apologize again if they're cold."

She felt a cool graze against her inner thigh and jerked on the table, the metal clanging beneath her in protest. He shushed her softly, pressing his palm to her thigh now, letting her feel the whole of his hand. He held it there a moment, then slid it further down between her legs. She tightened the muscles in her thighs, desperately trying to close her legs as the stirrups held them apart. His second hand touched the inside of the other thigh, then gently pulled her hands away from her shift. He did not lift her skirts or look down between her legs, but instead felt his way with his hands. His right hand found her folds, and with deft fingers he pried them apart, pressing his fingers against her body.

Liv shuddered violently, crying out in shock and near shame. Yet, the doctor did not flinch at her frightened response. He shushed softly, cooing to her as his thumb began to move against her. She gasped, imagining faces peering down from the landing above, and closed her eyes.

"That's right. Close your eyes, lass. But tell me when something feels good."

His thumb moved against her in circles, the pressure undulating and changing as his hands moved. She clutched the fabric of her shift, willing herself invisible.

"Now, I'm gonnae penetrate ye here."

She whimpered in terror, then gasped, feeling one of his fingers slide into her. He pressed his free hand against her belly, as though he might hold her in place as his other hand moved between her legs. She stifled a cry as his finger moved inside her, then felt her body tense against his touch. Something about the way he moved made her insides tighten, the places he touched growing hotter by the second. Suddenly, he quickened the movement of his thumb. She reached down, grabbing hold of his wrist.

"What's wrong? Does it no feel good?"

"No! Aye!" She clamped her eyes shut again, desperate to hide from his view as she lost the capacity to form words. Instead of express herself in English, the sound spilled from her lips in a long, 'ugh' sound. He doubled his speed again as her cries grew louder and higher pitched. Suddenly the heat shifted, and she felt exactly as though she might wet herself.

"Wait! Please!"

He hummed softly to himself. "There we are. Relax now, Livvy. There we go."

Her hips jerked and her thighs tightened suddenly, shaking the stirrups and table beneath her as her body convulsed. Muscles she didn't know she had contracted somewhere hidden as her pulse throbbed between her legs. The convulsion happened twice more, then subsided to smaller tremors as his hands began to slow. A moment later, he pulled his finger from inside her and turned to a nearby table, taking up a small rag to wipe his hands.

"There we are, lass. Now, just take a moment and relax. Let it subside."

She lay there on the metal table, breathless and panting, her legs still splayed, her sex cold against the open air. She could hear a strange rhythm in her ears, matched to the sound of her heart beating in her chest. She swallowed, exhaling in soft sighs.

She startled suddenly at the touch of Findlay's hands at her ankle. She glanced at him, unable to hold his gaze as he unlatched the strap and set her useless limb onto the table. A moment later, both legs were free and he was helping her to sit up.

She sat on the edge of the table, feeling her body throb in places she's never felt do anything of the sort before. She felt fluid rushing from between her legs and lunged up from the table. It felt as though her courses had come in a sudden rush.

She touched her hands to herself, thoughtlessly, squeezing her legs together.

"If ye feel a rush of fluid, that's entirely normal. Your body may continue to produce it for the next day or so."

"Am I bleeding?" She asked, panic stricken.

He smiled, touching her arm. "No, no, lass. It's completely normal. Seminal fluid may be clear or cloudy, but it isn't blood. Ye appear very healthy."

He gestured for her to take a seat and turned to his table, jotting something down into one of his many notebooks. After a moment, he turned back to her, his brow furrowed.

"May I ask how ye came to have those scars on your backside?"

Liv turned away, searching the stone wall for a means of escape from this question. She knew the scars he meant, scars she rarely saw herself, having never owned a full mirror. She remembered the last time she'd seen them, wide half circles of dark red, overlapping each other across her lower backside and thighs. She'd never thought to have to explain them. Her mother assured her she'd never marry, and no one would ever see them to wonder how they'd come to be there. Yet, here she was shrinking under the concerned gaze of Dr. Findlay Lennox. He came to stand just a stride away from her, watching in wait of response.

She took a deep breath. "Just birthmarks," she said.

He exhaled out his nose, pursing his lips. "They look like burns."

She paused, feeling his eyes on her. Finally, she spoke. "My mother always said I was a willful child."

He furrowed his brow. "They were from punishment?"

She nodded.

"I've never seen whip marks that look quite like that."

Liv shook her head. "They're no from whippin."

Findlay watched her face, waiting in silent expectation. Despite a desire to melt into the drain, she spoke. "She stopped whippin me when I was nineteen. I'd grown too old and it didn't have the same effect she wanted anymore. So one night when she was well in a mood, she pulled the bed warmer from the fire -"

Findlay inhaled sharply at this. "She beat ye with it?"

"Aye."

Findlay closed his eyes, touching Liv's hand gently. His face looked pained.

"She'd only take one or two goes with the pan each time, but it left those burns. Some of em took weeks to heal."

"Ye sweet girl. I'm so sorry. No wonder you've the melancholy."

Liv shrugged, giving a sad smile. "Aye. I imagine that'll be part of it."

Findlay leaned against the table beside her. "And what of your father? Did he agree with these beatings?"

Liv furrowed her brow. "He hanged himself when I was twelve."

Findlay exhaled.

"He had the melancholy, as ye say. Always did. Used to be troubled by dreams, as well. His were worse though. He believed they weren't dreams, said he was awake when they happened. That's why he – why he did what he did."

"Aye," Findlay said softly. "Seems he found an end to his troubles, no? 'To die. To sleep. To dream - no more.'"

"'To sleep perchance to dream – aye, there's the rub.'"

Findlay froze, staring at her as though she'd grown a second head. He swallowed, covering the startled response. "And ye have these dreams yourself?"

She took a breath, mulling this over. She'd never spoken of these troubles to anyone before, but Findlay's concern seemed honest – and he was a doctor. "His were different. He believed there was an angry man in the garden that would come to him at night, threaten him and the like. My mother would buy him whisky to help him sleep, as it was the only thing that stopped the dreams, he said."

Nobody believed him, but I did."

She stopped, faltering a moment with this tiny detail – a piece of her puzzle she'd never imagined sharing with another. Somehow, it felt safe to tell him her secrets now, in the wake of this strange serenity she felt from his expert touch.

"After he died, the angry man in the garden came to

me for the first time. But he wasn't angry at me. Told me stories as I fell asleep. I told my mother about him when I was twelve. I think she was glad to be rid of my father and his dreams. When she knew I had 'em too, she changed."

"Is that when she started beatin ye?"

"Aye."

Findlay leaned against the table, crossing his arms over her chest. "Ye have the dreams as well, then?"

Liv swallowed. "I'm afraid you'll think I'm mad if I say so."

"Ah, we all have dreams, Deliverance. Not all of us are mad."

Liv nodded. "Aye. Sometimes I do. Tonight was the first I've had in a long while."

Findlay reached for her face, brushing a strand of hair behind her ear. Then he seemed to catch himself, pulling his hand away as though her skin might burn him. "Well, you're safe here. No one'll lay a hand on ye. And if they do, ye come to me straight away, I'll sort them out. As for the dreams – we'll keep an eye, won't we?"

Liv smiled at the doctor for the first time, letting him see her face without an urgent desire to hide.

Findlay smiled back, offering a hand to help her down from the table. Then he made his way around the room, blowing out each lamp until the only light offered was from the single lamp in his hand. He escorted her up to the study, then the two of them made their way up to their chambers. Findlay stood at the bottom of the stairs as she made her way up to her room, her own lamp now cold.

"Get some rest, lass. Let me know how ye feel tomorrow, aye?"

Liv nodded down at him, then turned for her bedroom. She set the lamp on the bedside table, curled up under the piles of quilts and blankets, and was asleep in moments.

CHAPTER FOUR

"Oi, girl! Did ye no hear me?"

Liv jumped at the sound of Fionnula's stern tone, barking from across the kitchen. "I'm so sorry, I must've been off with the fairies."

"Aye, I'd say so. I need ye to bring tea down to Dr. Lennox and his guests before it gets cold, here."

Liv's stomach twisted, instantly. She had yet to see the doctor that morning, Findlay spending much of his day in his operating theater, as usual. Yet, she'd felt her heart race at every sound she heard from the parlor, every distant hum of a male voice in the distance. Patients and their family had come through, as well as several other men from the college, but Findlay had yet to show his face in the upstairs of the house. She was almost relieved at the distance, despite thinking of him constantly.

She'd slept better the night before than she had in many, many years, and her dreams were pleasant – unnervingly so, dreaming of the doctor and his infamous procedure until she woke with the familiar rush of fluid between her legs. She wanted to see him again, of course, but somehow the mere thought of him being close to her set her whole body on fire, face first.

"Are ye unwell? Your face is the color of a beet, child."

"I'm well. I am. Just a bit hot, is all," Liv said,

touching the back of her hand to her face.

"Well, get away from the fire, then. Bring the doctors their tea and come right back up. I've an errand for ye to run."

Liv nodded, lifting the heavy tray from the kitchen table. The office door was wide open, betraying the sound of voices within.

"Ah, I'll have to think on it," Findlay said.

"Think on it? I've a waiting list for my classes, lad. What is there to think on?"

This voice was unfamiliar, boisterous and excited. Liv hovered outside the door, working to build up the courage to enter the operating theater and lay eyes on the tall redheaded man within.

"I know ye have, Rab. I just haven't yet shaken the last time," Findlay said.

"Oh, aye. I remember. Understood, lad. Understood. Still, there's much to learn, much to discover."

"I'll consider it, then. Soon enough, I'll come round _"

Liv stepped onto the stairwell and the conversation stopped instantly as Findlay rose to meet her at the bottom of the stairs. She averted her eyes as best she could, which was quite the feat, as she'd only just begun her trek down two full flights of steps.

"Gentlemen, this is the new member of my household. Deliverance, I'd like for ye to meet my colleagues – here, let me take that."

Findlay snatched the tray from her hands and set it on a nearby table before taking her hand and pulling her toward the gathered men. They were glancing over several notebooks, sketches of various human forms and limbs, all open and flayed, showing bone and muscle beneath. Liv averted her eyes from that as well. She was sure she looked like a blind girl, darting her eyes about the place.

"This is Dr. Knox," Findlay said, gesturing to a bald man with brown sideburns that cut like ax blades across his cheeks.

He gave a dramatic half bow, taking Liv's hand in his. "What a delight, Deliverance. And may I say, what a glorious name ye have?"

She returned the bow with a short curtsy. "Thank ye, Doctor, sir."

"Aye, 'Doctor Sir.' I like that."

Findlay turned her to another man, this one older, and more stoic, his hair fully white at his jowls. "And this is Doctor Munro."

The older doctor nodded in her direction, giving a half grunt of greeting.

"It's a pleasure to meet ye both," she said, her entire body tense against the sensation of Findlay's hand, gently resting at her lower back.

Dr. Knox gave a flamboyant gesture, leaning toward Findlay. *"Morde meum globes! Numquid, cum crisas, blandior esse potes?"*

Liv spun toward the doctor, her brow furrowed. He met her scathing gaze with a mischievous smirk. She turned her eyes to Findlay who seemed quite curious, then curtsied to take her leave of them.

The latin speaking Dr. Knox dove for the tray of food, snatching up a small tea cake and devouring it with grateful moans of pleasure. "What a feast you've brought us, lass. Our Dr. Lennox will want to keep a close eye on ye, or he might find me stealin ye away, to my home."

Liv offered a smile and another curtsy as she turned

back toward the staircase, desperate to leave Findlay's presence so she might breathe again.

"Will ye excuse me, friends? I need to have a word with our Deliverance."

Oh god, what had she done? Fired. She was fired, finally. Shouldn't have dreamed about the tall doctor all night. Shouldn't have thought about him all day. Could he read it on her face?

Findlay followed her up the stairs and into the parlor, half shutting the door behind him. "How did ye sleep, then? Any improvement?"

She sighed in obvious relief. He noticed, and gave her a furrowed brow, though he was smiling.

"Aye, I - I did. Very much so," she said, nearly stumbling over the words.

"Is that so? Well, that's grand! Any trouble with dreams? Did ye wake at all."

"No, I slept like the dead through the night. The baby next door didn't even rouse me," Liv said, smiling.

He furrowed his brow again, but this time he wasn't smiling. "There's no bairns next door, lass."

"Oh aye. I heat the wee thing cryin each night. Keeps me up, poor thing."

He stood in the theater doorway, crossing his arms over his chest. "Are ye sure it's no a street cat, perhaps? Or a bird of some kind."

Liv chuckled, humoring him. "I know well enough what a bairn sounds like, sir."

Findlay turned toward the office door, shutting it fully. "Can ye tell me which direction it is coming from, then? I might need to check up on someone if they're cryin at all hours."

Liv crossed to the parlor window and pointed down

the narrow alleyway that separated their building from the neighbors. "Down the end of the close. Through the far wall of my room."

Findlay glanced down the way, his brow in constant furrow now. He nodded. "Well, alright then. I'll have a quick visit later this afternoon, then."

"Oh goodness. I hope the poor wee thing is alright."

"I'm sure she is. Thank ye again for bringing our tea, love – err, Deliverance."

She curtsied and turned for the kitchen. "Gratias tibi ago."

"Precare," she said, then stopped in the kitchen doorway.

Findlay chuckled to himself, running his hand over his face. "Ye speak latin, ye know Shakespeare -"

"I don't know Shakespe -"

"'To sleep perchance to dream.' Ye quoted him last night."

She swallowed, glancing around the room. "My father was fond of books like yourself."

"Of books and ancient languages, it seems. I apologize for my colleague."

"It's fine. I don't know what he said."

"Aye, I think ye do. Ye had a scandalized look to match a phrase like 'bite my balls.'"

Liv turned her eyes down and her nostrils flared, but she straightened, waiting to be excused. "Is that what he said. Well, I never -"

Findlay chuckled. "Fine, then. We'll pretend ye didn't understand him, aye." He watched her a moment, silently – appraisingly. "Ye seem a rather accomplished girl, Deliverance."

She curtsied, warily. "I thank ye, sir."

He nodded to himself, turning back for the theater door. "Let me know if you've need of anythin. I'll be downstairs for the afternoon."

With that, he turned for the office door, disappearing back into the recesses of his operating theater. The boisterous voice of Dr. Knox echoed off the high walls as he welcomed Findlay back.

"There ye are! Three shilling should do it. Take my coat."

Fionnula was in a state as Liv returned to the kitchen. Despite the rather uneventful afternoon, something about Findlay having company rattled Fionnula, fiercely.

Well, are they staying for tea, dinner, into the evening? Shall I prepare dinner, as well? Has he even a clue that we're no prepared for hosting?

Liv was wrapped in Fionnula's generous coat and being hustled out the door with three shillings in her pocket a moment later.

"Make your way to Grassmarket and bring home Haggis and a bushel of root vegetables, I don't care which," she'd demanded as she pushed Liv out the door.

Liv stood out on the street, watching as a covered carriage came down the way, the horse's hooves clomping against the cobblestone streets. She waited for it to pass, then followed it toward Cowgate, careful not to step in any droppings it left in its wake.

The Cowgate was bustling as she made her way through, many of the voices shouting in what sounded like Irish accents. She clutched her skirts, lifting them just so as she hopped over the unfortunate rivers of filth that ran down from the alleyways. Grassmarket was bustling, the familiar smell of livestock and horses drifting through. Liv scanned the faces, stalls, and storefronts, looking for a butcher of some kind. She spotted hanging sausages in a window front and barreled across the way, just before a line of three horses was brought through to the horse market.

The butcher wrapped her sheep's stomach in brown paper and made change, shooting her a grin of missing teeth as he handed the tied package across the counter. He offered her directions to the nearest stall for root vegetables, and she was on her way, feeling proud to be of use in the strange place. She dodged figures and farmers as they hurried through on their own errands.

"Deli! Very!"

Liv heard the sound of someone calling strange words, but was too keen on grabbing the stall owner's attention to recognize the voice.

"Rancy! Livvy!"

The last word caught her attention, stopping her mid-sentence. She turned to meet the beaming face of Janet Brown, her missing tooth offering a black cavern at the corner of her mouth.

"What, ye don't like our new names?" She asked, nudging Liv, then tugging at the tie that held her Haggis within its brown paper bundle.

"Oi, stop that!" Liv hissed, slapping Janet's hand away as Mary tilted and resettled the hat atop Liv's head. She shook her away, turning back to the now exasperated stall owner as she requested a bushel of root vegetables.

"Well, which ones, ae?"

Liv shook her head. "She said it didn't matter. Whatever you've got?"

He glowered at her, turning away to collect her order as Mary scanned down Liv's backside, as though appraising a prize heifer.

"I dunno, Janet. D'ye think she's had it done?"

Janet grinned. "Well, course she 'as. D'ye see the way her hips swivel when she walks, now?"

Liv jerked toward Janet, then Mary, her face burning hot, and both girls burst into laughter. Janet reached for Liv's ass and gave it a squeeze, causing Liv to shriek in the middle of the market. Several heads turned to eye her, but Mary offered them all a piece of her mind.

"Go bout your business, nosy bastards!"

An older woman with her young daughter harrumphed, rushing her child away, but a young man in shabby clothes smiled and made his way over.

"Is miss unwell?"

Mary put her arm around the young man's shoulders, giving him a squeeze as the stall owner took Liv's coins from across the table of produce.

"No, Jamie. She's right as rain. How are ye, then, lad?"

He nodded, excessively. "Well, well. Very well. Fine day, we're havin. Fine day."

"Aye, that it is," Mary said, then she planted a kiss on the young man's cheek and loosed him into the crowd of market goers, his face as flushed as a plum.

Mary turned to meet Liv's gaze, gesturing after the young man. "That's Daft Jamie."

"Daft Jamie?"

Janet nodded. "Aye. Poor lad is 'aff his heid.'"

Liv watched the young man go, offering up a greeting to strangers as he passed. He had a strange way about him, like blissful ignorance that made him kind to everyone he met. Liv felt for the young man, wondering what kind of person he'd have become, had he his wits.

"Am I to stand here all day, then?"

Liv startled around to find the stall owner holding her bushel to her. She took it, tucking the change into her coat pocket as she piled the haggis atop the bushel and turned back toward Cowgate.

"Where ye headin then?" Janet asked, following just behind her.

Liv hustled along, glancing to her newfound companions. "Just back home. Fionnula'll skin me if I don't get back soon."

"Ah, she is a right brawler, idn't she?" Mary asked, giggling. "Makes a splendid berry tart, though."

Janet groaned in agreement as they both matched Liv's pace, accompanying her into the dark streets of Cowgate. Mary and Janet both waved and beckoned to a few people as they made their way through, clearly recognizing some of the young men milling about.

After a few minutes of listening to Mary and Janet making snide comments on the prowess - or lack thereof - of each man they greeted, Janet finally slapped Liv's backside as they reached the corner toward Surgeon's Square.

"Tell us, then, Livvy – have ye had it done, then?"

Liv's cheeks flushed, and she tucked her head down, hoping her hat would hide her face. It failed, and the two women began to laugh heartily, their voices echoing off the high buildings of the medical college.

"That's our girl! Did ye enjoy it? Ye did, didn't ye? Best thing you've ever felt? Christ that man is a miracle."

Mary pretended to swoon, leaning into a nearby doorway.

Janet laughed. "Has he done it more than once, then?"

Liv shook her head. "No. Just the once. Said it'd help with my sleeplessness."

"Oh I bet it did!" Mary said, her voice bouncing back at them, startling a couple young men making their way into the college. "Our dear Dr. Lennox is a treasure, idn't he?"

"Doctor, my arse. What that man does is a bloody miracle! Should be Saint Findlay, I say!"

"Aye, Saint Findlay it is!" Mary agreed, turning into the small alley that led to Dr. Lennox's practice and home.

Liv stopped at the steps that led up to her door, giving a polite nod to the two women. She wanted to smile at them, perhaps engage this conversation, but she was so desperately shy, embarrassed at the thought of anyone knowing that a man had touched her in such places – that a man like Findlay had touched her in such places. And worst of all, that she'd loved it.

Janet reached past Liv, turning the knob for her to go inside. "Tell the doctor you're having trouble sleepin, for us. Countin the days til Wednesday, I am."

Liv thanked her, shifted into the hallway, and turned to say goodbye.

"Ye tell Skinny Malinky Longlegs we said Hullo, aye?" Mary said, pointing to the nearest window. Then she leaned in, whispering. "And next time he's fiddlin ye, I dare ye to grab his cock!"

Liv's whole body nearly imploded with embarrassment as Janet collapsed in laughter against the nearby building. Mary just gave Liv a tip of an imaginary hat and the two women sauntered around the corner and out of sight.

Liv fought with the bushel in the hallway, flustered immeasurably by Mary's boisterous words. *My god, what if he heard that?*

She shifted there, leaning her hip against the door until she heard it click. Then she headed toward the kitchen.

"She's hearing a bairn cryin?"

Liv stopped just outside the kitchen door, frozen.

"Aye. I asked Dr. Munro - asked after a bairn. He's said he thought it was coming from here. Thought I might have a patient that gave birth with no place to go."

"Findlay, she can't stay up there. It's only gonnae get worse, and ye know it."

"Well I can't rightly put her in the guest quarters. A young woman on the same floor as myself -"

"That's no what I mean, lad. She's been here less than a fortnight and she's already hearin -"

Liv deliberately stomped her feet on the hallway floor, bumping into the front door again to announce her arrival with a bit more sound. The conversation stopped, the kitchen door opening into the hallway as Findlay's face appeared, holding it open for her to come through.

"Ah, looks like you've got yourself quite a prize there. Tell me that's no Haggis."

Liv gave him a startled look. *Was I not supposed to get haggis?*

"Course it is! Looks as though it'll just be us

tonight," Fionnula said, snatching the bushel from Liv's arms and hauling it over to the kitchen table.

Findlay smiled at Liv, shrugging. "Aye, I apologize, Fionn. I didn't know ye were plannin a fancy dinner. I'd've had them stay."

Fionnula shook her head. "No bother. It'll make a fine meal. Go on then, lass. Go light the fires for the evenin. I'll get the veg stewin."

Liv did her best to eat with Fionnula in the kitchen, Findlay taking his supper in his office as usual. Despite it being some of the finer Haggis she'd ever tasted, her stomach was in knots. Fionnula seemed to not want her there, despite Dr. Munro confessing to hearing the baby as well. Where was the poor thing? It was as if Fionnula blamed her for being able to hear the child cry. It was so unfair, Liv nearly teared up as she leaned over her haggis, flattening the meat with her fork until it was spread thin across the plate. When Fionnula finally sent her off to make a final round of the fires, Liv was grateful to be out of the woman's company.

She checked on Findlay's fire, making sure it would last into the later hours when he finally left his work and took to bed.

Then she made her way up to her dark quarters and slumped into her bed. Much to her relief, there was no sound of the baby. Instead, she was kept awake by the constant thrumming of her own thoughts.

CHAPTER FIVE

It was too good to be true. However long she'd managed to sleep, the high pitched wail cut through her dreams, waking her instantly. Liv opened her eyes, staring up at the dusty beams of her ceiling. She took a deep breath and closed her eyes, willing herself deaf.

With each break in the wail, there would be an almost torturous prayer that this was the silence that would last, that this was the sound of the child being tended to. Yet, each time the duration would change, some silences long, some short, but all of them ended with the same desperate wail.

Liv growled to herself, pulling her pillow from under her head and covering her face. Though the cries were muffled there, they were no less painful. Liv closed her eyes and thought of the previous night, not just of the deep sleep she'd managed, but of the magic that caused her that sleep – the sleep of the dead.

She took a deep breath, smelling the lavender oil she rinsed in her hair now seeped into the fabric of her pillow. She let the pillow lay across her face and lost herself in memory, fighting to drown out the child. She remembered the way Findlay looked standing in his study doorway, his sleeves rolled up, the lamp light glinting off the satin of his vest. She remembered the way his chest looked bare, the curled ruddy hairs, the pale of his skin. She began to imagine him touching her again, but this time, his chest bare, letting her see his body and the way it moved when he was close to her.

She swallowed, wishing she could experience this procedure of his again, but never daring to go in search of it. Medical or no, she wasn't thinking of him as a doctor. She was thinking of him as a man.

No, if she was to find sleep as a result of that procedure – as a result of the release it offered – perhaps she could find it herself.

Liv turned her face toward the wall, letting the cool air reach her lips beneath the pillow, then with the quiet of a creature afraid to be caught, tugged her nightshirt up over her hips, and reached her hand between her legs.

She searched for the places that Findlay's hands played so expertly, touching her fingertips against wet places she'd never thought to explore for fear of reprisals from her constantly watchful mother.

God, what would she do to me if she could see this now?

She reached lower, trying to find the entry Findlay's hands had found, but fumbling to touch the same places. Though her hands felt good, each movement stilled the moment it began to feel truly pleasurable, as though her arms fell exhausted in response to sensation. She turned her face to the other side, arching her back to reach lower.

Movement in the room stilled her, instantly. She froze, staring out from under the pillow, too terrified to move it. She moved her hands over her belly, shutting her eyes tight. It was only then that she noticed the change in the crying voice. The muffled sobs were no longer those of an infant.

Liv shifted beneath the pillow, scanning the floor of the room. She saw the shadow cast on the floor by her bedroom door. It was open again.

Liv lifted her hand to her pillow, and slowly began to lift it from her face. The skirts were the first of the woman to come into view. Liv stifled there, slamming the pillow back down onto her face. There was a woman standing by her bed.

She waited, listening to the cries. They were long and low, soft keening that sounded at times closer to singing than it did to sobs.

She thought of the madwoman, thought of her breaking into the doctor's home and finding her way up stairs, watching Liv sleep, waiting to unleash something upon her. Liv turned her head toward her wall and closed her eyes tight.

"Deliverance?" Findlay called from downstairs.

Liv gasped from beneath her pillow. She dared not open her eyes, but she called back nonetheless. "Yes? I'm here."

Suddenly, she felt a heavy presence near her bed, as though someone was leaning over her, their face drawing close to hers beyond the pillow. Liv could feel their breath blow past the pillow and into her face. There were words hidden in the breathing, barely tangible, but there nonetheless. Deliverance opened her, and spoke the word that repeated over and over in her mind.

"Margaret."

Despite all her courage, this voice whispering from deep in the corners of her mind terrified her, and she screamed, flailing the pillow out and over her to fight the woman away.

There was nothing there.

"Deliverance, are ye no well?"

Liv turned toward the door just as Findlay appeared in the darkness of the hall outside. The shape of him startled her for an instant, causing her chest to tighten to such a degree that she kicked her legs out across the bed, fighting to get as far away from the figure as possible.

Findlay lunged down, touching his hand to her forehead. "You're havin a bad dream, lass. You're alright."

Liv shook her head, her eyes darting around the room as though she might spot the woman hiding in a corner somewhere. "I wasn't asleep! She was here! She was right here!"

She pointed toward the space beside the bed, the room aglow with gray light from outside. The room was empty, save for the concerned face of Dr. Findlay Lennox, settling himself at her bedside like the physician he was. He eyed her with austere curiosity before following her gaze around the room.

"You're in no danger, girl. There's nothin here."

Liv opened her mouth to protest, ready to assure him that she had indeed seen something - someone, even felt their breath. Yet Fionnula's words replayed in her mind instantly.

She can't be up there - Only a fortnight and she's already hearin -

The subtle gray light played across his face, etching the lines of concern there for her to see plainly. She frowned, and despite every ounce of desire she felt to share this moment, to make him acknowledge what she'd seen, instead she nodded. "Aye, just a bad dream."

Findlay forced a smile, running a hand over her

upper arm. "You're in a new place, a city, no less. It's no small adjustment. There's no shame in cryin, lass."

"I wasn't -" She stopped, then she took a deep breath. He'd heard it, too. "Alright."

Findlay collected the quilts from the foot of the bed where she'd kicked them and pulled them up over her as she turned onto her side. She wanted him to stay, wanted to beg him to sit by her until she fell asleep, as though perhaps his presence would stave off the crying woman – even the crying baby. Yet, he turned for the door, and she lay there silent.

He began to shut her bedroom door when Liv lifted her head. "Dr. Lennox?"

He turned back to her, smiling. "It's Findlay."

She nodded. "Findlay."

"What is it?"

Liv watched his face, the terror of that moment stealing any sense of fear she had of meeting his gaze. She watched his pale blue eyes. "D'ye know a Margaret?"

Findlay Lennox betrayed himself wholly in that single instant, his face falling with such sadness, she nearly crumbled to see it.

He recovered quickly, but not completely. "Where did ye hear that name?"

Liv frowned. "She was the one cryin."

Findlay's frown overtook his face, and he turned away. "We'll speak on this tomorrow, aye? Get some rest, now."

With that, he shut the door to her bedroom and was gone.

Liv listened to his slow footsteps retreating down the stairs and stared at the space her open bedroom door had hidden from view a moment before. There was a woman, her face obscured by shadow, standing in the corner of her room.

Liv felt her chest tighten as she watched the figure a moment, waiting for her eyes to adjust, for the impossibility of it to set in and somehow make the woman vanish. Liv quickly snatched up her box of matches and lit one, holding her shaking hand to the lamp wick and turning it up to its brightest. She glanced back toward the corner of the room, now fully bathed in golden light.

The figure was gone.

Liv placed the cover onto the still burning lamp and turned onto her side, her face toward the wall. Then she prayed softly to herself, watching her shadowed silhouette dance on the wooden planks.

CHAPTER SIX

"Come on, lass! Be quicker, will ye?"

Liv moved about the kitchen like a phantom, barely able to focus on any task laid before her. She hadn't slept in several days again, her lamp oil having burned down by the third night, leaving her to wake to the sudden gut-wrenching fear of knowing that someone was in the room with her – that if she turned, she would see them.

"What're ye on about, girl? Are ye no right in the heid, then?"

Liv shook her head, vehemently. "I'm sorry. I am tryin."

Fionnula shifted by her, hauling the hot kettle off the fire. She turned to Liv, giving her a stern glare. Then it softened. "Aye. I know ye are. Come now, carry this down for the examination and get out quick as ye can. The students will be arriving shortly."

This was a first in her time with Dr. Lennox. He'd seen many patients – husbands bringing their wives in; other women like Mary and Janet, volunteering their services for Findlay to perfect his approach. He'd not performed the procedure on her again, growing too busy to even notice her in his preparations of this class.

It was an exhibition – an unveiling of the procedure itself, of its impact on patient's behavior. Findlay had room for a dozen or so students to fit comfortably in his operating theater, but thirty had paid to attend. He'd not had time to even eat, let alone speak to his scullery maid.

Liv hefted the heavy kettle at her side, strolling down the stairs and into the exhibition room. Findlay wasn't alone below, a familiar figure standing by as Findlay bustled about with his notes.

"You've quite the attendance today, lad. I'm impressed."

Dr. Knox leaned back on one of Findlay's tables, his hip folding several note papers that Findlay left there.

"Aye, and I'll thank ye to no remind me."

Dr. Knox scoffed. "Ah, you'll be grand! It's a rather exciting breakthrough, if ye ask me."

Liv scooted past the two men, coming to the wash basin against the near wall. She poured the steaming contents in, letting the kettle run empty, then turned back toward the stairs.

"Ye will come to the next dissection, won't ye lad? It's only right that I return the favor."

Findlay made a soft humming noise, a mix between an affirmative grunt and a strange displeased sound he made when he idly sipped his tea and it was too hot. "That's kind of ye."

"Come on, now. It's been months since that girl – what was it? I forget her name, just now."

Findlay shot a quick glance at Liv as she made her way up the stairs, then averted his eyes. "Her name was Margaret."

"Ah, yes. Margaret. Rest her soul."

Liv slipped back into the parlor just as the front door bell clanged down the hallway. Liv made her way down the hall, pulling her apron from around her waist before opening the door to greet the figures outside.

They filtered in over the course of twenty minutes, the last of the men all huffed and disconcerted at the thought of being late and missing the class. Their voices rumbled under the floorboards, carrying from the upper landing of the operating theater, even with the door shut. Fionnula moved with fury again, a behavior she always exhibited when there was any sort of company. Liv simply followed her routine, giving Fionnula a wide berth.

Suddenly, Findlay's voice boomed off the high stone walls of his theater, and Liv couldn't help but smile. Despite his nervous demeanor just a few moments earlier, he'd clearly turned it off in time to teach his class. Liv moved about the kitchen, washing up and scrubbing pots, making a point to do so as quietly as she could, listening to the doctor below.

"As many of ye already know, the term Hysteria is derivative of the ancient Greek term, hysterikos, or 'suffering of the womb.' It was and is still believed that many ailments of the mind and spirit can correlate with ailments of the female reproductive system. I've discovered evidence of this best represented by the common flux of emotions during pregnancy, or even those women suffer during certain stages in their cycles. There are those, including myself, who are workin to better understand this correlation and the medical applications of such a theory, but as this approach grows in -"

"What are ye doin, girl?" Fionnula snapped, whipping a damp towel in Liv's direction. She'd stopped scrubbing the floor and was kneeling there, listening to Findlay's commanding voice, enjoying the clear attempts he made at a more 'proper' accent. She'd thought it proper enough, already.

"I swear, Deliverance, if ye don't stop with this nonsense, I'll take the belt to ye."

Liv recoiled, instantly, moving across the floor as though she'd spotted a rat scurrying by.

Fionnula stopped dead, frowning down at her. "Come now, love. Ye know I didn't mean it."

Liv's hands were shaking as she moved to rise from her knees, but Fionnula moved across the kitchen with surprising speed. She stooped to meet Liv's eyes, and searched every inch of her face. From this close, Liv could smell the tea on her breath, see the crow's feet etched into the corners of her eyes, and the amber-green flecks that gave her brown eyes their honey color. Liv swallowed.

"Are ye still hearing that bairn, then?"

Liv bit her lip. Say no, she thought. Say no, all is right as rain, or she might convince Findlay to let you go.

Liv shook her head.

"Come now, child. Don't lie to me."

Liv darted her eyes away, trying to turn her face, but Fionnula took it in her hands and turned her, making Liv return the gaze.

"Ye touched, then?"

"Pardon? No! I'm no touched – what d'ye mean by that?"

Fionnula glared into Liv's eyes, one at a time, then took a deep breath and rose to her full height. "It's no to be ashamed of. Your no the only one."

Liv stared at the woman, unable to argue with the knowing look. "How d'ye know?"

Liv had spoken before she could stop herself. The

strange relief she felt to hear Fionnula say such a thing pulled the words out as though they'd been tied to the end of a string.

Fionnula leaned over a small counter in the corner of the kitchen and began inspecting and picking at small bundles of herbs, pulling them together into her left hand. After a moment in silence, she turned to Liv and lifted the small bundle of green over an empty kettle and made a grand flourish of cracking the stems. She let the leaves fall into the pot. "How d'ye think?"

Fionnula made her way across the kitchen to fill the kettle, Liv still frozen there by the strange energy that now filled the kitchen. Fionnula brought the kettle to the fire and hung it from a spit.

"Have ye ever heard of a white woman?"

Liv gave a quiet gasp. Such a term was common in Highlands. She had heard it. Many times.

"I'll take that as aye, then. Well, ye know they're no evil, aye?"

Liv nodded. "Aye."

Fionnula stopped at this, giving Liv a surprised, appraising look.

"My Da spoke of them. Said there were many still up in the Highlands."

"Aye, that there are. Though not all are true to their word if they're claimin to be such a thing."

Liv watched Fionnula collect another small handful of herbs and drop them into the waiting kettle. "Is that what ye are?" Liv asked.

Fionnula smiled. "Aye. And I gather ye are, as well."

Liv startled at this, shaking her head in near fear at such a notion. "No, no me. I'm no like that."

Fionnula raised an eyebrow, then gave a soft grunt,

turning her attention to the pot over the fire. "If ye say so."

Her father's talk of white women became one of the reasons her mother later took the cane to Liv's back. Liv and her father had always earned smiles and gifts from the local eccentric, Mrs. Ferguson. She made poppets and drank mead, kept cats and took visits from the heartbroken and the ambitious. Every time they crossed her path on the way to church, or to visit relatives, she gave Liv and her father a small bouquet of herbs. Mrs. Ferguson began delivering them to Liv's door after her father died and Amelia began keeping Liv home from church.

'Abominations like ye have no place in the house of the lord,' she'd said.

Liv was beaten red for each visit Mrs. Ferguson paid her, never receiving the little trinkets she'd brought.

"Ye know there's no bairn up there, don't ye?" Fionnula asked, snapping her from her spell.

Liv swallowed. "Pardon?"

"The bairn keepin ye up nights. Ye know full well that cryin ain't comin from no livin thing."

Liv tried to shake her head, but the crying woman flooded her mind, hovering in the shadows of her room. The memory of it sent shivers through her, and she cringed to think of it.

Fionnula sighed. "Ye do know."

Liv opened her mouth to protest, but no words came at first. Then, a moment later she looked up to watch Fionnula return to the now whistling kettle, lifting it from the spit and carting it to the kitchen table.

"Who is Margaret?"

The kettle dropped onto the wooden table with a loud thud, and Fionnula turned her eyes on Liv as though she might set her afire with them. "And ye say you're no a white woman. What is this, now? Did Findlay speak to ye of her?"

Liv shook her head. "No, he hasn't. He wouldn't say either."

"No surprising, that. Here, drink this down, child."

Fionnula crossed the kitchen with a steaming mug cupped in both hands like some precious thing.

Liv took it from her. "What is it?"

"It's for your nerves. And for your spirits. I'll make another brew when your off to bed. See if we can't stave off the visitors."

"Visitors?"

"Aye, visitors."

The doorbell clanged in the front hall and Fionnula gestured for Liv to stay where she was. A moment later, there was a commotion in the hallway as a woman was led through the house, similarly distraught as the madwoman from a fortnight earlier. Liv listened to her wails and grunts, fighting to ignore the sounds as she stared into the contents of her mug. She'd taken no more than two sips, but already she felt warm, the strange haze behind her eyes clearing slowly, as though she'd found an hour's sleep in that single sip.

"Deliverance?"

Liv startled, turning to find Fionnula returned to the kitchen, staring at her with raised brows. She shook her head, mortified to think Fionnula had found her sleeping there, still upright, still holding her mug, but asleep.

The older woman took a deep breath as the sounds

of the exhibition suddenly shifted, coming to include a wailing female voice within the cacophony of male voices.

"Was your mother touched, then? Like ye?"

"I'm no touched," Liv said, defiantly. She didn't like this word now any more than she had when her mother used it. Being touched was a sin. Being touched was worthy of punishment and rejection. Being touched made her father kill himself –

"No, was your father, aye?"

Liv opened her mouth to protest, but the shock of Fionnula's confident tone stopped her. Had she read something on Liv's face?

"There's no shame in it, love. Tis a blessing."

Liv glared into her mug. "It doesn't feel like a blessin."

With that she slopped down the last three big gulps of her strange tea, cringing as the contents moved in her throat.

"Aye, I imagine it doesn't. What did your father tell ye of the spirits?"

The mug felt heavy in her hands, and Liv rose from her seat, setting the empty cup on the kitchen table before answering. "He didn't."

Fionnula crossed herself, something Liv found strange from a woman who proudly proclaimed herself to practice witchcraft. The mere notion of this would have turned Amelia Baird into a tempest of righteous and holy judgment, doing all she could to summon up the wrath of her beloved church and every member therein.

Liv felt almost comforted by Fionnula's strangeness.

"Did he no?"

"But he saw them, aye?" Fionnula asked, making herself busy by chopping some potatoes.

"Aye. He had terrible dreams when I was a bairn. Said they came - a man came - said angry things to him."

Fionnula moved toward the fire, turning the roasting pheasant on the spit. "Did ye ever see these angry things?"

"No til my Da died. The man came to my room then, but he wasn't angry with me."

Fionnula smiled to herself just so. "No?"

Liv shook her head. "No. He told me stories to help me fall asleep. I told mother, but I think she didn't like havin a daughter who suffered the same dreams as my Dad."

Fionnula gestured to Liv to keep going.

Liv swallowed, searching for the pieces of the story that wanted to be shared. She'd never told anyone these details of her life. She'd been too ashamed to want anyone to know she bore scars all over her legs and backside from a monstrous mother who treated her more like a dirty secret and slave than a child.

"Was the angry man the only one ye saw?"

She nodded. "Aye – til I came here."

Fionnula sighed. "Aye, seems they find ye when you're near."

"But why? Why me?" Liv asked and her tone betrayed more worry, more exhaustion than she'd ever intended.

Fionnula frowned, setting the knife down beside the tall pile of cubed white and orange vegetables. She took a deep breath. "Imagine a lighthouse - you've seen such a thing up there in Inverness, aye?"

"I have, aye."

"Well, imagine you've been lost at sea. You're floating there alone in the dark, sure you'll drown soon enough with no land in sight."

Liv furrowed her brow. "I'd rather no imagine such things. Sounds dreadful."

"Well, imagine ye spot a lighthouse near. Ye may be lost and tired, but ye see that light, you're gonnae do all ye can to get their attention, are ye no?"

"Aye."

Fionnula scooped the parsnips and carried them over to the stove, letting them roll of her hands and into the pot, each one falling with a tiny 'plop.'

"See now, to these poor souls, you're the lighthouse, ye ken?"

"I don't understand."

"See, they can see ye, can tell ye see them as well. You're their only contact with land, so they do all they can to make ye acknowledge them – save em from drownin, as it were."

Liv slumped down onto the bench by the hallway door. "How do I shut off the bloody light?"

Her hands shot to her mouth, shooting Fionnula a pained look of apology for the sudden salty language.

Fionnula smirked at her from across the kitchen table. "Ye tell em to bloody sod off."

Liv smiled at the matron of the house, feeling a sudden swell of affection for the wise creature. That moment of reverence was quickly cut short as the parlor suddenly burst to life.

The hallway filled with figures at a constant pace; young men making their way up from the operating theater, discussing what they'd seen in hushed tones as they collected their coats and slipped out the front door in groups. The voices were excited, many of them speaking of Dr. Lennox with admiration.

"Did ye see how she changed? Had ye any notion such a thing was possible?"

"Did ye ask about next class? Will he teach the procedure itself?"

Some of the voices were English and Irish, and she was sure she heard an accent that could only be American – though she'd never heard a real American before.

Fionnula returned to her work as though Liv wasn't there, keeping feverishly busy as the crowd filtered through on their way out. After the footsteps died away, the unfortunate woman was escorted through the hallway, her demeanor as docile now as a well fed bairn.

Liv moved toward the parlor door, listening for his familiar voice. Instead she could only hear the boisterous regaling of Dr. Robert Knox, holding court to the last of the idlers – students waiting to interview the innovator, Dr. Findlay Lennox.

"Go on down and ask the doctor when he'll take his tea. The nips are soft," Fionnula said after a moment. "I'll make ye another round of tea. Need to wake ye up, lass."

Liv curled up under her covers, her face turned to the wall as it was every night when she attempted sleep. The lamp was still spent, Liv being too shy to ask for more oil so soon after the last request. She began to envy the Jews of ancient biblical tales, with their eight nights of light. She curled into her pillow, feeling warm and heavy from Fionnula's tea. Perhaps, she would sleep tonight. Perhaps she'd sleep through the slow creak of her door opening, betraying the sudden arrival of her unwanted roommate. Liv lay there with her head on her pillow and closed her eyes.

The sound was high pitched and slow, like a breathless groan deep in the throat of some dying thing. Though she'd been asleep a moment before, the familiar sound woke her as though someone had blown a trumpet in her ear. She felt her heart pounding in her ears and throat, the sudden panic of being woken by something in the room – something that wasn't supposed to be there. Liv closed her eyes tight as the door finally stopped moving and the creak ceased. The woman would be standing there, her face shrouded by shadow, just as she was every night.

Yet, this time Liv clenched her fists and braced.

"Show your strength," Fionnula had said. "Tell them you'll no have them comin about. Command them to leave."

Liv had argued against such a proud and confident response to something that simply shouldn't be, but Fionnula assured her of her method.

"It is the only way. They are no of this world – no anymore. Command them to go, and they must. This is our world, no theirs."

Liv planted her hands against the mattress, and with another deep breath flung herself upright to face the terrifying figure in the doorway.

"I demand ye leave this -"

She stopped dead, staring at the female figure that stood hovering there. Despite her face in shadow, Liv recognized the dress, the light cream fabric with pink roses and green leaves. Liv fought to focus her eyes on the woman's face.

"Mary?" She whispered.

The bedroom seemed to vibrate, then the bedroom

door shifted on its hinges just so. Liv watched it, breathless. Then suddenly, with a force no living thing could have summoned, the heavy door slammed shut, rattling the beams overhead and the panes of her windows with a monstrous shudder.

Liv stifled a cry, fright shaking her to her bones, but concern - sudden overwhelming concern pushed her to move through that fear. She jumped up from her bed and went for the door. The knob turned, but the door would not open. She felt it shift in the doorjamb, the give and take of someone holding the doorknob on the other side, keeping the door shut. Liv banged on the door, hollering to the woman outside. "Mary! Open the door!"

She twisted the knob again, feeling the tension of someone just outside refusing to let it turn. She kicked the door, fighting with the person outside. The room changed suddenly. That same unmitigated panic surged in her chest, pulling up from her stomach and into her throat. She turned to look over her shoulder.

The crying woman stood just inches from her face, her eyes clouded by death.

Liv screamed with such fury, it shook the room. She lunged away from the figure, slamming against the door as the woman reached toward her own belly. The dark blue fabric of her dress grew darker, as though her body was open and bleeding beneath. The stain grew, bleeding out in all directions, soaking her skirts as it moved across her like some living thing. The woman pulled her hands away from her belly, her fingers covered in red.

My bairn? Please. Give her back to me.

This voice came from somewhere as distant as the moon, but as close as though Liv had said the words herself. She scrambled back to her feet, turning away from the figure for the door. She scrambled for the doorknob, pulling with all her might against the force that wanted to keep her within. The door burst open into her face, knocking her backward.

"Deliverance! Are ye no well?"

Liv fought to steady herself, the beams of the ceiling fading and focusing in strange pattern as she lifted a hand to her head. She touched the back of her head where she'd made contact with the hardwood floor. It was sore, but there was no wetness there – no blood.

Findlay took her arm gently as she tried to sit up. "No, no. Go slow now. Let me look at ye."

His cold hands slipped into the tendrils of her hair, now curled wildly and tangled from sleep. He touched his fingers against the egg that was swiftly forming on the back of her head, and she hissed.

"Ah, that'll be sore then, aye? What happened?"

"Mary…" She said.

"Mary? What of her?"

Liv pointed toward the door. "She was here. Why's she here so late?"

Findlay furrowed his brow at her. When he spoke it oozed patience. Almost too much for her to tolerate. "She isn't here, lass. There's no one."

"She was! She wouldn't let me leave the room. Then that woman – Margaret – she was here again."

"Stop, Deliverance. Please stop."

The words stilled in her mouth as she heard Findlay's tone. The mention of that name seemed to trouble him enough to become stern. He shook his head, as though shaking off the frustration that had played in his voice. "I'm sorry, but there's no one here."

Liv frowned, her lip beginning to tremble. "I saw them! They were right there!"

Findlay lifted her to her feet, steadying her there against him. "Shh, now. You're alright."

She touched the bump on her head and winced, her head still swimmy from the bump as well as Fionnula's special tea. She let Findlay move her back to her bed.

"We'll have to find a way to let ye sleep, won't we?" He asked, doting with medical concern as she lowered herself onto her pillow. He quickly turned for the bedside table, taking up a match and lighting it before taking her face in his free hand. "Look at me a moment?"

He held the match there as it burned down, directing her to stare at his moving finger as he waved it from side to side. When the match burned down to his fingertips, he blew it out quickly, tossing it onto the bedside table.

"I told ye she shouldn't be up there."

Liv and Findlay both startled at the sound, turning to find Fionnula in the doorway.

Findlay turned toward the open bedroom door, exhaling in exasperation. "Aye, thank ye Fionn. Get to bed!"

The woman hollered something else as she shuffled back to her quarters.

Findlay shook his head, turning back to Liv to check her further.

"Please don't make me go? I promise I'll no make a sound again. I'll no talk of seein things, I promise."

"Shh, lass. It's alright. You've done no wrong. I'll no make ye go for a bout of bad dreams. Get some sleep and come speak to me in the morning. We can discuss how to best put an end to these night terrors, aye?"

Liv took a deep, shaking breath, betraying her emotional state. She was shaken by what she'd seen, shaken by the stern tone Findlay had taken. She feared disappointing him, desperately. The only thing she feared more than the thought of disappointing him was that of making him angry.

"Aye, I will."

Findlay rose to his full height, towering over her bed like some gentle Goliath. "Come take your tea with me tomorrow, aye? We'll discuss it then."

With that, Findlay slipped out, shutting the bedroom door behind him. Before she could scan the room for that familiar, frightening presence, Liv turned toward the wall and tucked the pillow over her head. If she was to have company, she didn't ever want to lay eyes on it again.

CHAPTER SEVEN

"Ah, look at ye, sweet girl! What a sight for sore eyes ye are?"

Janet cast aside the young man she was chatting with under a bridge to join Liv on her walk to Grassmarket. Fionnula sent her on an errand for more lamb and a few bundles of the herbs that she stewed up for Liv's tea. Liv was happy to be out of the house.

"Given the ruckus of last night, I think we need a fair bit more, don't ye?" She'd asked as she sent Liv out the door with a basket and her hat tied firmly to her head. Findlay escorted her as far as the college on his way to one of Dr. Knox's dissections.

"Mornin, Janet. How are ye fairin?"

Janet skipped over, tucking her arm up under Liv's to walk together, their strides matching.

Liv glanced over her shoulder, searching the small crowd of people still milling about under the bridge. "Where's Mary?" She asked, trying not to betray concern.

Janet took a deep breath. "Dinnae ken. We took breakfast with this Irish fella we met once or twice in Canongate. Started havin a fair fight with his Missus, so I let out. When I come back, Mary'd left with the bastard. Haven't seen her, since."

"D'ye know where she went?"

Janet shrugged, but there was concern betrayed in

the wrinkles that appeared between her brows. "No, but it isn't the first time she's run off with some bloke, only to come home a fortnight or a month later with a black eye and a broken heart. I'll be here when she's ready to come home."

Liv took a deep breath. She'd wanted to see Mary, tell her of her dreams, but seeing the worry playing at Janet's brow, she thought better of sharing this tale.

"So what are we shoppin for today, then?" Janet asked as Liv slowed to ogle the colors at a paint stall. Liv leaned over the jars and containers, reaching her finger toward a splash of red on the wood table.

"Careful, lass. It'll stain your lovely dress," the man behind the stall said, his accent softened by a lack of front teeth. Liv smiled to the warm man and went along toward the rest of the market. Janet waved toward several familiar faces, introducing Liv at a distance without any intention of letting the people speak to Liv as they made their way through.

As they approached the butcher shop, Janet hollered down the way towards the familiar limping man, busy entertaining a small gaggle of children with a broad smile. "Ay Jamie!"

The simple fellow turned up just long enough to nod and smile, then turned back to a tiny girl with long braids, giving her a silly grin and a dance, much to her delight.

Liv ordered her lamb, paid the butcher, and let Janet take up her arm again as they returned to the busy market. Yet, her mind was elsewhere. She'd fought bravely throughout the day to still any frightened memories of the events the night before – of those strange, opaque eyes and the bloodstains that moved like a living thing.

'Where's my baby?'

It was this single question that troubled her most of all. Was this the baby wailing through the walls, crying for a mother that never seemed to come? The thought of a child alone like that, even in spirit, broke her heart.

"Where's your mind, Livvy, dear? Ye seem troubled."

Liv startled at the sudden attention. Liv shook her head. "I don't know. Bit distracted, I s'pose."

"Has our lovely doctor gotten his hands on ye again, then?"

"No!" She said, a bit sharper than she'd intended.

Janet ignored her frazzled tone. "Well, why on earth no, Delivvy? If I lived under the same roof as that talented bastard, I'd have my legs behind ma heid at all hours of the day!"

A couple young men in dusty brown jackets guffawed loudly as they passed, giving her cheeky grins in response to her comment.

"It's no like that. It's a medical procedure. I can't rightly ask for it like a cup of tea -"

"Aye, medical! And I'm a very sick woman," Janet said, giving Liv a hearty tussle as they turned back down into Cowgate. "It's only medical because it's a doctor who's doin it, aye? D'ye imagine he calls it 'medical' when he's havin a go at himself?"

Liv straightened at this notion. "At himself? How on earth -"

"Aye, on himself. Ye ken lads do that, don't ye?"

"But they haven't got -"

Janet's eyes went wide, then she rolled them in exasperation. "They've a cock, lass. And when it stands up, they can either think of their gran to make it go away, or they can pull on it til it spits!"

Janet exploded in laughter at her own joke, but Liv simply cringed, glancing around at the people near them, praying they weren't silently judging her along with her crass companion. She was sure they were.

"And I assure ye, love. Our Dr. Lennox is a man. Bet he pulls it daily!" With that declaration, she leaned in to Liv's ear, as though she meant to whisper this for just her to hear, but then spoke loud enough for lads at the nearby pub to catch every word. "Christ, what I wouldn't give to be the one pullin that man's cock!"

The small crowd of men all glanced over, their eyes growing wide.

Fancy a pull then, lads?

Two of the men stepped into the street toward her and Janet, one of them whistling as the other called, "From a lovely thing such as yersel? Certainly!"

"Jesus, lass! What are ye thinkin?" Janet grabbed hold of Liv, tugging her further away from the pub. She turned back to the approaching fellows. "Ye ken well I'll take care of ye later, lads!"

"Ay, it weren't ye offerin, Janny!"

"Aye, it was! Sod off, ye bastards!"

The men groaned and hollered a few more choice words, but Janet hustled Liv along, dragging her like a misbehaving child. "Deliverance! Ye can't say things like that! These lads aren't like Findlay. They'll hurt ye if they think you've led em on!"

Liv furrowed her brow, staring at Janet, confused. "I didn't say anything."

Did she?

"Aye, ye did! Christ, that's something I'd expect Mary to say, but no ye!"

Liv's face flushed, and she ducked around the corner toward Surgeon's Square with Janet's arm still firmly hooked in her own. She'd heard the words clearly, but had thought Janet their source. Janet kept glancing behind them, shooting flirtatious looks at the lads who'd followed to the corner.

Liv swallowed hard. How could she say something like that? They hadn't been her words. She didn't even know what they meant.

"Shall I walk ye back then?" She asked, and even with the mortification the woman caused her, Liv hefted the basket up onto her hip and nodded, silently. Despite her cavalier and distracted mannerisms that day, Liv had grown fond of Janet and Mary. She wondered as Janet pulled Liv tight against her, complaining against the chill there in the darker corners of the city, whether Janet and Mary were her friends. She hoped to think of them as such, but in her entire life, Liv had never had such a thing before.

She settled a gloved hand over Janet's, covering her from the cold.

Janet smiled at her. "You're a sweet girl, ye know that, aye?"

Liv smiled, ducking her head so the brim of her hat covered her face.

"It's a rare treat to meet such a thing these days. Shall I come in, then? Perhaps the doctor is free for an appointment?"

Janet gave her an exaggerated eyebrow waggle, and Liv laughed. They turned into the small alley that led to Dr. Lennox's practice. A tall figure in a dark suit stood just outside the door, his red crown bowed there as though he were praying to the doorbell.

"Dr. Lennox! Have ye time today? Mary's off and about and I've all the time in the world -"

Findlay turned and his expression stopped them both at the bottom of the stairs. His eyes were red and his face flushed, but he forced a smile down at them. Liv fought to curtail the strange surge of need; a want to go to him and salve whatever thing seemed to ail him.

"Ah, my sweet Janet. Are ye well? I'm so glad to see ye."

He came down the steps toward them and Liv moved aside as Findlay leaned in to kiss Janet's cheek. Though Liv flushed a moment with what she could only identity as jealousy, Janet flashed her a shocked and excited expression. Liv forgave her instantly.

"I'm sorry though, dear. I can't take ye at the moment. I've a full schedule today. Will ye come Thursday, perhaps? Round noon?"

"Of course, Dr. Findlay. I would love to," Janet said, reaching for Liv. She took her hand and gave it a tight squeeze before turning back down the narrow alley. Liv watched her go a moment, almost afraid to meet Findlay's pained gaze. When she did, he stood in the open doorway, holding it open to her.

He didn't speak, disappearing into his operating theater before anyone could so much as greet him. Fionnula took the basket, pulling the papered bundle of lamb before shooting Liv a wary look.

"Where's the herbs I sent ye for?"

Liv's eyes went wide. "Ah, I'm so sorry! I completely forgot! I'll go back! I'm sorry!"

Liv turned for the door, but Fionnula just made a soft tsking sound. "It's fine, love. We've enough for the night. I'll go round tomorrow when I'm on my errands, then."

Liv apologized again, turning her attention to cleaning up the leavings of that morning's breakfast. The two women worked in silence a moment, Liv scolding herself for her forgetfulness.

"Deliverance, love. Did the doctor speak to ye on the way in? Did he say whether he'd be staying long?"

Liv stopped, searching Fionnula's face. Though she kept an airy, uninvested tone, she was certain Fionnula felt Findlay's strangeness when he came into the house.

"No, he didn't speak to me."

Fionnula gave a soft grunt, returning to her work by the fire. Liv glanced into the parlor as she made the evening rounds to tend the fires. Tea would be soon enough, and she was expected to meet with the doctor and take her meal to discuss her nightmares. She wondered if he would still want her company. If his expression was any inclination, Findlay Lennox was not having a good day.

CHAPTER EIGHT

The silverware clanged against plates on the tray as she set it on one of the small tables in the parlor. She came to stand on the steps leading down to Findlay's exam area, searching the stone floor beneath for a sign of the man.

"Dr. Lennox? Your tea's ready," she called, her voice echoing in the expanse of the theater. There was no response.

Liv turned into the house. The light outside was fading, leaving the house to be lit only by lamp and fireplace. She saw a sign of gold flitting under the doorway of the study, the door closed for the first time since she'd first set foot in the house.

She wrapped her knuckles on the door. "Dr. Lennox? Are ye ready for your tea, then?"

Beyond the heavy door, she listened for any sign of a presence there. There was nothing for a moment. Finally, she took hold of the doorknob, and with a second polite knock, entered the study. Findlay's long frame was sprawled across a settee that only held half his length, his head fallen back in sleep, a book open on his chest. Liv spotted the open bottle of whisky on the table before him, a half empty glass still glowing gold in the lamp light. Instead of calling his name she moved across the room, collecting the book from his chest before touching her hand to his shoulder to wake him. Despite losing her father when she was twelve, she still remembered how rough being woken could be on a mind full of alcohol.

"Findlay? Dr. Lennox? It's tea time, sir."

Findlay stirred, taking that deep, startled breath many make when they first awake. He wiped the back of his hand across his lower lip. "Christ, was I asleep? Sorry! Pardon my language."

Liv smiled at him, waving the word away. Then she slipped out into the parlor to collect his meal, making slow progress through the study door as she fought to keep the plates and silver from clanging together.

"Ah, thank ye, sweet Deliverance. What would I do without ye?"

This passing comment triggered something deep in her belly, and she blushed bright red, the color spreading across the bridge of her nose for even her to see plainly. She turned her face away to hide the blush, but she was sure he saw it.

He made a gracious sound, a groan of pleasure and excitement as he straightened on the settee, taking in the meal before him. "I've admitted many times, growin up with Fionnula has spoiled me rotten when it comes to food."

Liv leaned over the table, pouring him a cup of tea and pushing it closer to him, willing him to drink without pressing. Another habit she'd learned from her father. "I didn't know ye grew up with her."

"Oh aye! She ran my father's household as well. Took care of my mother in her later years. I had no one when I first acquired this property, but when mother died, good ol' Fionnula came to save me," he said, then leaned in, lowering his voice. "There was a time once or twice where I called her mum without thinkin. She's been with me for a very long time. Oh!

And she's made one of my favorites, has she no? Is that a pork pie or lamb?"

"Lamb."

"Christ – Damn it -"

It was Findlay's turn to blush as he swore, then swore again in realization of his course language. Liv watched him in his inebriated state, finding it strangely endearing. She'd only ever seen him drink twice, but this was the first time she saw the alcohol have an effect. She imagined a man of his size would take a considerable amount of drink before he could be considered drunk.

"Please, Livvy. Pardon me for my behavior. I know we were meant to take tea tonight, I just – I've had a rough day."

Liv shook her head, moving toward the parlor door. "It's fine. I can speak with ye another time."

"No, no! Stay! Dine with me, talk with me. I think I may benefit from the company."

He gestured toward a chair along the side of the settee, and Liv moved to take her seat, letting him pass her a plate before cutting into the steaming hot pie. He groaned again as the smell overtook the room.

"She is a wonder, our Fionnula. Mhmm!"

A moment later, Liv had a slice of lamb and kidney pie on her plate, a fork in her hand, and a cup of tea with a splash of whisky in it - Findlay's insistence.

They both began eating, Findlay humming and groaning into his meal with every bite. He was loose and at complete ease there, the whisky clearly still strong in his system. He didn't seem drunk, but he seemed easy. Liv was happy to see the mood change from that afternoon.

"Now tell me, lass – how're ye findin Edinburgh?"

Liv held a hand over her mouth as she chewed, fighting the urge to moan in unison with Findlay. She swallowed finally, wiping her face with her napkin. "I'm finding it very well."

"Are ye? That's grand. You've been out into the city I take it? Seen the Grassmarket and the castle, aye?"

She nodded, waiting to take another bite until she was sure Findlay was done with his current branch of conversation. "The castle only from afar."

"Oh, it's worth exploring up the Royal Mile, Livvy. Worth it most certainly. So, ye find it better than Inverness, I take it?"

Liv gave a half laugh, exhaling out her nose. She turned her eyes down in apology for the gesture, but Findlay just smiled.

"Anywhere would be better than Inverness," she said, lifting her fork for another bite.

He stopped and searched her face, breaking from his ravenous assault for a moment. "I take it that's no to do with Inverness itself, then?"

"No, no to do with Inverness. It's rather lovely up there, if I'm honest."

He nodded, wiping his face with his napkin. "Well, you've been a right blessin here, Deliverance. Had I know what Inverness had hidin in its walls, I'd have advertised in their paper instead."

Liv smiled. "I'd've never seen it. Mum didn't believe in newspapers. Said it was full of filth and pish – pardon my language," she said, catching herself. She'd been spending too much time with Janet and –

Liv frowned.

"Well, she's probably right about that, at least. Though no about much else, from what I gather."

Findlay glanced toward Liv's lower half, nodding in

acknowledgement of her burns. She fought to still the blush that traveled up her throat.

The two of them ate in companionable silence, Findlay still groaning and grunting through his tea and his pie. When Liv couldn't finish her slice, Findlay happily added her serving to his own. Liv watched him, eyes wide with shock to see how much food he could eat. He was tall, quite possibly the tallest man she'd ever met, but he wasn't a giant, and he wasn't heavyset. Still, the pie disappeared as though thrown to a pack of wild dogs. When he was done, he downed his now lukewarm tea, then poured himself a second cup, adding another splash of whisky in for good measure. He turned the bottle toward Liv's cup, but she waved him away, thanking him.

"I apologize to be drinkin in your company, Livvy dear. Isn't my usual behavior, assuredly."

She smiled. "It's fine. Ye seemed somewhat distraught this afternoon when I saw ye, so -"

"Aye. Aye, that I was."

Findlay lifted his teacup and stared into its contents a moment, as though he'd become some fortune teller, working to read the leaves within.

"Ye asked me the other night – who's Margaret, ye said."

Liv swallowed, her stomach dropping. "Aye."

He stared into the teacup, seemingly lost within. "I know who ye mean."

She didn't speak, waiting for him to continue.

"She was my patient," he said and took a sip of his tea. Then he slumped back onto the settee as though defeated. "I've been a doctor for a few years now. We're ten a penny round here, but I'm one of the few that many would consider an expert in my field."

"What is your field?"

He gave a side nod, his eyes half closing as he did. "Women's health, I s'pose. I can treat anyone, but most of my patients are women."

Liv felt a strange pang at this. She knew it well, but somehow the declaration of his contact with other women made her feel strange. Was this jealousy?

"Why?" She asked.

He raised his eyebrows and his heavy lids barely moved. "Why women?" he chuckled. "Well, I can't say I don't appreciate women, like any man, but -"

He stopped, letting his head fall back on the settee. Then he blew out through pursed lips and sat up.

"I was born by what is called a caesarean section. D'ye know the term?"

She shook her head, taking up a sip of her own tea and cringing, having forgotten the whisky. "No," she said, fighting not to cough.

"It's when a surgeon delivers the baby by cutting open the mother's abdomen."

"Really? My God!"

He nodded raising his eyebrows as though he'd just confessed to fighting a bull, not being cut from his mother's body. "Aye, no surprise she couldn't give birth to me, I mean look at me."

Liv smiled at him and made a theatrical point of shuddering at the thought. He grinned.

"My mother survived the surgery, but survival isn't common. Oftentimes, the caesarean is a death sentence to a mother. Though she had health troubles all her life as a result, her survival was considered a bloody miracle. Pardon me."

She waved the language away.

He continued. "When I heard the stories of my

birth, I felt protective of my mother. I felt as though I'd almost done her harm just by bein born, and the only way I could do right by her was to become a doctor and help other mums – like her. So, though I was fair bothered by other lads in college for it, I turned my focus in later years."

"I heard a bit of your exhibition the other day. It was very interesting," she said, fighting against shyness to give the confession.

"Oh aye? Did ye now? Well, I'm glad. That's no something I publicly profess to quite yet. It's still in early stages – research and the like."

She nodded. "Well, it helped me. Very much so."

"Did it?" He asked and his face brightened so much, she felt her own face flush. She turned her nose into her tea, nodding.

He gave a long exhale. "Well, that makes me glad. It makes me glad…"

He drifted off then, staring at the grandfather clock that stood ticking in the corner of the room. Liv waited with him in silence. The quiet stretched so long, she feared he may have fallen asleep again.

"Ye know the girls from Cowgate – Janet and Mary? They're friends of yers, aye?"

Liv startled, furrowing her brow. "I know them, aye. I think – I think they are my friends."

He nodded. "Margaret was one of them. Girls from Cowgate – or Canongate. She came to the city for work – was a midwife back in Dumferline before she was forced to move. Sadly, there's no a great deal of work for the Irish and poorer crowds, so - some women turn to selling themselves to make a wage."

Liv swallowed. She felt almost naïve. She hadn't realized what Janet and Mary were.

"When I first began to research this procedure, I requested volunteers. Women who wouldn't be bothered by such an act, as long as it was their choice and they were compensated for their time. I was surprised by just how many turned up for the job. Margaret was one of a dozen of my earliest volunteers."

"Like Janet and Mary?"

He took a deep breath. "Aye. Like Janet and Mary."

He tapped one of his long fingers against the teacup in his lap. "She came for her appointment every few weeks. I learned a great deal from those first volunteers. They answered my questions, and helped me better understand anatomy in ways ye can't learn from a dissection table. Over time, I perfected my approach and began to implement the procedure into my practice."

"Like the women those men brought from the asylum?"

He smiled, nodding. "Then, just a few months ago, Margaret came to me in trouble."

He stopped, closing his eyes a moment.

"What kind of trouble?"

"She was with child," he said, his eyes still closed as he spoke. "She was unmarried. Didn't know who the father was. She didn't want to have the child, so she came to me."

Liv inhaled sharply, and Findlay cracked an eye to look at her.

"It's no somat I do often, but Margaret wasn't the first woman to come to me in that sort of trouble. I've done it maybe three times in my career, each time knowin it could ruin me if anyone found out. But these women were suffering, and – well, I pitied them."

The grandfather clock ticked softly to fill the silence as Liv waited for him to go on.

"I relented finally. She came to my office late one night, lay down on my table, and as I went to begin the surgery, she had a change of heart. Decided then and there that she couldn't give up the bairn. She left my office that day terrified, but hopeful - on her way back home to Dumfries."

Liv thought of the woman in her bedroom, thought of the opacity of her eyes, heavy in their lifelessness. This woman he spoke of didn't sound like the terrifying thing in her room.

"I didn't think I'd ever see her again. Went about my practice without another thought," he said. Then he sat forward, clutching the teacup as he pressed his hand to his face. "Ye know the medical college, aye? One of the best in the world, and Dr. Knox is renowned in his field. Gets cadavers from the prisons and the unclaimed, and holds classes so immense he has to sell tickets."

Liv nodded, urging him onward.

"I attended them whenever possible. Robert is a friend as well as a mentor, and I've learned so much from his classes over the years. I know ye find it horrific, and I s'pose it is, but to truly learn anatomy one must see it firsthand. Only way ye see it, is if there's a body to dissect."

Liv cringed, taking a sip of her whisky to hide the gesture. The burn of it caused her to cringe more.

"When someone dies with no family or connections, they might end up on the table if the body goes unclaimed, but for the most part, the college only receives cadavers after a criminal execution. So most the cadavers are mostly men. But he assured me I simply must attend that week's dissection – that it was a woman on the table. I arrived with my notepad and pencils, ready to sketch and take notes like a complete arse."

He stopped suddenly, and his breath grew shaky. He blew out slowly, then took a new deep breath.

"Midway through the dissection of her abdomen, Knox makes a grand show of having discovered that the woman had been pregnant when she died." Findlay took a long pause, and the emotion of it made Liv feel as though she betrayed him just by being present. "All the lads surged forward, craning for a closer look. I hadn't bought a ticket, so I stepped aside, letting them all take the better vantage. I regret it to this day."

"Why?" Liv asked, and her voice felt foreign in the quiet space.

"Because from my new vantage point, I could see her face."

Liv touched her hands to her stomach, remembering the frightening sight of the bloodied woman in her room. "It was Margaret?"

He frowned and it was so honest, Liv almost moved to the settee to sit beside him - comfort him in some way. Yet, she didn't move. Comforting was not in her job description. She had to know her place.

"I haven't attended one of Knox's exhibitions since, though he kept askin me to. I finally let him convince me this week. Assured me I couldn't miss this one, as it was another female specimen. Female specimen," he said again, and the words were dripping with disgust. "I shouldn't gone. I just shouldn't."

Liv leaned forward in her chair, nervous. "Why?

What happened?"

Findlay gave a sad laugh. "I knew her. Another girl from Cowgate."

Liv fought with this news, searching for words, but not wanting to hear the answer they might bring.

"I couldn't stand the thought of watchin another woman being butchered like that, thinkin the whole time that I might know the poor lass. But I go, and lo and behold -"

"Was it Mary?"

Findlay startled, slamming his teacup onto the table with a bit more force than he'd intended, splashing a small amount of its contents onto the saucer. "What? Why d'ye say that?"

"Because I saw her. Last night, in my room."

Findlay's mouth hung open a moment and he stared at her. Then he shook his head as though shooing away a fly. "No, no, Livvy! Those are dreams, lass. Nothin more. Wasn't Mary. Was no one ye know."

Liv watched him there, settling the contents of the tray, wiping up the spilled tea despite it being her responsibility.

She searched his face, wanting to believe him. "Would ye tell me? If it were Mary, I mean?"

Findlay stopped, holding out his hand to her. She faltered just so, almost afraid to feel his touch again. His warm fingers wrapped around hers. "I would, love. I promise I would tell ye."

She pursed her lips and exhaled. Then she nodded.

He turned his attention back to his teacup, swigged down the last of its contents, and stood to his full height, slapping his hands against his thighs. Then he turned for the parlor door. "Well, that was a lovely meal, despite the dower mood. I'm sorry for puttin my troubles on ye, lass."

"No, it's no bother."

He smiled, hovering by the door. "Never got round to discussing your troubles, did we?"

Liv shook her head, but before she could assure him, he continued.

"I wanted to discuss the possibility of scheduling an appointment for ye. Twice a week would be best, I think. We can adjust the times and the frequency based on how ye fair?"

"If ye think it's best?" She was frozen there, unsure what was happening, but certain she should agree with anything the doctor said.

"That is, if ye feel comfortable with the procedure. I know ye said it helped last time."

"Oh, aye! It did."

She cringed at the high pitched fervor of her response. She fought to steady herself, but the memory of the last time he touched her instantly set the place between her legs tingling.

"Well then. Given the trouble ye had last night, why don't ye come find me this evening. Wait until about an hour after Fionnula's off to bed, if ye would. She's no exactly keen on some of my methods, sadly. She's no the only one."

He shot her a grin and turned, leaving her surrounded by the smell of whisky, lamb pie, lamp oil, and books. She turned for the clock.

Fionnula wouldn't be in bed for another hour. Liv pinched her thighs together to fight against the strange sensation, and carted the tray into the kitchen.

CHAPTER NINE

Her stomach twisted as she made her way back down the stairs to the study. She turned her eye to the grandfather clock; it was well over an hour since Fionnula had bid her goodnight. Liv stood in the doorway that separated the study from the parlor, staring at the line of gold that framed the door to the operating theater. Her stomach twisted again.

When she felt sufficiently brave enough to knock on the door to his theater, she looked at the clock once more. It had taken her fifteen minutes to build up the nerve.

Liv knocked softly. Despite almost praying he didn't hear, Findlay's voice echoed from somewhere distant.

"Come on in."

Liv stepped down onto the first step and turned to shut the door behind her.

"Lock it, if ye will?"

Her insides lurched at this command, but she did as she was told. She made her way down the staircase, unable to look at the doctor as she reached the lower level.

She glanced at him out of the corner of her eye, and stood nervously by the stairs. Findlay was hunched over one of his tables, scribbling notes into one of the many notebooks strewn there. She waited, fidgeting with her fingers at her waist.

"Deliverance, come on over and climb up on the table for me, please."

She inhaled sharply, but did as she was asked. Findlay still hadn't so much as glanced at her, too ensconced in his scribblings.

She sat there for a long moment, praying the cold of the metal would warm beneath her backside.

"Ah, bollocks. I forgot to have ye bring hot water again. I'm sorry, dear. Cold hands it'll be."

Liv made to hop up from the table, desperate for the reprieve on her nerves. "I can go get it now. It's fine."

"No, no. There's no need. Unless you'd prefer it."

She swallowed. She didn't know what she'd prefer. Cold hand and get it over with, or prolong this fire in her belly. Why was she so nervous? She'd done this before.

She shook her head. "I'll be fine."

Findlay was now fully focused on her, coming to stand at the side of the table. "Well then, same as the last. Lie down for me, please. And place your feet in the stirrups."

"The what?"

The table shifted and clanged beneath her as he lifted the first contraption into view. He smiled at her, tapping a finger to the metal claw. "The stirrup?"

She swallowed. "Right."

A moment later, Findlay was tying her second leg into the stirrup.

"Right, now how did we find the effects last time? Did it help with sleep – with the dreams?"

Liv nodded, barely moving her head as she did. Her hands were tightly clutched together over her belly, and her knees leaned toward each other, though they did not touch.

"D'ye have any concerns about the procedure – things ye might have me do differently?"

"What? No?" She said, but it was as much a question as a declaration.

He chuckled softly. "Well, alright then. Ye know if ye find you're havin trouble sleepin again, ye can always come down. I'm up most nights well past midnight."

Liv took a deep breath. "I don't want to impo -"

"Ah, it's no imposition. It's what I do. Relax your legs for me, Deliverance."

She swallowed, closing her eyes tight as Findlay lifted her skirts to her knees. Then instead of touching her, he turned back to one of his tables, shuffling something about. Liv felt the air cold against the place between her legs, wanting nothing more than to lock her knees together and shield herself from view. The silence began to draw out too long. She stared up at the open beams far overhead.

"I did try to – well, I thought I might be able to to do it myself, but it didn't work."

Findlay stopped what he was doing, but did not turn to look at her. "What's this, now?"

She froze, feeling as though she'd confessed to stealing the silver. "I know I'm no doctor, but I was desperate to sleep, so I thought I'd try and – but it wasn't -"

"Ye attempted the procedure on yourself?" Findlay asked, turning back to the table. He came to stand alongside Liv, looking down at her face as he waited for her to respond. She could only nod.

"Ye need no be a doctor to perform it on yourself, love. You're no the first lass to tell me so. Though, ye are the first lass of -" He stopped, glancing down toward her open legs, view of her shielded by her skirts. "Well, did ye succeed, then?"

Liv shook her head.

"Why no?" He asked.

"I don't know."

Findlay moved around the table, coming to stand between her legs. He hoisted her skirts up just enough to glance down at her. She felt so exposed, yet in that sense of helplessness, the tingling sensation grew a thousand times worse.

He stood there a moment, silent, his hand coming to rest on her ankle. Then he took a deep breath. "Will ye show me?"

Liv jerked her head upward to look at him and he pushed her skirts past her knees. She yelped, as though her thighs being bared was far more scandalous than him staring down between her legs. "I'm no good at it. I told ye it didn't -"

He smiled at her, patting her knee. "Aye, I know. Show me."

She lay there, her heart beating so hard, she could feel her chest pounding.

"Ye don't have to if ye'd rather no -"

"No, no!" She blurted out. Despite the shock of his request and her fear of being seen in such a way, neither sensation could overpower how troubled she felt at the thought of disappointing him. He sounded both curious and clinical in his request. She was almost afraid to have him see how fumbling and useless she was, given his expertise.

She moved her hands down the length of her belly, fidgeting and faltering with each inch she moved. When they finally reached her thighs, she stopped again, frozen a moment. Findlay turned back to one of his tables, grabbing up a notebook and a pencil and setting them on a shelf her.

"It's just me, here. There's no to be ashamed of."

She nodded, but her hands remained frozen.

Findlay leaned forward, pushing her knees aside. "It's fine, love."

He touched his hand to her thigh, the way he had a week before; the initial touch to prepare her for his cold hands. Before he took his hand from her thigh, she slipped her hands between her legs, pressing her fingers to the place that felt hot to the touch. Findlay inhaled sharply, but did not speak as Liv closed her eyes tight and let her fingers move against her body.

She was not an expert, as she reminded herself over and over again, but she knew the place that felt the most sensitive, and the direction that made it more intense. She moved her fingers, picking up speed as she did, trying to replicate the way Findlay's hands felt. She would fail again, and she knew it, but she wanted to make him proud somehow, show him that she'd paid attention.

"Is that the spot that feels best, then? D'ye mind if I take notes?"

Her eyes shot open and she turned to look at her. He pulled the notebook from beneath the table, and jotted down a few scribbled words. "Keep going, love."

She swallowed, letting her head fall back again onto the cold metal of the table. She moved her fingers from side to side, picking up speed as the sensation began to build. Somehow, the sensation was far stronger there on the metal table – with Findlay there. Her fingers moved in the same way they had before, but with each movement of her wrist, she found herself getting warmer. She turned her head to the side as though willing herself invisible, and tripled the speed of her fingers.

"That's it, love. Keep that pace, you'll be right there."

She whimpered involuntarily, and her hand stopped as her face burned. Yet, before she could recover from that sense of humiliation, Findlay tossed the notebook across the room and pushed her thighs apart. Without a word, his hand touched hers, moving her fingers under his. She writhed against the table then, the sudden cool of his fingers doing something to further amplify sensation.

"Here," he said, pressing one cool hand against her thigh as he pushed her legs wide. She turned to look at him for the first time since she'd started, and just as her eyes met his, he slid his fingers inside her.

She jerked on the table, her body clenching around his fingers. He nodded to her, cooing softly. "Keep going, love. I'll help."

His fingers moved inside her, and the sensation felt as good as before – or perhaps better. She did as she was told, rubbing her fingers flat against the place that grew hotter and hotter with each moment. Suddenly, Findlay doubled his pace, watching her intently. She fought to keep her own pace, that familiar sensation of heat and pressure building under her fingers.

Findlay stepped into the table, tossing her skirts up over her stomach as his free hand pressed on her belly. She cried out then, feeling close to that strange release. It was then that her hand lost all use, shaking from effort and exhaustion. Findlay gently moved her useless hand aside to take up the work. He doubled his pace again. Liv arched her back, turning her face away as her mouth fell open in a silent scream.

"There ye are, lass. Right there."

She cried out, feeling his body pressed against the table between her legs, the fabric of his trousers touching her bare backside. She moved her hips to meet his hands, letting her head fall back, and she held her breath.

The wave came with such fury that she convulsed in the stirrups, the table clanging and shaking beneath her as she shuddered. Findlay's hands didn't still. They didn't even slow as sensation reached the point of violent. She cried out, reaching down to his hands to still his movement, her body too sensitive to take further manipulation. Yet something about Findlay had changed. His brow was hard with concentration, glistening just so with sweat. His whole body hummed with tension. His lip curled just slightly as his hands moved, building up speed as she cried out against it, clutching the sides of the metal table to brace against him.

Suddenly her body opened to him. She gasped for air as the same sensation as before returned, but this time a thousand fold stronger. Liv screamed, her voice echoing off the walls like a prisoner in some torture chamber.

"Findlay!" She cried, and he made a sound, almost imperceptible as her body tightened around his fingers, clenching and throbbing in rhythm to her heart beat.

His hands slowed now, still moving, letting the strange contractions build, then recede before he slipped his fingers from inside her. He turned to wash his hands in the basin of cold water. Liv lay there, breathless and panting, feeling a trickle of sweat move between her breasts. She stared at the staircase, desperate to look at Findlay, but unwilling to do so. She feared he would see something in her eyes that shouldn't be there.

Livvy, damn it. It shouldn't be there!

Findlay turned to his table of notebooks and papers and snatched up the tossed notebook, scribbling something into its pages. "Deliverance, would ye say ye felt release twice, or was it a continuation of the first?"

She startled at being interrogated about the experience. "What?"

"I apologize. D'ye mind if I take some notes?"

Liv licked her lips, trying to still the sudden dryness of her mouth. "No, no. It's fine. Ehm, I believe it were twice."

"How far did sensation recede before peaking again?"

He gestured in the air, waving his hand as though going up a hill, then back down and up again.

She shook her head. "It didn't go down at all."

His brow shot up just so, and he turned his attention back to the notebook. Liv almost felt more exposed now than she had with him standing between her legs. She made to move, craning to lift her ankle from the stirrup. The table creaked and clanged beneath her, but did not release her leg from its hold.

Findlay turned to the sound and lunged forward. "Ach! So sorry, love. My mind was reelin. I wanted to get it down on paper before the thoughts left me. Here, let me help ye."

He took her leg, his hands cold and damp from the water, causing her to flinch as one of his hands touched the back of her knee. He shot her a grin before apologizing, then turned to the other leg. A moment later, she was sitting upright on the edge of the table, her heartbeat still pulsing in her ears.

He was back at the table, jotting something down when Liv shimmied to the edge, lowering herself onto the stool. Her leg nearly buckled beneath her and she stumbled hard, careening toward the stone wall of the exam space. She slammed head first into a soft, but solid shape.

"Go slow now, love. Ye needn't rush."

Liv looked up at Findlay, straightening herself there as he held her. She didn't want to shake off his hands, but she was embarrassed to have him see her weak in the knees like that. She steadied herself, the place between her legs throbbing as she pressed her thighs together.

"I expect you'll sleep well tonight. And for future reference, you've a good deal of sensitivity just inside and at the perimeter of the vaginal orifice. If ye should attempt it on yourself again -," he paused, holding his hand in the air. "- insert these two fingers as well as external stimulation. Should amplify sensation. Otherwise, I'll suggest we have two sessions a week for as long as the sleeplessness continues. Tonight is Thursday, aye? Shall we say, Sunday? Ah, you're family's religious - no Sunday. Monday, then?"

"Sunday would be fine," she said, trying to hide the fervor she felt. Sunday was sooner. Sunday was one day closer than Monday. She preferred Sunday.

"Ah then. Sunday it is," Findlay said, offering her his arm and walking her to the stairs. "You've got your legs under ye now, aye? Will ye be alright going up the stairs while I finish my notes?"

Liv nodded, vehemently, still wanting to hide her weakened state.

"Grand. Ye have a good night, then."

With that, he turned back to his notebooks and Liv took her first few steps up the stairs. She was slow moving, her legs exhausted and still shaking from the work of pulling against their restraints, but she was moving, and she was steady.

"Ah, my manners left me. Here."

She turned, startled at the sound of his voice so close again. Findlay had followed her up the first few steps and was beside her now, offering his arm. Despite wanting to hide the flush of her cheeks, Liv took it and let him escort her up the stairs.

Her room was as dark and cool as it always was, but somehow, she didn't feel the need to search the room for unwanted guests. She felt calm, with a tinge of nervous excitement deep in her belly. She shut her bedroom door, turning her eye to the windows and the dark sky beyond. She curled up into her bed, tucking the covers up to her chin as she listened to the distant sounds of Findlay turning in for the night. She found herself smiling there, her cheek planted into her pillow. Yet, her feet were growing uncomfortably cold. She pulled her legs in close to her backside, but the cold felt almost bone deep, and unwilling to loose its hold on her.

She woke twice, despite the furious call of sleep, and soon realized that if she didn't make due, it wouldn't be night terrors and screaming babies that kept her up, but the simple state of cold feet.

Liv rose from bed, collecting the bed warmer from the corner of the room. Then with bare feet, she tip toed down the stairs to the ground floor, making her way into the dark kitchen to fill the pan of the bed warmer with hot coals from the kitchen hearth.

She was halfway across the upstairs hallway when she heard a strange sound. It was a voice, muffled and softened, seemingly in distress. Coupled with the soft sounds was another strange rhythmic clapping. She stopped in the hallway, listening a moment longer.

The sounds were coming from Findlay's room.

Liv set the bed warmer down on the stairs and moved closer to his door. He sounded as though he might be in distress or pain, but the sounds were soft. She didn't dare knock and disturb him. What if he was crying? He wouldn't want to be discovered in such a state.

Yet, what if he was in need? What if he *was* in pain? Or even troubled in his sleep? Should she disturb him?

Liv moved closer to the door, pressing her ear to it to listen as the softened cries grew more guttural - almost grunts.

Liv dropped to her knees just outside his door and pressed her face to the keyhole. She searched through the small opening, the light of the fire glowing across Findlay's now tussled bedclothes. Then she gasped, her hand moving instantly to cover her mouth as she took in the sight of Findlay Lennox's naked body, prone across his bed, his hands between his legs, moving in quick rhythm. She remembered Janet's comment, of how a man touched himself, pulling on himself. Liv watched him, frozen, knowing how wrong it was to watch, but unable to look away. His hand moved up and down the length of him as he exhaled in soft grunts. They were growing in intensity, and Liv found his face, his head back, eyes closed. Suddenly his expression changed, a look of almost pain and frustration, then his other hand moved to between his legs, catching something as it poured from the end of his cock.

Liv's stomach was in fiery knots as she watched. He slowed, turning to clean his hands on a handkerchief by the bed. She lunged away from the door as he swung his legs down, turning back toward the stairs and her own bedroom.

The clatter echoed through the dark space like betrayal, and she yelped as one of the hot coals toppled out of the bed warmer and burned her ankle. She recoiled from the stairs, searching for the fiery pieces, willing herself anywhere but in that dark hallway. She closed her eyes as light cast across the space.

"Are ye alright, Deliverance? Ah, Christ! Here, let me help ye."

A moment later, Findlay appeared with the shovel from his fireplace, sweeping up the hot coals and tipping them back into the bed warmer as she held it open for him. She took a deep breath, unable to meet his gaze as she bowed her head in thanks and turned for the stairs.

"Good night, ye."

She glanced over her shoulder, catching sight of him. He was bare chested, clad in only his long johns.

She nodded. "To ye as well."

Then she scurried up to her room, tucked the bed warmer under the lower half of her mattress, and crawled into bed.

That night, she dreamed of only one visitor – a naked redheaded doctor.

CHAPTER TEN

"Ye best hurry that up, lass, or I'll club ye," Fionnula said, chuckling to herself by the fire. Though her words were a bit terse, her tone was jovial, a strange state for her to be in, indeed. Though she'd never been a cruel woman, she was not a ray of sunshine by any means – until now.

Fionnula was going on holiday.

Even she found it to be a strange notion.

The summer had passed with hardly a warm day to proclaim it, and October was upon them, the brisk weather getting crueler with each passing day. Despite the bite in the air outside, Fionnula had ventured to Grassmarket herself that afternoon, a lightness to her step that even the passing doctors made comment on. Now she was home, and the contents of her famous pork pie were stewing away in the pot as she prepared the dough, letting Liv watch and learn as she went.

"Ye know I haven't gone back to Leith since poor Mrs. Lennox passed, god bless her. Been tending the poor woman's son all this time. It'll be nice to be home again."

She'd crooned for days, finding little details about every third parsnip that reminded her of a tale, or of an old grumpy neighbor's oddly shaped head. By the day before she was due to leave, Liv had heard some stories no less than three times.

"Will ye get any rest while away, then?"

"Och no!" She exclaimed, still as joyous as ever. "My lad, Angus, has a new bairn. I'm sure his Missus will need some time with her hands free, and I've tended more bairns than I can count."

"Including me," said a deep voice from the parlor door.

Liv didn't turn around to meet his gaze, her face flushing from just the nearness of him.

"Aye, most of all ye – the most troublesome of the bunch!"

Findlay sauntered across the kitchen, leaning over the stove to groan at the smell of that night's meal. Then he made his way across the room, snatching up an apple from the kitchen table. He leaned against the counter, pulling a small knife down to carve the apple.

"What time will ol' Angus arrive? Has he sent word?" Findlay asked, punctuating the end of his sentence with the sharp crunch of an apple slice.

"Should be round 'bout nine, he says. And he's said he's bringin a surprise for us."

"Ah, Christ. Sounds ominous."

Fionnula threw a piece of parsnip at him. "Language, ye scoundrel!"

He smiled, shooting Liv a quick glance before bringing the knife up to his lips with another slice of apple. Despite the many months they'd known each other now, Liv still found it difficult to look him in the eye. Especially on Thursdays. Or Sundays. Or Tuesdays, as he'd added after a month of their twice weekly appointments.

She was responding well, he said. Despite all the madness of her dreams, she'd learned to quiet them. There was no longer a weeping infant to wake her in the night – only the faceless woman, hovering in the corners of her bedroom, or opening her bedroom door in the middle of the night. She'd learned to sleep through the sound, learned to sleep through the painful sense of someone watching her. They'd rewarded her progress by appearing around the house during the day more than once, standing at the windows, watching the quiet or busy streets outside. They never cried anymore; they simply hovered nearby, letting her know of their presence. Still, Liv did not pain their company. She'd grown accustomed. Much like the angry man from the garden in her father's house, they'd grown companionable and calm.

It didn't hurt that Findlay's regular attention inspired restful hours, and constant pining dreams, filled with the memory and fantasy of his touch.

Today was Thursday, and it was as though she could feel him, no matter where he was in the house.

"Ave any further appointments this evenin?" Fionnula asked, and even without looking, the smile was clear in her voice.

"No, all sorted." *Crunch.* "Bit concerned with Mrs. Kilbride's state this afternoon."

"Oh aye? Is she no due soon?"

Crunch. "Aye, she is. Bairn doesn't seem to know it, though."

Findlay and Fionnula continued their conversation as Liv carved the pork leg for the pie. Her hands were bloodied from the haunch and her knuckles raw from slamming into the table, but she listened, lost in the familiarity of the moment.

"Well, off with ye, then. I'll have our Deliverance bring your tea down."

Crunch. With that, Findlay tossed the core into the

waste basin, crossing in front of the kitchen table as he bid Fionnula goodbye. Liv fought not to stifle as his hand grazed her lower back, a silent gesture to let her know he was there. Her hands stilled for just a moment, holding her breath as he passed.

"Ye know, I have half a mind to take my tea with ye two lovely ladies. Be a nice way to send ye off, no?"

Liv startled at the thought, but Fionnula instantly accepted the invitation, crooning with delight at the gesture. Then Findlay was gone, the spot on her back still tingling from the tiny graze of his hand.

Tea was sensational, and Findlay spent much of the meal groaning and fawning over every bite as Fionnula regaled them both with further stories of Leith, Angus, and all the trouble he and Findlay got themselves into growing up together around the Lennox household. Then as though spring loaded, Fionnula headed to bed for the night, eager to begin her holiday the next morning. As per usual, Liv was left with cleaning up and setting the house to sorts before her appointment with Findlay.

When the time came, she found him as she always did; hunched over his table, studying his notes in quiet contemplation. She no longer waited for invitation during her appointments. Liv sauntered across the exam floor, setting the kettle of hot water beside the wash basin, then hopping up onto the metal table with her legs dangling off the side. There she waited, inspecting the mortar between each brick of the wall.

"How are we this evenin, love?"

She smiled. "Very well. And yourself?"

He paused, staring down at the papers. "Well enough."

He shuffled something aside, staring down at long dingy pages in an old notebook. After a moment, he finally turned to the hot water, washing his hands in the basin. He wasn't his usual attentive self. Liv felt almost disappointed to find him so despondent.

"Ye seem troubled," she said finally.

He startled. "Do I?" He asked, then as he watched her face, he sighed. "I must, aye? Just a bit bothered, is all. Isn't to do with ye, Livvy. Pay me no mind. Lie down, feet in the stirrups, please."

She did as she was told, coming to rest her arm under her head. Findlay wasted no time lifting her skirts, pressing his warm hand to her inner thigh as he always did.

"Is it that Mrs. Kilbride woman?"

Findlay startled again, meeting her gaze over her bare knees. He pinched his lips between his teeth and frowned. "Aye, it is."

Liv pulled her ankles from the stirrups before Findlay could remember to strap them away. "Is something wrong with the bairn?"

He leaned his hip into the metal table, coming to stand just at her knee. Liv searched his face, waiting for response as she pretended to be oblivious to the touch of his leg against hers.

"I'm no rightly sure. Lorelei's full term now, but she's showin no signs of dilation or contraction. And the bairn isn't in the right position for comin into this world easily."

Liv let her hand fall onto the table beside her, grazing her thumb against his arm as she did. He stood there silent, his arms crossed over his chest. He stared at the knuckle of his right thumb. Liv watched him a moment longer, waiting to see if he had anything further to say. After a long moment passed between them, she shifted off the table, her bare feet padding onto the hard stone floor.

"Where ye off to, then?" Findlay asked, his voice betraying honest surprise.

Liv made her way across the room, coming to stop at the bottom of the stairs. When she turned to respond, he'd given chase, standing just a step behind her on the exam room floor.

"I know you've got a great deal on your mind. I'll let ye get back to it."

"No, no. Deliverance, it's fine, love. I'm fine -"

But Liv continued up the stairs, fighting to still the smile on her face as she reached the upper landing. "We can reschedule for another time. I'll no keep ye."

With that, she made her way up the last steps, fighting to ignore Findlay's further protests from the floor below. She wanted nothing more than to turn around and let him remind her of his expert hands, but something about the way he looked, the heaviness to his brow made her feel as though it was him that needed the procedure, not her. Still, Liv didn't know the first thing about medicine or how to touch a man. Even if he'd let her, she'd make a mess of it, for certain. She shut the door to the operating room and stood in the dark parlor.

"Was the doctor in need of something?"

Liv shrieked, spinning to face the kitchen door. Fionnula stood there in her cap and night dress, a look of suspicion on her face.

Findlay's footsteps echoed up the theater steps and the door burst open, Findlay's tall shape framed by the light within. "Are ye alright, love?"

"Love?" Fionnula asked, and the furrow to her

brow deepened.

He turned toward the kitchen, and Liv was certain his expression mirrored her own. "Fionn, what are ye doin about?"

She stared at him a moment without answering. "Am I disturbin somethin?"

"No, no!" Findlay exclaimed, and his tone betrayed an almost youthful excitement. "Deliverance was just askin if I'd be to bed soon. She was turnin the fires on her way to bed, wanted to know –"

"I see," Fionnula said, turning into the kitchen without a word before Findlay could finish his lie.

Liv swallowed as the two of them stood in conspiracy. Then with a quiet good night, Liv turned for the study and made her way upstairs to turn Findlay's bedroom fire before heading to bed.

"Come on now, child! We mustn't keep him waitin!" Fionnula exclaimed, wrapping her shawl around her shoulders by the door. The older woman had wailed and keened at the sight of her son, the sound of it traveling through the house as she embraced him by the door. It took Fionnula several moments before she could introduce Liv to her son, Angus Tully as she'd been too focused on her surprise – Angus had brought his eldest son, little three year old George Tully. Fionnula had snatched up her young grandson with the strength of a much younger woman.

After Liv served the four of them breakfast, Findlay gave Angus another brotherly hug by the door, then dropped down to the little boy. "Ye take good care of your Gran now, Georgie? I'll need her back here soon enough."

"Aye, sir," the little boy muttered, turning his face into his father's hand.

Fionnula reached for the young boy's cheek, giving it a loving squeeze. "Och, what good manners he has, my lad."

A moment later, the house felt massive and lonely, the Tully family having piled into their carriage for the long ride to Leith.

Findlay shot Liv a smile and turned back for the parlor, snatching up his satchel and coat to make his way out. Liv watched his expression as he returned to the front hallway, standing by the door a moment as though he didn't want to leave.

"Will ye be well enough, then?"

He scoffed, quietly, but nodded. "Can only hope."

And with that, he slipped out the front door, the sound of constant patter announcing the drech day outside.

Liv made quick work of the morning's chores, determined to meet all of Fionnula's expectations. She'd written a lengthy list of details to tend to. Everything from cleaning chamber pots and stoking fires as she often did, to stewing suppers from recipes Fionnula assured her were older than the very house in which they slept. Within an hour of Findlay's leaving, Liv had an early steep of pork bone and peas on the fire, and the scullery was scrubbed down and tidy. Liv was fretting her way through the piles of books in the study when a shape passed across the parlor door. She stopped by the table of books, turning to watch for a second pass, waiting for the strange shift of light to explain itself.

Had it been a bird outside the window, or a passing of something in the road outside, perhaps reflecting off the puddles. Yet as she stood there with a copy of *Pride and Prejudice* in her hands, nothing gave itself explanation, save for the heavy feel in the air. Liv set the books back down on the table, their pages marked by ribbon.

Liv took the first few steps toward the parlor door. She touched her hand to the doorjamb and leaned in, dreading what she might see. As the room came into view, the familiar shape of dark skirts swayed on the floor beneath the window. Margaret was watching the rain outside. Liv stopped, leaning back into the study slowly, unwilling to look further into the room to see the whole shape of her. This wasn't a shadow in the corner of her eye. Margaret was standing like some solid thing. Liv dreaded her visits, but this was the first time she'd seen the figure while home alone. There was no one to call to, no one to come into the room and break the spell of this vision by just their presence. Liv stared at the skirts as she moved out of view of them.

Then, just as Liv was almost free of the sight, the skirts swirled around their center as the figure turned toward the study door. Then with unearthly speed, they darted toward her, forcing her to lunge back from the door, willing herself blind to the face that would soon appear in the doorway. She stumbled over Findlay's footstool, toppling onto the hardwood floor just as the front door bell rang, filling the house with its shrill clang.

Liv startled, frozen on the floor as she listened. The parlor door was clear. There was no woman standing there glowering down at her with a face Liv had fought for months not to see. She moved slowly across the floor, letting the parlor inch into view. It was empty. She was alone.

The doorbell clanged again, this time it didn't stop. Whoever was at the door was adamant that they be answered. Liv pulled herself to her feet and hurried down the hallway toward the door.

"Is the doctor in, lass?" The man said, his words punctuated by the sudden rise of his wife's high-pitched scream.

Liv startled at the sight of the man, his hair clinging to his forehead from rain as he held his very pregnant wife upright. Liv stepped aside of the door. "No, sir. He's gone off to the college."

The man's eyes darted across the street, then back into the house. "Will he be back soon? I'm afraid we need him!"

Liv gestured for him to enter, the woman clutching her belly in what looked like anguish. "Come now. I'll show ye to the operating thea -"

"We know well where it is! Where's Dr. Lennox?" The man cried, his tone betraying the worry of a man who cared very much for his wife.

Liv offered Mrs. Kilbride her arm, leading the couple down the hall to the parlor. They turned for the theater door, and Liv surged forward, making sure that someone was on the stairs to catch the ailing woman should she lose footing. Mrs. Kilbride stopped twice on the stairs, clutching her belly as she screamed. There seemed to be no sense to the timing of her wails – as though the pain was constant, rather than rhythmic as she'd learned from conversations with Findlay. They brought the woman to the table, helping her upon it before Liv turned back to the stairs.

"I'll set the kettle on the fire and go cross the way.

He's with the Dr. Kno -"

Liv stopped dead. Standing just before the stairs, her dark eyes set with powerful intent, was the woman Liv called Margaret. Her navy blue dress was impossibly still around her, and the fabric at her belly was dark with blood, but she did not cry now. She simply stared into Liv's face, a glare to chill her very blood.

"Are ye no gonnae do anything, lass?!" The man cried, exasperated.

Liv startled, turning to apologize as she forced herself to move forward, coming to stand at the foot of the stairs, mere inches from the scowling face of a woman only she could see. Liv turned her eyes to the floor and pushed forward, her chest tight with fear.

The figure seemed to move closer as Liv passed, and suddenly Liv felt compelled by a thought. It wasn't hers, yet this sudden overwhelming fixation drove her up the stairs, heading for the liquor cabinet.

Liv felt flooded by a sudden knowledge, as though it had been her own. Mrs. Kilbride was in agony, and the cause of that agony could harm the baby. The pain needed to be dealt with and eased, and without the doctor there to administer any other treatment, whisky was the best possible option. She rushed through the parlor, no longer frightened of the figure by the stairs, but propelled by it, careening through the study, and prying open the liquor cabinet. She cared little which bottle was best, but simply grabbed the decanter with the most to offer, and hurried back down the stairs.

"Here! Have her drink."

"What, now? Are ye mad?"

Liv opened the bottle as the woman reached

toward, gratefully. Liv shoved the stopper into the man's hands and held the bottle for Mrs. Kilbride, who took three massive gulps of whisky before slumping back onto the table in a wail.

"Keep it close. Give her more if she needs it. I'll be back!"

As Liv moved back toward the stairs, she realized the glaring woman was gone. Liv rushed through the parlor toward the front door, barely taking time to wrap her shawl around her shoulders. She threw open the door and rushed out into the rain.

The medical college was immense, consisting of several buildings and doorways leading to all manner of hallways and classes. She'd seen Findlay head down toward Cowgate and rushed in that direction, stopping two young students as they passed. They pointed her toward Dr. Knox's Anatomy School, but assured her the class was well and full.

She barely acknowledged their warning as she barreled into the building, the door slamming against the wall as she entered. The high ceilings echoed with the clamor of it, but she left the door wide behind her, throwing open the first two doors as she moved down the hall. Finally, one of the rooms contained a man with his face in a book, startled awake by her intrusion. He wiped spittle from the corner of his mouth.

"Where will I find Dr. Knox?" She asked.

The young man shook his head, then mumbled his response, pointing down the hallway. She turned further into the building, rushing down the hall to a foreboding black door.

The hallway felt heavier here somehow, the air harder to breath as a booming voice echoed off the walls in the space within. Liv opened the door, and the air, only hinting it in the hallway outside, now overtook her. She stopped just inside the door, shocked by the sudden intrusion of the smell, and turning her face away as though she might deny it. She fought the urge to gag, pressing her face to the doorjamb for an instant to regain her composure.

"May I help ye, lass? I do believe ye may be lost, aye?"

Several of the young men around her laughed, but she straightened, turning to look down into the theater. This room was similar to Findlay's operating room, but grander in scale by fivefold or more. There wasn't a single seat in the viewing parlors open, and below them all on the lower level, the familiar figure. Dr. Knox stood beside a metal table, his hands and the front of his apron covered in blood.

Liv stared down at the horror below. There on the table lay a young man, his body bared to the room, his middle open like a meat pie split by a fork, pieces of his insides laid out on a nearby table. One of his legs was removed, showing bone and blood within, and his head was no longer attached to his torso. Liv stared at the gore below, suddenly realizing the source of the smell that filled that room; that all present seemed oblivious or immune to. She suddenly felt violated. Dr. Knox set a lump of red and brown onto the table before him, blood dripping from his fingers as he let it go. Suddenly a young man from one level down turned toward her, rushing past her into the hallway. Clearly, they weren't all unaffected by the smell and sight. She stepped aside to let him pass, catching a sudden view of the head that now lay separated from its owner. For a moment, all she could comprehend – why she was there, who she sought, it was all gone – all she knew was the dead man's face.

"Lass? Are ye unwell?"

She swallowed, tasting the sickly sweet stench of the room in her throat and wanting to gag. She straightened, fighting to hide her sickened state. "I'm here to fetch Dr. Lennox?"

There was a sudden commotion in the hall below, just out of her view. Then Findlay's tall shape appeared, stepping out from beneath the landing. He took one look at her and his expression changed. He snatched up his things and ascended the stairs, taking three steps at a time.

"Are ye unwell?" Findlay asked, repeating Dr. Knox as he moved her back through the door and shut it behind him. Though the smell faded instantly, the subtle sting of it lingered in the back of her throat. She wanted nothing more than to return home and steal a drink of Mrs. Kilbride's whisky.

"I'm no – aye. You've an emergency at home."

With that, Liv turned back toward the front of the building, hustling down the hall as much to get away from what she'd seen as to bring the doctor to Mrs. Kilbride.

"What's the matter? What's wrong?" Findlay asked, tugging his coat up onto his shoulders.

Liv slammed her shoulder into the front door of the college and stepped out into the rain. "It's Mrs. Kilbride."

No sooner had the words left her lips that Findlay surged past her into the street, running across the way and disappearing down the alley to his home. When Liv arrived shortly thereafter, he'd left the front door wide open.

"Let us have a look then, aye?" Findlay said as Liv appeared on the stairs of the operating theater. She remained above, unwilling to intrude, despite her desperate desire to be of aide. What good could she do? She wasn't a midwife, wasn't trained as Fionnula was to help in moments like this. She was a scullery maid, good for cleaning and tending fires.

Findlay settled there, his hand under Mrs. Kilbride's skirts as Mr. Kilbride cooed to his wife softly, brushing her matted and sweaty hair away from her brow.

"How much has she had?" Findlay asked, gesturing toward the whisky bottle.

"Christ knows," Mr. Kilbride said. "Your lass told her to drink, and she did as she was told. First time this morning she's no been screamin."

Findlay glanced up the stairs at Liv, his eyes wide. She feared reprimand, but something in his expression betrayed gratitude. He didn't speak to her, but his words were pleasing nonetheless. "That's grand. She's more comfortable, then?"

The two men spoke of Mrs. Kilbride as though she wasn't there, but as Liv watched, it was clear the woman could no sooner speak for herself than walk on the ceiling. She was dripping sweat and pallid like the sick, her woozy state now keeping her calm. Findlay moved between her legs again, pressing a hand to her great belly. Then he shot Liv a look, and instantly his fears were betrayed.

Liv turned for the parlor door. "I'll get the hot water!"

"Come right back!" He called, and his tone startled her. Liv reached the kitchen, touching her hand to the kettle that hung near the fire all day. Though it hadn't been screaming hot, it was still steaming, the water sizzling against the sides of the kettle as it swung out on its spit. Liv gripped the handle with a kitchen rag and hauled it back down into the theater. Findlay was there, sleeves rolled up high, hunched over his patient in careful assessment. She was moaning now, but with far less horror than before.

Liv set the hot kettle down by the basin. Findlay appeared at her shoulder, startling her. She turned to meet his gaze, his blue eyes crystalline and clear.

"I need ye, lass. Can ye attend me?"

Liv swallowed, startled by such a notion. "I've no trainin. I don't know what to do, I've no -"

"I know that well enough, but given her state, I've no choice but to ask."

She glanced back at the woman on the table, her face contorting with pain as her husband whispered to her.

"Will she be alright, then?" Liv asked.

Findlay looked down at her and his eyes clouded just so. She could read the answer without word. Findlay stooped lower, coming to whisper in her ear. "She's in constant contraction and the bairn isn't in position. It's more to ask than I should, and I know it, but this bairn isn't comin out without help."

Liv swallowed. "What d'ye mean, help?"

He frowned. "I'm going to have to cut it out."

Liv tried to step away, bumping into the basin behind her, the hot kettle singing the knuckle of her pinky finger. Findlay took her by the shoulder, steadying her.

"I know you've seen enough blood for one day, but if she strives for too long, the bairn's going to die -"

"Oh lord, no," she said, unable to keep the words

silent.

Liv's throat grew tight, but she fought to still it, not wanting the Kilbrides to see her grief. They knew only that Mrs. Kilbride was in labor, not that she may well be in the last moments of her life. Findlay stepped toward Mrs. Kilbride, coming to stand at the head of his metal exam table. He lowered himself onto his stool, staring between Mrs. Kilbride's legs as Liv moved to stand beside Mrs. Kilbride, touching a cool cloth to her forehead.

Findlay moved at the end of the table, and Mrs. Kilbride tensed, whining against the pain. Findlay pressed on her stomach with one hand, and Liv caught the movement of his other arm as he reached his hand inside her. Mrs. Kilbride clenched her teeth, clutching both her husband and Liv's hand. Liv felt her knuckles grinding together, but did not protest. Findlay pressed on her stomach, pushing into her, then repositioned and tried again. The third time, Findlay stood to his full height, leaning his weight over her belly as he pushed. When he pulled his hand away, his expression had fallen. Liv fought back tears as he turned back toward one of his tables — the place where he kept his instruments.

Liv watched him a moment as he unfolded his tool satchel, the sharp metal within glinting across the stone walls. Liv turned her face away, unwilling to watch him choose his knife. She turned her eyes toward the theater steps and instantly regretted it. The woman in the bloody dress had returned, watching the drama with glowering eyes.

"Dr. Lennox? Tell me you'll no cut her, lad. Please!" Mr. Kilbride begged.

"Jacob, I've no -"

Mrs. Kilbride took a deep breath and closed her eyes tight. In the moment Liv glanced away, the figure by the stairs was gone. Yet, Liv could still feel her, like some strange mist in the room, cool on the skin. Liv wrapped her second hand around Mrs. Kilbride's to comfort her, leaning an elbow onto her massive belly. She felt the shape moving beneath the mother's skin, and suddenly by some unspoken compulsion, Liv shoved her weight down onto the striving woman's stomach. Mrs. Kilbride gasped in shock, her eyes going wide.

Mr. Kilbride and Findlay both turned on Liv, demanding to know what she was doing, but all Liv could hear was the same familiar voice, growing in agitation and urgency.

Now, now. Now!

Liv pulled her hand from Mrs. Kilbride's, stomped up onto the footstool beside the table, and leaned over the woman's belly. Then with blind intent, she pressed her elbow into the woman's side, and then her fist down from into the woman's ribs. Mrs. Kilbride gritted her teeth as Liv pushed harder. She felt resistance, like stubborn horses pulling at their reins.

"Findlay!" Liv demanded, and despite his confusion, he moved with speed toward the head of the table. He reached his hand between Mrs. Kilbride's legs just as Liv pressed her second elbow down into the woman's belly. The shape beneath her moved, shifting so suddenly that she was knocked off balance. Liv slumped over Mrs. Kilbride as Findlay roared with startled relief.

He shot Liv a rapturous look. "There we are, Lorelei! There we are. Push for me now."

Mrs. Kilbride took Liv's hand, seemingly drunk enough to forgive her violent handling. Mrs. Kilbride pressed her chin to her chest as she curled into herself, bearing down.

Findlay chuckled, his eyebrows shooting up as he smiled. "One more for me, Lorelei."

Mrs. Kilbride did as she was told, and a moment later, Findlay stood from his seat at the head of the table, a tiny, slimy, and quiet thing clutched in his hands. Liv rounded the table, snatching a cloth from the counter to take the tiny thing from him. Findlay handed the little boy to her, then turned back toward his tools, returning with a metal pod. He stuck a strange rod into the baby's throat, and with a gurgle and a strangled cry, the baby screamed in protest, unleashing a furious wail. Mr. Kilbride clutched his wife's hand, pressing her knuckles to his lips as he kissed her hand over and over. Then he bent to her forehead, and kissed her there, watching as Findlay settled the tiny baby across her chest. Mrs. Kilbride wrapped her arms around the tiny thing and let her head fall back onto the metal table, sobbing in relief.

Liv turned back toward the stairs, searching for Margaret somewhere in the room. Even the lightness of the air betrayed her absence. She was gone – for now.

Findlay stepped away from the table, wiping the sweat of his forehead onto his rolled up shift sleeve. He hovered nearby, his energy that of a man whose job is not yet done, but he gave them a moment. After a couple more striving pushes from Mrs. Kilbride and a long while to rest and recuperate, Findlay let Liv clean the little boy, then sent her to set the guest bedroom to sorts for the new parents.

There was no way Findlay would allow Mrs. Kilbride to travel, and despite the couple's protests, he prescribed two or three days of rest and recuperation before she attempt the carriage ride home.

Liv hustled up the stairs, collecting extra quilts from the closet and fluffing the pillows before turning down the bed for the Kilbrides. She knelt by the fireplace, making quick work of bringing the waiting logs to a nice burn. She listened to the fretful sounds of Mr. Kilbride and Findlay escorting the new mother up the stairs. By the time they were leading her through the door, the room was cozy and warm, filled with the sound of wood crackling in the fire and rain pattering against the warped windowpanes. Findlay gave orders of rest and showed them the bell to call for help should they need it. Then Findlay slipped out the door as Liv made the final touches.

"There'll be a pea soup come tea time, if you'll have it," Liv offered. Mr. Kilbride made a point of clutching his belly to show appreciation. Liv smiled. "I'll bring it up for ye, shortly."

She helped position rags beneath Mrs. Kilbride for the blood, then a pillow under her arm to help her hold the tiny infant to her breast. As Mr. Kilbride knelt beside the bed to watch his wife and son, Liv took her leave of the quiet couple, shutting their bedroom door with the lightest click.

She stood there in the quiet hallway a moment, her hand still pressed to the door as she listened to contented grumbles of the tiny person first discovering his mother's breast. Liv smiled to herself, turning into the dark hallway to go check on their tea, praying it would be worthy of houseguests.

Something stopped her at the stairs, a sudden

pressure at her wrist, pulling her in the dark. She spun toward the figure, his hand held tight on her arm, and as she stumbled through the bedroom door, she slammed face first into the solid shape of Findlay's chest. Before she could apologize or even speak, she felt fingertips at her jaw, turning her face upward.

She barely had a chance to meet his gaze before he kissed her.

Liv's legs went weak and she slumped against him, held aloft by his arms alone as his lips pressed to hers, soft and warm. He pulled from the kiss, just so, then returned with twice the intent, clutching her hair in his hands as he loosed a quiet groan from deep in his throat. She curled her fingers into the fabric of his shirt, pulling at him as though she might draw him closer.

Then he released her, standing over her a moment as he searched her face. "You're a wonder, my Deliverance."

She fought against the comfort of his touch, and forced herself to let him go. She wanted desperately for him to kiss her again, but didn't dare say so.

Findlay searched her face for a long moment, as though seeing her with new eyes. Finally, he released his hold on her, touching the back of his knuckles to his lips. "I apologize, lass. I don't know why I did that."

Findlay disappeared out into the dark hallway. Liv listened to his footsteps travel down the stairs and into the parlor. It took her another ten minutes to finally leave the warm embrace of his room.

CHAPTER ELEVEN

Findlay seemed to evaporate after the kiss. Despite moving throughout the house, bringing their new guests three meals a day and making the rounds of cleaning, chamber pots, and tending fires, he was nowhere to be found – as though he made constant effort to not be where she was.

The Kilbrides were gratitude itself, and their small son – a boy they named Oliver Lennox Kilbride – was sweet and easy, calming to the breast whenever something troubled him. Mr. Kilbride fawned with constant affection, making a point to moan and praise Liv's pea soup, even when eating it for a third time. By the third day, with Dr. Lennox's blessing, the Kilbrides packed their new bundle into a hired carriage, and waved their final farewells as the horses trotted down toward the Royal Mile.

As the carriage disappeared out of sight, Findlay turned toward Liv in the front hall, acknowledging her presence for the first time in days. "I'll be expectin a call from Dr. Knox this afternoon. Will ye have some tea ready, in case he happens to stay a while?"

Liv nodded. "Of course. I can hurry down Grassmarket now, if you've a preference of something -"

"No, the soup is fine. Is it still fine?"

Liv exhaled out her nose in a half laugh. "Well, Mr.

Kilbride seemed rather pleased with it last night. I can't say whether it will be at its best much longer."

Findlay nodded, keeping his eyes to the ground. "I imagine he'll be satisfied with that, then."

He stood there a moment not speaking, but gratefully not rushing to leave her company either. He nodded to himself, as though preparing to speak once or twice, but no words came. Finally, he spoke. "Thank ye, then. I'll be at work. Ye may send him down when he arrives."

Then he was gone, disappearing into the depths of his operating theater to pour over notes and sketches again.

Dr. Knox arrived shortly after lunch time, bowing to Liv as he stepped into the front hallway. He made several comments of her keeping the house well in Fionnula's absence, apologizing for her fragile composure in the dissection two days past. Liv politely showed him into the parlor, nodding and agreeing with everything he said. She felt uneasy in the man's company. She'd met him before. He'd always been a bright character; boisterous and dramatic and funny, but still – Liv felt on edge near him, as though the air around him was somehow humming softly, like the buzzing of a dozen flies.

"There we are, Lennox! I expected you to call on me after your sudden disappearance last I had your company."

Liv watched as Dr. Knox shut the operating theater door. She stood alone in the parlor with the memory of his strange energy.

The two men remained downstairs throughout the afternoon, leaving Liv to her chores. The scullery was cleaner than ever it had been, and though the meals she cooked were rather simple, they were well made and took far less time and preparation than Fionnula's usual fair. Liv didn't dare attempt something profound in a kitchen that felt more Fionnula's than even Findlay's. The soup was eaten for lunch, leaving her to work on her lamb and parsnips for tea. Knox was still in heated discussion with Findlay when they finally emerged from the operating theater to sit for their meal. It was one of the few times since attending to Dr. Lennox that the man took his tea in the dining room, a beautiful and well-lit room just off the study toward the back of the house.

"You've never answered my question, Rabbie. Come now," Findlay said, offering Liv a nod of thanks as she set his plate before him.

"Ach, ye know well enough where I get them!"

Findlay waited for Dr. Knox to receive his plate before the two men dug into their meals, forgetting or deliberately refusing to say grace beforehand. Liv had set out a decanter of Findlay's preferred whisky, but set out a bottle of red wine for the two gentlemen as well. She wasn't the least bit surprised when they favored the whisky.

"I'll no believe Margaret was sentenced to any dissection."

"Well, of course no, but she was certainly of the lower classes – a vagrant often meets an ill end in this city. And who is there to claim them then, ae?"

Findlay shook his head as Liv circled the table to set the platter down.

"And what of the marks? Three now have shared the same bruising pattern."

Dr. Knox scoffed into his whisky. "Oh, you've gnawed this bone long enough, Lennox, my lad -"

"I'm simply askin ye. Where are ye findin your specimens?"

Specimens. This word made Liv's stomach turn. She turned for the study door, ready to take her leave and allow the two men to eat in conversation.

"They're unclaimed or they're sentenced. Ye know as well as I – if they end up on my table, they've no family to speak of and no connections. Simple as that."

Liv stopped in the doorway. "That's no true. Jamie's mother lives in the Cowgate."

The sound of a fork hitting a plate announced the surprise of her audience. She barely turned to see the two men, watching as Findlay fought to finish chewing before he spoke. Knox seemed oblivious, inspecting a parsnip on the end of his fork.

"What's that now, Deliverance?"

She turned, averting her eyes from Findlay's. Despite missing his company the past few days, now that she had his attention, she felt herself shrinking in the wake of it. She swallowed. "The lad on the table two days past – I knew him."

Findlay took a deep breath, turning to look at Dr. Knox. The doctor's brow furrowed in sarcastic disbelief. "Ah, ye must be mistaken, lass. He wasn't somebody ye'd know -"

"James was his name, but everyone down in Cowgate called him Jamie – Daft Jamie. He was down the Grassmarket many times when I was on my errands."

Knox shook his head, wiping his mouth with a napkin in preparation of speech.

Findlay beat him to it. "Jamie! Aye, isn't that what the young lads in the dissection called him – Daft

Jamie? They said they recognized him!"

Knox shook his head vehemently, but Findlay's voice began to rise. Liv felt her stomach turning as the men's conversation grew more heated. There wasn't anger between them, but shared frustration with the other and a healthy flow of whisky. That and the strange uneasiness she felt in Knox's company inspired her to take her leave, grateful neither man noticed or attempted to stop her leaving. She reached the kitchen, turning her attention to scooping up the skins and scraps of the evening's meal, collecting them to be brought out to the garden for composting.

She scrubbed down the kitchen for the evening, then made her way through the house, stoking any fading fires, and adding wood to Findlay's bedroom fire before checking in on the two men. They were still at it by late evening, the first decanter now empty, replaced by a second that Findlay must've fetched from the cabinet. She slipped into the dining room just long enough to bid Findlay and his guest good evening, then made her way up to her bedroom.

As she did every night, Liv glanced around the room quickly, searching for shapes or shadows hiding in the corners. She took a deep breath and relaxed, grateful to find herself alone. Yet, despite her empty room, Liv felt cold in the small space. Though the windows were shut tight, the air seemed to only grow colder the longer she stood there. The hair of her arms prickled upward and she slipped down to Findlay's bedroom to steal a few coals for her bed warmer. Then she hurried back up the stairs, settling the warmer under the foot of her mattress. With another glance around the room, she untied the stays of her dress, letting it fall down the length of her body, leaving her in her shift. She settled into her bed in the dark, turned her face to the wall, and closed her eyes. The boisterous sounds of the gentlemen just a couple floors below felt strangely comforting as she curled up against the chill of the room. Then, as their laughter and roaring conversation faded with the evening, Liv fell asleep.

The sound seemed to drift through the walls; a distant wailing sound, calling her from her bed. Liv listened to the distant keening, trying desperately to understand the sound. It was high pitched, but strangely masculine. She turned toward the sound, waiting for it to settle in her ears and make sense of itself, but before she could decipher its source, she saw the figure across the room.

It was Jamie, his shoulders hunched into himself, shaking as he cried in a mournful wail. Her brow furrowed as she stood from her bed, setting her feet to the cold cobblestones of the street. She rose to cross the square and go to him. Yet with each step she took, he seemed to moved further away. He didn't retreat, didn't move at all, yet the distance between them grew. She stepped faster, fighting to catch up until she found herself running down Surgeon's Square toward Cowgate.

"Jamie!" She called. "Jamie, it's alright!"

But he only cried louder, the shape of him disappearing under the bridge. She stood there in the empty streets, her shift useless to shield her from the cold air. She strained to see into the darkness of the bridge, but could make nothing out.

"Jamie! Come back! You'll be alright -"

Figures surged from the darkness around her, coming toward her with impossible speed. Their faces appeared at her shoulders, both glaring and full of rage, both just inches from her own. She knew them instantly and closed her eyes tight, willing herself invisible to their gaze. She'd seen them many times – out of the corner of her eye, or hiding in the corners of her room, but now they set their eyes on her – just as Margaret had in the operating theater. Yet, now she was sure Mary was with her. Sure that one of those angry faces belonged to a woman she'd once thought of as a friend. She couldn't understand why they were so angry – why they wanted so badly to frighten her. "Please, Mary! Leave me alone."

The sound of Jamie crying returned, accompanied now by hissed words, slithering into her ears from both sides. They spoke in tandem, garbled and stumbling over each other, making it impossible to understand a single word. She scrunched her shoulders up over her ears, trying to shrink away from their assault, but she instantly felt their icy touch, moving up the length of her arms. She screamed, jerking away from them as the bed creaked beneath her weight.

Liv gasped, waking in the dark cold of her own room. Then she exhaled shakily, tugging the blankets up to her chin as her heart raced. She took a moment, fighting to still the pounding in her ears.

Liv wiggled her toes, rubbing her feet together to warm them against the bone deep cold of the room. She kept her eyes shut a moment as consciousness creeped in. The room felt heavy, the way it often did when she woke in the middle of the night, startled to consciousness by some terrible dream, or often worse; by sounds in the room. She frowned, realizing quickly what that familiar heaviness was.

As if the dream wasn't enough, Liv quickly realized she wasn't alone.

She curled her feet closer to her body, willing the room warmer. The bed warmer had been filled with hot coals, she thought. There was no reason for it to have gone cold already. She stared at the knots in the wooden planks of the wall, fighting with her nerves to do the thing she always dreaded doing – turning to face the room. She remembered the glare of their faces, the anger they seemed to harbor toward her. She didn't want to turn and see those faces – didn't want to hear those frantic whispers again, demanding her attention while leaving her helpless to understand.

She felt the bed vibrate and realized she was beginning to shiver. She would have to refill the bed warmer if she wanted to sleep, have to slip downstairs to refill it and make her way back up, always averting her eyes from the shadows, always with her head down. No matter how many times she saw something in the night, it never grew any less frightening.

She lay there a moment, stilling her breath to listen. A floor plank creaked in the hallway outside her door.

She froze, holding her breath. This was new. No matter what she'd seen before, how many times the figures visited, they'd never made that noise. The door opening, the crying, whispered words – all of these things had declared their company before, but never the sound of their weight on floorboards. Someone was there. Something solid was there.

Liv flipped over in the bed, willing herself brave enough to face whatever new horror it was that had come tonight. She stared at her open bedroom door, seeing the outline of a figure there, swaying in the shadows of the hallway. This one was different. This one was bigger, looming just outside the door like some stalking beast. She kicked her frozen feet out, scrambling away from the figure as she pressed her back against the wall. The figure moved, stepping through the doorway toward her as she screamed.

"Shh!" He said, lunging across the room toward her, coming to grab hold of her shoulders as his familiar face lowered to hers. Findlay's eyes were sleepy with drink, but his voice was soothing and soft. "Shh, love. Ye were havin a bad dream, it's alright."

She gasped, the tightness in her chest shifting from terror to relief with such speed, she feared she may cry in the wake of it.

"I'm sorry, love. I didn't mean to scare ye. I heard ye havin a fit in your sleep. Wanted to come wake ye. Shh. Shh, love. Breathe."

Liv did as she was told, letting his features come into focus as she settled there, the hard wall freezing against her back. He rubbed his hand along the length of her arm, feeling the gooseflesh beneath.

"Ach, you're frozen. Here," he said, and in a flash, disappeared out into the dark hallway, the sound of his footsteps retreating down the stairs the only sign he'd been there. A moment later he reappeared, a massive bundle of quilts in his arms. "Come on, there we are. Isn't that better?"

The blankets and quilts were all warm and heavy with the smell of him.

"I can't take these, sir. You'll catch cold without them."

He smiled. "No. I've the fireplace. You've no but a lamp up here."

She made to protest again, but he simply wrapped one of the heavy quilts around her feet, rubbing them through the thickness of blankets. She fought to still the yelp that nearly escaped at the sensation of his hands.

"You've no had one of those in a long while now, ae?" He asked.

Liv nodded, pulling the blankets around her shoulders.

He took a deep breath. "Here I thought our appointments were makin better progress."

"Oh no, they certainly were – are! I've no had any trouble for some time."

She wasn't lying. Sometimes, she could see the shape of something from the corner of her eye, catch movement down a hallway or across a window, but the sleeplessness, the night terrors had all but left her – or perhaps she'd learned to ignore them. Until Mrs. Kilbride.

Still, this dream was different. This time she felt threatened.

He turned his face toward the floor, his brow furrowed.

"I'm sorry I disturbed ye. Twas just a bad dream. Here," she said, trying to offer his pile of blankets back to him. He rose from the bed, ignoring her offer, and pulled the bed warmer out from beneath the mattress. He left the room with it, returning a moment later to lift the end of the mattress and restore the bed warmer to its place. Then he lifted the blankets up, holding them out as he waited. "Come now. Let me help ye settle, then."

She stared up at him a moment, feeling exposed and strangely warm under his gaze. She moved down the length of the bed, stretching her bare legs across the mattress, pushing her shift down as she did. She could feel the heat of the bed warmer beneath the mattress, and she rubbed her feet together gratefully.

Findlay spread the first blanket over her, tucking the ends of it under the mattress. She pulled it up under her chin as he leaned over her to straighten the second quilt across the bed. With him so close to her, his face just inches from her own, she could smell the whisky on his breath. She watched his face in the dark, remembering the way his lips felt, the way they tasted when he kissed her just days earlier. She wondered whether she'd taste the whisky if he kissed her now. She tugged the blankets up, watching him as he straightened over her.

He stood there a moment, motionless and silent. He seemed to sway there, as though pulled by indecision. Then he turned toward her bedroom door, wordless.

Liv called her good night to him, turning on her side to face the wall as she always did; her only protection from whatever things might visit her room as she slept.

She snuggled into the warmth of the blankets, and pressed her nose to the fabric, inhaling the smell of him as she closed her eyes.

The mattress shifted at her feet with the weight of something. She startled, turning to find Findlay now seated at the foot of her bed, taking great care not to crush her feet beneath him.

She turned to him. "Are ye alright? D'ye need the blankets back? Ye can have em, I'm sorry."

He shook his head, as though shaking her off like some fly buzzing at his ear.

She fought with the blankets to turn, sitting up to watch him. He stared across the room, his expression pained. He opened his mouth to speak more than once, but seemed to think better of it, leaving her to sit in the heavy silence of his presence. Finally, he took a deep breath and spoke. "Will ye sleep well enough tonight, then?"

Her chest tightened. She felt pulled to speak, but wary of the response she might draw. If she said the right thing, he might touch her. Yet, a stronger part of her searched deeper, for the magic spell she might cast to make him *kiss* her again. Despite the pleasure that he could give her as a physician, the way he kissed her felt like something more — something she wanted more than anything.

She swallowed. "I don't know. I hope so?"

He turned his head toward her just so, but didn't look at her. He exhaled sharply out his nose once or twice, as though scoffing at some notion that only he'd heard. Then he licked his lips.

The cold air against her legs was the first thing to betray his movement. He lifted the blanket from the edge of the bed, the cool of his fingers running over her ankle bone as he turned on the mattress to face her. She recoiled just so. Despite having experienced this so many times in the sterility of his exam room, somehow his touch there - in the quiet of her bedroom — brought a depth of intimacy the might completely change the act that would transpire there. His hand took hold of her ankle and pulled her leg aside, causing her to lean back on the bed. He shifted onto his knee, pulling the blankets aside in a rough movement, leaving her legs bared to the cold. She moved her hands down, tucking her night shirt between her legs to shield herself from view. Why did she feel so exposed now, as though this man was new to her, as though he'd never touched her before?

Findlay set his hands on her knees and pushed them apart, lowering himself down over her as his hand slip up the inside of her thigh. His fingers found their mark and she stifled a cry. She turned her face to the wall, willing herself invisible to the intensity of his stare.

Her legs were open and limp on the bed, one knee leaning against the cold planks of the wall, the other was pressed across his hip. She couldn't decide why this felt so different. Was it because her back wasn't on a metal table, her legs not restrained in stirrups? Or was it because the last moment she'd been alone with this man, he'd kissed her? That kiss had changed things. It must be that kiss.

Findlay moved closer to her, rising on his knees as his hand moved. His touch was different as well. The focused precision of the procedure was giving way to exploration. Instead of maintaining his usual rhythm, he moved his fingers from inside her, touching and exploring every inch, humming softly to himself.

"My God, you're aroused for me already."

She inhaled in almost embarrassment as his fingers slid against her, his eyes trained on the work of his hands. Suddenly he pulled her right leg up from the bed, settling it over his shoulder as he leaned over her, forcing her leg high. She felt pinned there, helpless, but the new position amplified all sensation. He set his hand over her sex, pressing his knuckles to the most sensitive place, and began to slide his fingers from side to side with such speed and force that the muscles in her leg strained against him. He held steady, unmoved by her efforts. She grasped his wrist, fighting to slow his movements, but he simply leaned further over her, his lips twisting in a wicked smile.

"I want to hear ye. Let me hear ye."

His voice was hoarse, a whisper that sounded as foreboding as it did pleading. She feared what refusing would bring, but she almost feared ascension far more. She bit her lip, keeping still. Findlay's fingers slid inside her with enough force to elicit the sound he wanted. He chuckled, moving his fingers inside her. "Say my name."

She gasped, her hips beginning to move with him, completely out of her control. "Findlay," she whispered.

He groaned, pressing himself against her thigh, pushing her leg higher. Her chest tightened as she felt his body, something hard beneath the fabric of his long johns rubbing against her bare leg. She startled at the sensation, pressing her hand against his hip as he leaned a little too far, pushing her leg higher than she could manage. He started at the touch of her hand, turning his head down. Then with his brow set, he reached down and took her hand, and pressed it to the hard shape between his legs. Liv recoiled, stifling a cry of shock and almost fear. She'd never touched such a thing, and had only ever seen one through the keyhole of Findlay's bedroom door. Yet there it was, so close to her, almost threatening in its forbidden nature.

His fingers returned to their usual purpose, stroking and filling her the way he knew would bring her to release. She exhaled in a shaky cry, watching the way his body moved. He gripped her bare thigh, moving his hand over her skin, pressing his body to her in rhythm. He glared down at her, watching her face as she grew close to release.

"Cry my name," he said, his breathing growing hoarser as the bed creaked beneath them.

"Findlay," she said, the word trembled on her lips.

He lowered himself toward her, and she feared he might kiss her again. She opened her mouth.

"No. Call me Dr. Lennox."

She met his gaze, sensation tripling at the dark look in his eyes, and she did as she was told. "Dr. Lennox. Oh, please!"

He growled, grabbing her hand again and pressing it firmly to the shape beneath his long johns. This time she didn't recoil, letting him cup her hand around a softer shape there, kneading her hand around it as his hips moved. He would know she was close, and knew well how to finish this work of his, but he seemed to be drawing it out, relishing in it in a way he never had before. He smiled down at her, leaving her hand on him, watching her touch him.

Liv's hand was shaking as she rolled her fingers around the soft shape that seemed to be beneath his cock. She felt so inept, so useless, but she wanted desperately to please him. She rolled him in her hand, kneading gently like dough, watching for response. When his eyes closed and his head fell back, she reached for the waistband of his long johns. Despite the trepidation she felt, she would overcome it to see him sigh like that again.

He bare hand grazed against the hard shape of him. He startled at her touch, glaring down at her a moment as he exhaled. Then without a word, he shifted on the bed, grabbing her hips and yanking her to the edge of it. He pulled at the drawstring of his long johns and dropped to his knees on the floor. She watched in rapt attention, frightened and excited to see what he would do, but before she could ever guess his intention, he spit into his hand and grabbed ahold of his cock, stroking himself. Then with his free hand, he pressed her knees up toward her chest, and without any warning, slammed his open mouth between her legs.

Liv screamed, slamming her hand against the wall, fighting to brace herself against what was happening to her. She wanted to pull away from him. The shock of it scandalized her as much as the feel and warmth of his mouth aroused her. What must she smell like, or taste like? How could he want to put his mouth there? Yet as she grabbed hold of his hair, trying to pull him away, spare him the displeasure of committing such an act, he slid his fingers inside her, growling as he devoured her.

And he was devouring her. His mouth and tongue moved with the fervor of a starving animal feasting on prey, all while his fingers stroked madly, the folds of his shirt sleeve billowing with the movement. Liv screamed over and over, unable to stop him, and unable to deny how good it felt. The familiar heat of release was building at a pace she couldn't brace against, and she was left to watch him, breathless and silent as the first wave hit. Her body jerked beneath his mouth, and she tightened around his fingers. He doubled his efforts as the release washed over her, leaving her crying out in desperation with each new surge she felt. His hand moved fiercely on his cock as he panted against her. He gave a sharp cry, turning his face to her thigh and biting the flesh there hard enough to make her cry out. Then he sighed, panting there, his forehead resting against her thigh.

The two of them remained there in breathless

silence, Liv unable to find a word in any language that could rightly fill it. She swallowed, unable to settle the shaking of her legs.

Finally, Findlay moved, rising from his knees with a soft groan. He tied the drawstring of his long johns and lifted the hem of his nightshirt, wiping it over his mouth and face. Then he slumped down onto the foot of the bed, sitting there between her legs.

Several moments passed between them until the room seemed deathly still.

"Dr. Lennox?" She asked, forcing herself to sit up.

He almost startled at the sound of her voice, turning to face her. "Findlay," he corrected her.

She searched for words, but there were none. She stared at him, at the cool color of his eyes, blue even in the dark of the room, and her heart ached. She didn't have words to express what she felt, just that she wanted to take hold of him, pull him toward her and feel him surround her, living there in the warmth of him forever. But that kind of affection came with something she couldn't have. The kind of affection she wanted was to be found in a husband, not a master. He knew her only as a maid. How could she ever hope for more?

They stared at each other a moment, and when the urge grew too strong to combat further, Liv shifted on the bed, coming to kneel beside the long shape of him. He turned his eyes away, but he didn't protest as she slid her arms across his chest, taking him in an embrace that he lifted his arms to accept. Then, summoning every ounce of courage she had, she opened her mouth to speak.

I love you.

Yet the words stilled in her throat, terrified to be

heard. She felt her throat grow tight around them, as though not saying them might choke her. Yet her courage failed. No matter how true the words were, no matter how long they'd been true, she could not speak them. Instead, Liv pressed her nose to his cheek, rooting at him as she clutched her arms around him. Finally, he turned to her, and kissed her, his fingers getting lost in her dark ruddy curls.

He breathed her in there, kissed her again, then spoke in a whisper she almost couldn't hear. "My beautiful Deliverance. Please forgive me."

Then with that, Findlay rose from the bed and disappeared into the hallway, leaving her to remember the warmth of him as the cold of the room settled in.

CHAPTER TWELVE

The next day was Sunday, and even in the usual quiet of the house on a Sunday, the house took on the air of a tomb. It felt lifeless. Liv made her way through her chores, taking time for prayer and contemplation as was often allowed on a Sunday, but by tea time, she'd grown concerned with Findlay's absence.

When evening rolled around, she settled her nerves long enough to make her way toward the operating theater for one of her three weekly sessions with Findlay. She opened the theater door to find Findlay crouched over a table with a book, the massive room lit only by the single candle he had burning on the table beside him.

He barely glanced her way as she reached the bottom of the stairs. Unlike any other appointment, she felt a new trepidation, as though the air itself bid her unwelcome. She swallowed, stepping forward to announce her presence.

"I hope ye managed tea, alright? I left it for ye, but I didn't see ye come up."

He shook his head, making a soft grunting sound deep in his throat. "Wasn't hungry."

She swallowed, coming toward the table in cautious steps. By now she'd usually be atop the thing, waiting like the obedient patient she was, but after what happened in the quiet of her room, she felt apprehensive. His demeanor was so changed now, so

162

unwelcoming. She stopped there, waiting by the table.

"If you're too busy, I'll leave ye be."

"What's that now?" He asked, barely glancing up from his book.

She swallowed. "Our appointment?"

He sighed, setting his palm on the pages of his open book. Then he rubbed his hands over his face. "I think it best we cease the appointments."

Her stomach turned, a pain she couldn't contain nor understand. "If ye think it best," she said, the words coming as though scraped from her throat.

He nodded. "I do."

With that, he leaned over his book again, ignoring her as she turned back for the stairs. Yet, she stopped there, her hand on the railing, listening to the candle flicker in the grand space.

"Have I done something – something wrong?" She asked. She cringed at the girlish upset she betrayed in her tone, but she simply couldn't leave without knowing.

He took a deep breath. "No, Deliverance. You've done nothing wrong."

"What if the dreams come back?"

This wasn't a question of if, it was when, and she was sure they both knew it.

"We'll have to make due, lass. I can't have ye as a patient anymore."

She turned then, crossing the room towards him. "Why? What have I done?"

"You've done nothing!" He said, and his voice echoed off the high ceilings. "I am to blame. I can't be your physician anymore."

"I don't know why? If I've no done anything -"

"Because I can't -" He paused, glancing at her for

the first time. "Because. It's what is best. Now if you'll leave me please? I've a great deal of work to do."

She stood there just a few feet from him, staring into his back as though she might move him with her eyes, but he did not turn. She stood frozen in wanting for a long while, then finally turned from him, fighting to still tears as she made her way up the stairs and into the parlor. She succumbed before she made it past the study.

The whole of the empty house grew cold with more than the autumn air. Findlay disappeared, leaving Liv in the expanse of the house to mumble to herself as she completed chores and stoked fires. She became so accustomed to his absence over the next three days that she began to sing quite loudly as she scrubbed down the scullery or trudged the chamber pots.

Despite his absence, she heard him in the evenings, making his way back into the house or coming up from the operating theater in the smaller hours.

Liv felt hurt beyond words. She felt as though something powerful had been shared between them, but in an instant, he'd returned to that distant, almost non-existent creature he'd become after kissing her. Yet, now it was far worse. Now it was as though she bore the plague. She fought hard to still tears some mornings when she made her way down to offer him breakfast and found him already gone from the house for the day.

She began to wonder if he might prefer her gone, and it very nearly broke her heart. Still, she bustled away about the house, setting it to sorts in his and Fionnula's absence.

The fourth morning, she heard him come downstairs, making his way directly out the front door without greeting her in the kitchen. Her stomach hurt to think of it, but she set her jaw and focused on her tasks, collecting a list of things she needed from the Grassmarket. By mid-morning, she was wrapped in her shawl and gloves, hustling down the road toward Cowgate. She glanced at some of the familiar faces, having made the acquaintance of many of the Irish immigrants that made their homes there. She gave a nod to a rather thuggish young man with jet black hair, a habit she'd learned from Janet.

"If ye let em think you're afraid of em, they'll give ye reason to be," she'd said. Ever since, Liv made a point of passing the small crowds of men with her head held as high as a queen, often giving them a quick glower if they ogled her for too long. This worked well. She only hoped someone else's words wouldn't leap from her mouth and get her in trouble again.

This morning, the young man startled her with a tip of his hat. "Mornin, Miss Livvy."

She straightened, unable to hide her surprise. It had been a long time since someone spoke to her in the street like that. She quickly curtsied and continued along. The Grassmarket was quiet on that Wednesday afternoon, leaving her to run her errands with far more ease than she would like. She wanted to be kept from the house as long as possible, the heaviness of deliberate distance growing harder to withstand with every day that passed. She saved the butcher for last, floundering through the stalls to inspect junk or carved spoons. Liv found herself glancing around the Grassmarket frowning to herself each time she saw a small child or an empty corner where Daft Jamie might have been drawing attention to himself for the benefit of the gathered crowds.

Liv stood aside as a carriage came down from the Royal Mile and after a moment's consideration, set her jaw and turned up the road. She marched toward Canongate with determination, drawing glances from some of the more proper individuals as she passed.

The White Dog had a boisterous air from within, betraying the flowing drink and the regular crowd. Liv shouldered the door open and stood just inside, scanning the faces around her. She caught the attention of a couple gentlemen, one she recognized vaguely. He waved to her, offering a seat at his side. She nodded politely and continued to scan the faces until she found the one she sought. Janet met her gaze and was up from her seat in an instant.

"Well dearie, ye look a right state!" She said, coming across the public house with her dress half draped off a shoulder. She tucked her arm under Liv's, giving a dramatic shiver at the touch of her. "Bloody cold out there, ae? What're ye doin all the way down here, then?"

Liv took a deep breath, ready to speak, but before a single word could come, Liv broke down in tears. Janet made quick work to lead Liv into one of the back corners, tucking her into a table with her back to the room to shield her from the ridicule of prying eyes.

"Come now, love. Tell Janny what's wrong. Whatever it is? We'll make it right as rain."

Liv fought to still her sniffling, taking several deep breaths before she could finally speak a word. Then with the fury of someone possessed, Liv poured out her heart. She told the wide-eyed Janet everything.

"And now he won't even look at me! He must hate me, and I don't know what I done!"

Janet was slumped down in the seat beside her, clutching Liv's hand. Liv wiped Janet's kerchief to her eyes as she finished her tragedy, and waited for Janet to respond. Her friend simply stared at her in disbelief.

"When was this, like?"

"What? Which part?"

Janet leaned in closer. "When he used his mouth, like ye said."

"Oh, ah – three nights past."

Janet shook her head, taking a deep breath. "Ah, love. He doesn't hate ye, I know that much."

"But ye haven't seen how he's been the last -"

"Livvy, love. It doesn't matter. A man doesn't do that unless he's right fond of ye. Or he's a pervert, and our Findlay isn't a pervert."

"No! He's no a -"

Janet patted her shoulder, urging her to lower her voice. "Christ, our Dr. Lennox – diddlin the maid. Explains why he stopped our appointments those many months ago."

Liv swallowed, searching Janet's face. "He didn't."

"Oh aye. He certainly did. Takin no more volunteers for the time bein, he said."

Liv turned her eyes to her hands, nervously fidgeting in her lap.

Janet leaned into her, drawing close to whisper. "D'ye truly fancy the lad?"

Liv's face contorted before she could respond, and Janet patted her shoulder again. "Aye, then it's settled. We've got to convince im to stop bein such a prick."

"He's no a prick!"

Janet scoffed. "Oh aye, he is. A proper prick, but a prick nonetheless. The lad fancies ye as well as ye do him, ye know that, ae?"

Liv shook her head. These words felt warm to hear, but accepting them felt naïve – wishful thinking more than logic.

"Look, he's your master, and he's your doctor – and then he up and takes ye as his lover? If that isn't the most scandalous thing I've ever heard -"

"It's no like that!" Liv pleaded, but Janet waved her away.

"I'm no sayin so, I'm tellin ye what he must be thinkin. He's a good man, ae? In his mind, he thinks he's taken advantage, he says?"

Liv swallowed. "I don't know."

"Oh, I do. Well, if Mister High and Mighty wants to be proper, you'll just have to show him that what ye want matters, too, aye?"

Janet hopped up from her seat and conferred with the bartender a moment. Then she returned, snatching Liv up and leading her into a backroom. "You're gonna go home, then, and be the proper lady that ye are, but when you've a chance to have him alone – the old bag is still away, aye?"

Liv nodded. "She won't be home another week."

"Good. Ye wait until ye have him alone, and then here's what ye do -"

The house was bustling when Liv arrived home; young students coming into the hallway for private tutelage from the great Dr. Lennox. Liv pushed past them into the kitchen to set down her basket, then returned to greet and show the men through the parlor. She glanced down into the operating theater as she showed them in. Findlay was busy below, conferring with Dr. Knox and the sterner gentleman, Dr. Munro.

There were more men than the time before, the doorbell clanging in announcement of their arrival every few minutes. She greeted them all, led them down the hall to the parlor, and instantly took her leave to return to the door to greet the next. Once the traffic died down and the theater door was shut, she stood in the kitchen a moment, listening to Findlay's voice as he took command of the full room. She turned her attention to settling the day's purchases, tucking away the large wooden spoon she'd used her own wages to purchase for the kitchen.

She worked mindlessly, listening at all times to Findlay, though his words were too muffled by walls and distance to understand. She could hear the room laughing from time to time, the vibration of it carrying through the floorboards, and it made her smile. He sounded to be a very engaging teacher, indeed.

The doorbell startled her at half past, and despite the notion of late stragglers, Liv knew exactly what she would find when she opened the door.

The two men held the woman by her elbows and shoulders, her long hair matted to her forehead. She glanced up at Liv, then lunged for her, hissing and spitting. Liv darted back, taking up her apron to wipe the spit away as she welcomed the men inside. They both apologized profusely as they passed, showing the mad woman to the examination room.

Liv watched them go, listening to the crowd in the operating theater go silent as the woman entered, growling and screaming at all of them as she was led down the stairs. Liv stood in the hallway and watched as one of the students inside shut the door. She wanted to return to her work, settle into her cooking and cleaning, but her feet refused to move. She stood there staring down the hall at the theater door, imagining what was going on within.

This woman – a patient of Bedlam who knew Findlay no better than any other stranger would soon know his touch in a way that Liv was now denied. She would have his undivided attention, and he may not even know her name.

Liv's chest tightened as the screams of the woman stifled, then Liv turned for the study, running up the stairs to her room, desperate to be out of earshot of what was taking place in the lower levels of the house. She threw herself onto the bed and cried.

Despite her frazzled state, Liv made her way back downstairs to complete her chores. She was angry, but she was by no means going to neglect her duties. What would Fionnula say? The woman was led back out of the house not long after Liv returned downstairs. Another half an hour later, and the gentlemen began to filter up from the theater. She stood over the kitchen fire, pulling a meat pie from the oven as she listened to the young men's excited banter on their way out of the house. She'd heard all of this before, but this time she loathed their comments and excited tittering, wanting nothing more than to run out and box their ears for speaking praise of what Dr. Lennox had just done.

Bastards, she thought, and her face flushed.

By tea time, Dr. Munro and Dr. Knox were still in the theater with Findlay, the three of them conferring when Liv leaned in to announce the meal. The three men came up to the parlor, the two older doctors taking their leave. She was startled that they didn't choose to stay. She was even more surprised that Findlay didn't offer.

Liv stood in the kitchen waiting for Findlay to call for his supper, but instead he seemed to stand just inside the parlor, silent. The two of them remained there a moment, separated only by a wall, both silent and still.

Finally, Findlay came through the kitchen door. "Sorry, Deliverance, but I believe I would like to have a bath before I dine, if that is alright."

Her eyebrows shot up in irritated surprise. What right had she to disapprove her master's designs? "I'll bring the water up, then."

Findlay nodded, muttering a thank you as he stalled in the kitchen doorway. Then a moment later, he was gone. Liv made quick work of settling the basin and kettle over the fire. The first kettle was already steaming hot, and she mixed the scalding water with cool until she had a large basin of steaming water to carry up the stairs to Findlay's bath.

She fought with the heavy metal basin all the way up the stairs, careful not to jostle it so much to have it spill at her feet. She reached the bathroom door and bumped it open with her hip. She nearly dropped the bucket on the floor when she turned to find Findlay standing by the bathtub without his shirt. He quickly tugged his shirt back over his head, his pale skin flushed pink across the whole of him. Liv frowned to see him startle so, quickly moving across the room to pour the first basin into the tub.

"That'll do well enough, lass. I needn't anymore."

Liv scoffed, turning back for the door. "No, the tub will have chilled the water considerably. I've got two more on the fire that'll be ready in but a moment."

She didn't look at him when she spoke, but simply stormed back out of the bathroom.

So desperate to be outside my company that you'd choose a cold bath? You bastard, she thought.

She almost cringed then. She wasn't one for thinking ill thoughts of others, but that day, she'd muttered the word bastard in the direction of almost every man she'd met. Still, she hustled down the stairs to the fire to find the kettle already whistling away. She filled the second for another round, snatched up the first, and turned back for the stairs. She found Findlay still fully clothed, sitting on the edge of the tub in wait of her, his bathrobe hanging by the door.

Liv poured the scalding water into the tub, tendrils of steam whispering up from the massive copper basin. She turned for the cabinet, pulling a washcloth and bath sheet to lay across the back of the tub to keep Findlay's skin from touching the cold metal. Then she turned back toward the door without a word.

"Thank ye," he said softly as she slipped back out the door.

The basin wasn't roiling yet, but the water within was hot to touch. Liv pulled the basin down, then the kettle, combining the two for a final trip up to the bathtub. She slammed her hip into the door, irritated to find that he'd shut it while she was gone.

When she turned to look at him, his pale body was bared to her as he sat slunked down into the recesses of the copper tub. They both froze at the sight of one another, Findlay's hands moving quick to cover himself, though the side of the tub was too high to see anything beyond.

She swallowed. "I'm sorry, sir. I thought ye knew I'd be bringing another round."

"No, no. I'm sorry. Here," he said, pulling the washcloth into the tub to cover himself. Liv faltered by the door, both desperate and terrified to move forward and see the shape of him. She'd seen his chest before, but the long shape of his legs, lightly fuzzed from thigh to ankle with light red hairs – that was a sight to unsettle her. She thought of what it would feel like to run her hand over his skin there. Or over the sparse hairs of his chest. She took a breath and stepped toward the tub, setting the massive basin on the rim of it.

"This may be hot," she said, letting him shift his legs aside for her to pour the water in.

"Wait," he said, sitting up in the tub. "Will ye pour the last of it over my head?"

He met her gaze for one of the first times in three days, and she nodded. Then she poured the steaming contents of the basin into the tub as he groaned gratefully.

"Ah, that's perfect."

Then just as he'd asked, Liv moved toward the head of the tub, averting her eyes as best she could from the bundle of white that Findlay held over himself under the water. She poured the rest of the hot water over him.

She watched every ripple and droplet flow over his smooth skin, and she ached.

"Thank ye, Deliverance. Och, that water's perfect."

She gave a slight curtsey and turned back for the door, the basin clanging loudly against the doorjamb

173

in her haste to leave his company.

She shut the bathroom door and stood in the hallway, her heart racing.

"When you've got him alone, you're gonna touch him," Janet had said.

"What? Touch him how?"

"The way he touched you. I promise ye, whatever propriety that man possesses, he'll throw it all out the windae when he feels your mouth on his cock."

Liv had blushed a shade of crimson at these words, but Janet's orders surged through her mind at the sight of him there in the tub. He'd been bared to her, open in ways that had she wanted to, she could have touched him, though perhaps not in the way Janet prescribed. Still, she remembered the night when he'd put her hand on him, the way he showed her how to make him feel good. She wanted to try again.

She wanted to know the feel of his bare skin. Yet, she stood there in the hallway, scolding herself. Janet would be hugely disappointed that she hadn't taken the opportunity when it presented itself.

But what if he doesn't want me?

What if he pushes me away? Fires me for being so forward?

"Ah, but what if he doesn't?" Had been Janet's response. "Look, if he's gonnae fire ye for wantin him, then it's only a matter of time now, whether ye act on it or no. Best get a good time out of it before it happens."

Liv startled at the sound of the water sloshing within. She'd been standing just outside the bathroom door for so long, he'd finished his bath. She imagined him standing there, dripping wet, naked from head to toe, crossing the small room to grab his bathrobe.

Liv's hand loosened on the basin handle and it clattered to the hallway floor.

She was through the bathroom door in an instant.

Findlay froze there by the tub, looking her dead in the eyes as she shut the bathroom door behind her. He was exactly as she'd imagined, but somehow a thousand fold more beautiful. He held his hand over his cock, unable to cover the tangles of coarse red hair that framed it. She exhaled at the sight of him, searching her brain for an impulse that might make her move or speak, but nothing came.

Findlay swallowed. "Deliverance?"

Liv crossed the distance between them in three strides. He stiffened, but did not recoil as she pressed her hands to his chest. The water made his skin slippery to the touch, and she felt muscle beneath the soft skin, tensing as she pushed him backward toward the chair beside the tub. He slumped down into it, his hand still covering his sex. Liv dropped to her knees before him, feeling the water of the floor saturate through her skirts. She remembered Janet's exact orders, and pushed his knees apart, grabbing hold of his hand to pull it away. He let her, and her stomach leapt into her throat.

His cock was framed by red hair, half rigid across his thigh. She'd never seen this part of a man before, and the sight of him nearly terrified her. She startled just so, searching for the courage to do what Janet had demanded of her. Yet for a moment, the thought of moving closer to this part of him almost stole all her courage.

"Deliverance, love. Ye mustn't," he said. Yet his voice was husky and low as he spoke, his hands motionless at his sides. She ran her fingers through the hairs of his thigh, shuddering to feel the very thing she'd just moments before fantasized. Her hands moved upward.

Liv couldn't bring herself to touch him without his permission. She turned her eyes up to his, her breath catching in her throat. "But I want to," she said.

He frowned at her. Then a moment later, his brow furrowed and he grabbed hold of her wrists, pulling her up to her feet to stand before him. He didn't push her away, didn't retreat from her. Instead he wrapped his arms around her waist, pulling her against him. "Ye want me?"

"Aye," she said, the word shaking in her throat.

He bent to her, his nose rooting against her jaw. She ran her hands over his wet skin, curling her fingers until her nails dragged over his shoulders. She pressed her face to his chest.

He stiffened. "We mustn't."

She clutched him to her, fighting against his words.

"I can't take advantage -"

Liv felt his grasp on her change, but before he could push her away, she dropped to her knees before him. Then just as Janet had instructed her, took hold of him in her hand, and took as much of him as she could into her mouth.

Findlay unleashed a sound that she'd never heard a man utter in her life; a growl and a whimper combined. She felt his hands at the back of her head, taking hold of her hair gently as his fingers hooked at her jaw, gently trying to push her away. She grabbed his hand and ripped it away from her, sucking at him firmly. He tasted like water, with a subtle hint of something sweet and bitter beneath it.

"Please, love. Oh god, please! I can't -"

But the pleas died as he groaned. The muscles of his thighs tensed as his fingers got lost in her hair. She moved up and down the length of him, sucking at him as Janet showed her, careful not to let him feel her teeth.

"Get it right, and the lad'll be helpless to ye," Janet had said.

The sound of Findlay's voice left her feeling certain that if she wasn't quite getting it right, she certainly wasn't getting it wrong. She felt his body move, this hard thing in her mouth suddenly moving of its own accord as Findlay's hips surged forward just so. She settled her hands on his hips and left her mouth open to him, feeling him thrust there, gently. He filled her mouth, brushing her hair aside as he looked down at her. She pulled away then, breathing deeply before she moved to return to her work.

He grabbed hold of her hair then, making her look up at him. His blue eyes burned into her, the expression something so intense and unreadable that she felt she might shrink under its weight.

"Ye want me?" He asked again.

"Aye!"

Suddenly, he flared his nostrils and shoved her back, knocking her onto the floor. Before she could straighten, Findlay was on her, bearing his weight over her as he pushed her down.

She did not protest, opening her legs to him as he tore up her skirts. Yet, his hand didn't go to his usual work. She felt his fingers slide against her, then return to fighting with her skirts, pulling them up over her chest as the wet floor soaked her back.

Then he gave her an almost sad, but lustful look. "I'm sorry I can't make this hurt any less."

She gave a small whine of question and fear, but was stifled instantly by the hardness of him, pressing against her. She curled into him, clutching at his bare shoulders as he pushed inside her, causing her to kick her legs around him. The pain grew more intense and she whimpered, desperately. He responded by retreating, glancing down between them as he ran the head of his sex over her, giving her a moment's reprieve. It was a moment only. He pressed his fingers to her sex, rubbing where he knew she most enjoyed, his fingers playing at her with purpose. She sighed at the sensation. Then, he pushed himself into her again, deeper this time, to the point of that pain and a little past, his fingers still rubbing in tandem.

"Findlay! It hurts!" She cried, clutching him desperately.

He lowered himself over her, his breathing hoarse in her ear. "I know it, beloved. Forgive me."

With that, he opened his mouth to her ear, letting her feel his breath and the warmth of his tongue. Then without warning, he clamped his teeth down on her earlobe. She cried out against it just as he drove his cock into her as far as he could. The scream was lost in the shock and confusion of all the different sensations, leaving her to throw her head back in silent protest. He retreated slowly, his fingers still stroking her, kissing her as though asking for silent forgiveness.

She held her breath, Findlay's fingers drawing the familiar sensations as he pulled his cock from inside her, letting her muscles find relief.

"My sweet Deliverance. Forgive me," he said over and over. Then after a moment of whispers, he slowly pressed himself inside again. Her body yielded to him, and she whimpered. The pain left her shocked, unable to respond as he moved over her. The look of concern in his eyes was the only thing that could still the sting. She inhaled shakily as he retreated again, then thrust into her deeper, watching her closely for response. The pain was subsiding, leaving her to the feeling of his closeness, of the solid shape of him. Yet another thrust and he found a rhythm, the two of them sliding on the wet tile floor. Liv opened her legs wider to him, cautious in every movement.

She stared up at him as he moved, feeling his hands on her, his fingers, his breath on her face and in her ear. He looked at her with unwavering focus, and affection. She realized she would happily take this pain every single time if it meant he would look at her like that.

Findlay pulled her legs around him and pressed himself into her, grinding her into the tiles. She cried out in rhythm, startled by the sensation of it. His body weight pressed him to her in such a way that all the familiar places he touched in their appointments were now firing from the friction of his body. She reached down the length of him, clutching at his backside to pull him against her, building the pressure of his body on hers. He groaned in response, meeting her eyes with an almost grateful smile.

His breathing grew hoarser and he wrapped his arms around her, lifting her shoulders from the floor as his hips moved. She lifted her legs, unable to make a sound as the familiar sensation began to build, drawing heat to the place where he moved in her. She buried her face into his shoulder, clutching him tightly as his thrusts grew more desperate, loosing angry growls from deep in his throat.

Her body seized in familiar rhythm and she gasped. Findlay seemed to feel it, his growls growing louder, then shifting. Finally, he almost whimpered, thrusting into her three more angry times. He stilled then, slumping down onto her, breathless.

They held each other there, Liv unable to hold him tight enough to satisfy this strange desperation she felt. This was unlike anything she'd ever imagined. How could she be this close to him, feel him still inside her as he was, and still want desperately to be closer? It was an impossible want, and that knowledge made her heart ache.

"Ah, my sweet Deliverance. You'll be the ruin of me," he said, lifting himself just enough to meet her gaze and kiss her. His tongue slipped into her mouth and it fueled her desires anew, digging her fingernails into his shoulders, wanting to devour him all over again.

They lay there on the wet floor of the bathroom for a long time. When Findlay finally lifted himself from atop her, she felt almost cold in his absence.

He settled there on his knees, groaning from the stiffness in his legs. Then his hands slipped up the length of her thighs, parting her legs for him to look at her.

Liv startled at the sudden inspection, pulling her skirts down to shield herself.

He raised a brow at her. "I've seen ye many times, love. I want to see whether you're bleeding. Are ye in pain, still?"

"Bleeding?" She asked, sitting up with an even more desperate desire to shield herself from view.

"Aye, bleeding -"

"I'm a wee bit sore, but no bother. Please, Findlay.

Ye can be a doctor any other time, but no now."

He gave a half laugh, but his expression shifted somehow, betraying silent thoughts within. He helped her to her feet, making comment about the soggy state of her dress. Then he led her across the hall, startling her as he opened his bedroom door and waited for her to enter. Without a word, Findlay unbuttoned her dress, helping her out of it before turning to hang it by the fire to dry. Then he pulled back the covers of his bed, and invited her to lie down.

"What? In here?"

His brow furrowed and he set his eyes on the floor, but he nodded. "Aye. You're a soppin mess. You'll catch your death upstairs. Come now. Settle in and get warm."

Liv did as she was asked, curling up under the covers, hissing softly from the pain as she sat down on the mattress. He seemed to fret at the sound, but she simply smiled at him, trying to assure him in some wordless way that there was no trouble to this pain she felt. She was grateful for it. She loved every tiny part of the man that caused this pain.

He held the blankets aside, assuring her he'd return with some tea as he pulled on a dry, clean shirt. He went for the door, stopping as she groaned in contented gratitude. She rubbed her legs and feet together under the mass of quilts enjoying the warmth, the fireplace cindering away on the other side of the room. Findlay turned back toward her, coming down to meet her gaze at the side of the bed. He ran his thumb over the hair at her temple, his eyes darting from feature to feature over her face as though committing them to memory. Then he rose to his full height and ducked out of the room without another word.

She was asleep before he returned to his bed.

CHAPTER THIRTEEN

Liv woke with a start, straightening in the bed. She was coming from the depths of deep sleep, the air warm and light in the growing light of the room. The bed, the blankets, the air itself felt warm and cozy and safe. Such sensations were as foreign as an unknown language to her. She turned to find the bed empty, the other side of the bed still well made, evidence that neither she, nor anyone else tossed and turned in their sleep that night. She brushed the loose strands of her hair out of her face, listening to the low hums of male voices in the distance.

She knew not the time.

Had she overslept? Such a notion seemed absurd on any other night in her life, but in that bed, in the space that wore Findlay's sent like pearls, she suddenly thought it possible. Liv launched herself from the bed, snatching her dress down from over the fire, the fabric well dried and toasty warm.

The distant hum of voices rose as laughter betrayed their tone. She was dressed and settled in but a moment, the place between her legs still sore from the night before.

"Ah, there she is! Fresh from morning chores," Dr. Knox said, gesturing his greeting to her as she descended the stairs into the study. Findlay was there, but he did not look up. "We were hoping for a pot of tea, if ye wouldn't mind, dear?"

Liv nodded, glancing toward Findlay for a greeting; a passing look of something silent and deep. Still, he kept his back to her, inspecting the notes across the table. The kettle was empty, and the cinders were well faded, but a good stir with the poker and a couple fresh logs, and the fire was back to crackling in just a few moments. Rather than wait for the fire to gain power, Liv filled the kettle upon entering the kitchen and set it directly on the coals. By the time the flames had gathered strength, the tea kettle was hissing softly, warning of a coming whistle. The tea tray was set on the study table just a moment later, coupled with a few small biscuits.

"Lovely this, well done. I'll have two sugars, dear."

She furrowed her brow at this request from Dr. Knox. He'd come to tea several times since she first took up residence with Findlay. The man had never required her to fix his tea before.

"Now, have ye many bags to bring along, then? Or just the one?"

Liv stared at him. "The one what?"

Before Dr. Knox could respond Findlay turned around, his eyes still fixed on the floor. "I believe she just has the one. Deliverance dear, if you'll go gather your things -"

"Why would I do that?"

Findlay touched his finger to his nose. "I recall ye hadn't much when ye arrived. Dr. Knox's household will supply ye with better clothes, I am sure."

"Oh indeed!" Dr. Knox said, eyeing her dingy dress. "She'll be well taken care of."

Findlay swallowed. "I've arranged for ye to take a position in the Knox household from here on -"

"But I've no desire to leave here."

Dr. Knox nearly choked on his tea. "Oh my! Quite the willful thing, isn't she? That'll no do in my household I assure ye -"

Liv stepped toward Findlay. "What is it I've done? Why are ye doin this?"

Findlay took her by the arm, leading her into the back of the house toward Fionnula's quarters. His hand was gripping her arm tight as they moved, but not enough to hurt.

As they rounded the corner, she yanked her arm free of his hand and turned on him. "I'll no leave! Ye can't make me!"

"Ye will, Deliverance. Ye must."

Her nostrils flared, the cold air at the back of the house stinging the inside of her nose. "Why are ye doin this to me? I didn't do anythin wrong!"

The tears were coming fast, but she fought to still the tightness in her throat as Findlay turned away from her.

"I know well you've done nothin wrong, but *I* bloody have."

"Rubbish!"

"It isn't rubbish, girl. There's a line I've crossed, between master and servant – Christ, between doctor and patient! I betrayed your trust," he said, and the misery of his tone only drew her throat tighter.

"You've done no such thing! I'm no a child, Findlay. I knew well enough what I was -"

"No! Ye knew nothing of what ye were doin. I should never have touched ye."

She took a breath. "How can ye say that?"

He turned to meet her gaze, his breath short and sharp. "I was your doctor – I exploited the trust ye bore me as such. From the very first time I laid a hand on ye, I wanted ye. Not as a patient, as a woman. Whatever ailments I claimed to want to relieve, the most powerful one was my own. I knew well what I was doin. I did it anyway."

"I wanted ye, too!" She said, pleading, but he pretended not to hear.

"Now, because of me, you're no longer – Christ, you're no longer a maiden, Deliverance. That's my fault. I did this to ye!"

She swallowed. "And now ye punish me for it?"

"No! This isn't punishment. I've crossed a line – I've betrayed your trust and I can't take it back. Ye don't know what I've done."

"I don't want to go!"

Findlay shook his head, forcing the emotion from his voice as though suddenly unaffected. "Dr. Knox makes a far better income than I. He's offerin a better wage, a more comfortable life. I've Fionnula, I've no need of a scullery maid. It's putting far too great a strain on my household to pay your wages."

The strangely businesslike way in which he was conducting himself, as though ending the employment of a gardener to whom he never spoke, broke her heart. She grabbed hold of his shirt, pulling close to him, fighting to speak words that caught in her throat more than once before. "Don't do this, Findlay. You've no betrayed me. I love ye."

He rolled over her words as though he hadn't heard them. "You're young and naïve. Ye don't understand the position I'm in. The position this affair puts me in. The decision has been made."

Liv stepped back, glared up into his beautiful, sad face, and slapped him. He took it, wordlessly. When he didn't react, she slapped him again. He didn't look at her.

"Will she be ready soon, then? I've a lesson at noon and I'd like to take my tea at home this afternoon," Dr. Knox called from the study.

Liv's lip was trembling as she glared at Findlay, daring him to look at her – to give her any cause to slap him again. He didn't move.

Her heart was pounding in her chest, searching for the magic words that would change his mind, but she could find none. Even as they stood still, she felt a distance growing between them. She swallowed, steadying herself to face her new employer. She wouldn't give any other man the satisfaction of seeing her pain as she'd let Findlay see it.

She took a deep breath and spoke softly. His expression showed that he heard her. "You're a bastard, Findlay Lennox."

She turned on her heel, lifting her chin as she made her way down the hall and back into the study.

Liv curtsied to Dr. Knox. "I'll be down in a moment, sir."

"That's a good lass! I'll be with the carriage just out front. Hurry now."

She promised him that she would and disappeared up the stairs to her cold, attic bedroom, packing the little she owned into a single carpet bag.

"Mary! Jessie! Come down, will ye?"

The house on Newington Place was quite respectable, betraying the surgeon's good fortune. He regaled her with all the common responsibilities expected of her on the way through town – nothing she wasn't already accustomed, too. Yet, unlike Findlay's home, he informed her of the constant presence of his two sisters within the home.

Liv stood just inside the door, waiting for the Knox sisters to join them downstairs, her small bag clutched in her hands.

"Well now, isn't this a lovely surprise," the lighter haired sister said. She wasn't young, and was by all means plain, but she had a light and sophisticated air, betrayed heavily by her attempts to stifle the Scottish accent when she spoke. The woman stepped forward, waiting for Liv to curtsy. She did so. "I've been telling brother for years how desperately we needed attending. Good help is so hard to come by."

"Aye, grateful to have ye, child." This was the second sister, the darker haired one that went by Jessie. Both women looked to be in their forties, their hair still holding on to its youthful color beneath a strong flush of gray and gold. Liv curtsied, but didn't speak, letting Knox lead her through the house, informing her of her place and her chores. Despite the larger size of the home, the kitchen was in a shambles compared to the well-kept system of Fionnula's scullery. She took in the sight of each room, the flowered wallpaper and curtains betraying the presence of a woman's sense of taste. When Knox finally showed her to her quarters – a tiny room just behind the kitchen – he left her to her own devices, informing her of what he felt inclined to having for dinner – an encore performance of her pea soup. She would need to visit the Grassmarket for that.

Liv tucked her bag under her cot, and set to work, doing her best to breathe deep and slow as she went about each simple task. Yet, even lifting her hand to pin her hair up left her exhausted. Simple things became arduous when all her will was aimed at stilling the urge to weep. She ached in everything she did, in every glance toward a portrait or book – the portrait wasn't of Findlay's family, and the books were tucked away in their shelves, not strewn across tables.

Still, she was determined to show a brave face and make the best of her situation. Knox assured her he could pay her two pound more a year, and her room was next to the kitchen, offering warmth in the night hours, making the room cozy enough, despite its complete lack of windows and natural light.

Yet, even in these moments of stubborn determination, the house felt wrong. Findlay wasn't there to leave papers and have scribbled notes on every surface, yes, but beyond that, there was a heaviness to the space, the way grief hangs over the home of a widow. Liv greeted her new household in the parlor, offering Dr. Knox a list of required ingredients for his chosen dinner. He handed her three shillings, and she made her way out into the cold Scottish air, walking well out of her way to avoid coming anywhere near Surgeon's Square.

"Deliverance, the entire house smells of pork."

"Come now, lass. The tea's gone cold."

"Has my brother not bought you a new dress? This one is in shambles. We must have him send out for a new one."

Mary and Jessie took no time getting Liv accustomed to working for the Knox family. They spent the afternoon huddled in the parlor, sipping tea, working at needlepoint, reading, asking questions, making complaints, and between all of that, demands. Liv did not trouble at such needy charges, she'd grown up with a mother who demanded far greater, with far more troubling reprimand when Liv didn't meet expectations. Some part of her was grateful for the distractions – the busier they kept her, the less she could get lost in thoughts of Findlay.

Despite the lackluster gratitude of Knox's sisters, Robert Knox was courtesy itself when he sat down to take his tea. He found the pea soup just as savory as he'd remembered. The three Knox siblings took their meal, conversing over their dinner. Liv sat to eat her own meal in the kitchen, the bowl of soup growing cold before her on the newly scrubbed counter. Her stomach wouldn't allow a single bite. She'd barely been able to cook the soup, her stomach so rebelled against the notion of food. Still, she went about the act like a marionette in a pantomime, staring into the bowl as though it might tell her fortune.

Deliverance.

She straightened, hopping up from her seat and rushing into the dining room to greet her charges. "Yes?"

Robert turned to face her, eyebrows up, soup spoon to his lips. The two women turned lazily, a similar look of disinterest on their faces.

"Have ye need of something?" She asked, waiting for explanation.

The two women shared a soft chuckle, but Dr. Knox just smiled. "Why no, girl. We're quite settled. Though now that ye mention it, I might like a bit of brandy. The cabinet is in the parlor."

Mary gave the doctor a glower, chiding him as Liv turned for the receiving room in search of the liquor cabinet.

Deliverance.

"Aye! I'll be right there," she called, only to hear an

exasperated response from Mary Knox. She returned with a decanter and three glasses, making sure to be prepared for one of the sisters wanting a drink.

Mary's eyebrows shot up at the sight of the glasses. "Oh for heaven's sake, I didn't request brandy, child. Take that back."

"Aye, I've no desire either, thank ye."

Liv quickly set the brandy in front of Dr. Knox and hustled back out of the dining room, taking the two extra glasses back to the liquor cabinet. She opened the doors to the cabinet, setting one back on its shelf.

Deliverance!

She startled, turning toward the sound of the voice. A pair of angry eyes glared at her just inches from her shoulder. She screamed, losing hold of the second brandy glass and stepping away from the familiar face of Mary Paterson as it shattered on the floor.

"What on earth!?" She heard as a commotion betrayed her charges' approach. Liv glanced toward the door and back to the frightful sight of Mary. Mary was gone.

The three Knoxes appeared in the parlor door, Dr. Knox quickly turning a shade redder. He crossed the room, standing over the broken glass, making a disappointed tsking sound as he stood over the shards, his nose turned up as though the scene smelled of dog excrement.

"Ah, Deliverance. I'm sorry to say, but that will have to come out of your wages."

"I'm sorry. I'm so sorry, I'll sweep this up. Clumsy me."

The sisters disappeared from the doorway, their voices carrying in, scoffing at her behavior on her first day. Dr. Knox made a soft grunting sound deep in his throat, then took his own leave to finish his dinner. Liv hurried to the kitchen for the dustpan and broom. Dinner came and went, drawing the Knoxes to bed, but Liv was set to a list of chores that kept her up well into the night. She spent the rest of the evening glancing over her shoulder, the heavy weight of being watched following her from room to room.

"Deliverance, my chamber pot needs emptying!"

"This room needs a good round of dusting. I don't think you've done it thoroughly enough."

"Deliverance! My bed warmer's gone cold! Where are you?"

"Goodness, what a lenient master Dr. Lennox must've been. You aren't the most efficient, girl. Are you?"

The days passed much the same as the first. Nothing Liv could do was good enough, save for cook. Liv silently praised Fionnula's name with each passing night, when the only moment's peace she found was when the three Knox siblings sat about their dining room table, stuffing their faces. Pea soup, Pork pie, Haggis and Parsnips from the Grassmarket. She may be useless as far as the Knox sisters were concerned, but when it came to the evening meal, Dr. Knox considered her worth every penny. She was grateful for this, given that as the days passed, she found herself displeasing the sisters more and more.

This was in no small way impacted by her complete lack of sleep.

The visitors were coming again. Even without a window to offer light, she knew them to be there. Shadows seemed to form at her bedside, figures standing over her, moving in the corners of the room. Sometimes she would hear them – breathing, or muttering softly to themselves. So softly that words could not be deciphered. She woke at all hours, her heart racing with the strange heaviness of some unseen company. By the third night, Liv knew that if she continued without sleep, the Knox sisters' ire might turn even the well-fed Dr. Knox against her.

Liv made sure her bedside lamp was full, and turned it down low as she went to sleep that evening. The room was warm from the turned over fire in the kitchen, and though the lamp light made her shadow dance on the wall, exhaustion called her to sleep soon enough.

She woke with a familiar start. Her heart was racing and her body shook with a familiar chill – there was something there. She swallowed, her eyes set on the wall just inches from her face, watching her silhouette dance as she chanted to herself, 'Go away. I demand you go away. Leave me alone.' These were the words Fionnula told her would be enough, if she only meant it.

Yet no matter how desperately she thought them, this unseen guest remained. Liv curled into a ball against the chill, willing the thing gone. Was it Mary again? Why was she in Dr. Knox's house? Why did they follow her to a new home?

Liv chanted softly, drawing her courage enough to whisper the chant aloud. The dancing shadow on the wall began to fade – the lamp was going out. Liv stilled her whispers, clutching the blanket to her chin and going silent. She felt as though this coming darkness was punishment for having spoken them.

Please, please, please, don't go out! She thought.

The light dimmed to near dark, then returned, still wavering on the table behind her. Liv knew if she turned over, if she simply turned the knob on the lamp, the light would burst to full power, fill the room and drive out any guest that might be there. If only she could be brave.

Be brave, Livvy. Be brave.

Liv sat up quickly, reaching for the lamp. Despite the cover being firmly atop it, no sooner had her hand touched the knob than the flame went out. Liv stifled a whimper, feeling the strange weight in the room grow heavier with each passing moment. She scrambled for the matches, running her hand over the surface of the table until she felt the tiny box. She snatched it up, pulling a single stick from within and striking it.

The figure was inches from her face, angry and open mouthed, crouching down beside her bed to bring its face close to hers. Liv screamed, flinging the match as she kicked and flailed toward the figure, bringing the room back to full dark. She clawed at empty air to make it leave her be and lunged from her bed in the darkness, careening out into the kitchen to look back into her bedroom and see the figure whole. Though she could see nothing, its presence was there, still heavy and stifling.

The kitchen was warm, almost oppressively so, unlike the bone deep chill of her room. She stood there in the kitchen breathless, unwilling to go back into her room, to be in that small space with whatever was there.

It's just dreams, she thought, replaying Findlay's attempts at comfort. Dreams? No, she was awake. She knew it to be true. She'd always been awake. For every visit, for every cold night, when these figures came to her, she was always awake. They made sure of it.

Liv exhaled finally, scanning the kitchen for a new source of light. She took a candle from the mantelpiece and lit it in the cinders from the kitchen fireplace. She stood there in the golden glow a moment, fearful of every shadow and corner, as though they all held murderous intent. She felt as though they waited for her to blow out the candle and let them loose. She swallowed, backing out of the dark kitchen and into the main hallway. She knew one answer to her troubles – the same answer her father had chosen so many nights. If she could not be woken, she could not be troubled by these ceaseless things.

Liv scurried down the hallway, her night shift billowing behind her as she rushed into the parlor and opened the doors to the liquor cabinet. She scanned the bottles of gold and amber, settling on the bottle with the most to offer. The whisky was a light amber color, sloshing quietly in the bottle as she pulled it from its perch. She pulled the stopper out, and without pause brought the bottle to her lips and took two long swigs on the burning liquid, letting them roar in her belly as she breathed deep between each one. She stood there a moment, the candle flickering softly in her hand. Then she brought it to her lips for one more long drink, and set it back on the table. The stopper was in place and the bottle back in its proper shelf, when she stepped her bare foot down on a tiny shard of glass, somehow missed by her broom days before. She stumbled, tipping over onto a nearby ottoman as she lifted her foot for inspection.

"Brother, she's in here."

Liv startled, turning for the parlor door just in time to see a stern faced Dr. Knox appear there, his sister

Mary clad in her shawl and shift, a displeased expression to match his own. Liv stood instantly, glancing from his angry face to the still open liquor cabinet.

"I'm sorry! I'm so sorry! I couldn't sleep!"

He crossed the room in two strides, grabbing hold of her arm and yanking her to her feet. "Is this why Dr. Lennox was so keen to be rid of ye? You're a bloody thief?"

"No, sir! No!"

He yanked her toward the parlor door, forcing her to walk on the injured foot as the glass drove deeper with each step. He hauled her down the hallway and through the kitchen, pushing her back into her room. "Stay there!"

With that he disappeared, leaving her to settle on the edge of her bed, fighting with the dim light to find the glass cutting into her foot and pry it free. She winced, digging her fingernails in to retrieve it. Then turned the candle to her lamp, relighting it just as Dr. Knox's footsteps betrayed his hasty return. She stood quickly, ready to greet him and apologize – explain herself anew.

"I'm sorry, Dr. Knox. I swear I'll replace it. It's just the only thing that helps me sleep some -"

He let something fall from his hand, long and glinting black in the lamp light. The sight of it stilled the words in her throat. She swallowed.

"A thief *and* a drunkard. I will speak to our Dr. Lennox about this tomorrow. Kneel down, girl."

Liv splayed her fingers before him, a gesture of supplication. "Please sir. I promise it'll never happen again!"

"You're bloody right it won't. Kneel down and

lower your shift."

She stifled a sob, but she did as she was told. When her shift didn't fall far enough down her back for his liking, Dr. Knox grabbed the hem of it and tugged it down roughly. "Now, I'm sorry you've given me reason to do this. It isn't my nature."

"Please," she begged.

His tone had betrayed caution, a displeasure at the thought, but despite this, her word had no sooner crossed her lips than the belt whipped across her shoulders, drawing a cry of pain. She braced for the second strike, and it came with precision, drawing more pain than the first. Liv pressed her face into her hands and grit her teeth, fighting to silence her sobs as he whipped her over and over again. She fought not to scream, not to make a noise, just as her mother had always demanded.

"You'll no behave like that in my house, ye hear me?" He asked, winding up for another swipe.

Liv nodded, sobbing her ascension as he struck her again.

He lost steam by the fifth pass, and stopped at eight, wrapping the belt around his hand He turned for the kitchen, disappearing into the depths of the house, winded from his exertion. Liv knelt there for a long while, sobbing. She was afraid to pull her shift up over her sore back. She wanted Findlay. She wanted to feel the safety of his company, to have him protect her from these frightening visitors, the fear of the dark and of being alone. But he wasn't there. Findlay had sold her to a man with a belt.

Liv stood up from the floor, hissing as she forced her shift over her back. Then she pulled her bag from beneath the bed, and slid her arms into her dress.

CHAPTER FOURTEEN

The streets of Edinburgh teemed with a strange energy in the wee hours of the night. Liv careened through Old Town, the whisky kicking in with enough force to cause her to brace against walls and fences every few steps. Still, she was determined enough to keep moving. She left the Knox house deathly quiet, her back now throbbing in a constant heat from her lashings. She reached the College, catching sight of some of the taller builders as she crossed a muddy street. There was a ruckus down a side close, betraying the lively crowd of a public house, still serving in the late hours.

Liv shifted on the corner, her carpet bag throwing her off balance as she stomped into a divot in the road. A couple young men called to her, one surging across the street as the others laughed.

"Had a bit too much, ae, lassie?" He asked.

She turned on him, glaring with all her fury. His clothes weren't shabby, but the smirk betrayed intentions she wasn't welcome to. She swung the carpet bag around, slamming it into his shoulder.

"You're no wanted! Get gone!"

He threw his hands up as his friends laughed across the way. He turned back to the pub as he muttered a few colorful words in her direction. Liv ignored him, turning toward the Royal Mile, fightin to avert her eyes from the College.

She was alone there, more alone than she'd ever been, and had nowhere in the world to go. She couldn't go to Findlay, he'd cast her out like some meaningless lodger who didn't pay her rent, and she refused to return to Dr. Knox.

The last person to give her a lashing was her mother, and she'd traveled halfway across Scotland to make sure the woman never laid a hand on her again. She'd vowed then, even if it killed her, she'd never go back. She certainly wasn't going to live with anyone else who'd treat her the same. No matter the wages.

Liv stumbled through Cowgate and into Canongate, met with the boisterous sound of a public house still at full sail.

"Is Janet no here?" She asked, leaning against the bar to catch her balance. She didn't feel drunk, but her head felt as though it lobbed from side to side between her ears.

The bartender gave her a puzzled look.

She glared at him. "Janny? Janet? Janet Brown!"

"The blondie?"

"Aye?" She said, half asking half agreeing to anything in hopes it would result in her meeting with a familiar face. The bartender furrowed his brow in concentration as he poured another drink, but he nodded, gesturing for her to wait.

"Fancy seein you here, then! What an hour for it, as well."

Liv turned toward the round and friendly face of a man she'd seen more than once before. Despite his friendly demeanor, each time she'd met him, she couldn't for the life of her remember his name.

"Will? You remember me, don'tcha?"

She focused on him a moment, then nodded. "Aye,

of course."

"Livvy! What on earth ye doin here, love?"

Liv turned to find Janet standing before her and almost burst into tears. Janet moved her over to a stool before Liv could collapse there on the pub floor.

"Good grief, have ye been drinkin, lass?" Janet asked, pulling Liv's bag from her curled fingers and setting it on the floor. Before Liv could answer, a man called Janet from the corner of the pub, waving for her to return. She waved to him, then turned back to Liv, inspecting her. "And you've been cryin. What's the matter, my girl?"

Liv's lip began to tremble, and Janet slumped down on the stool beside her, waiting to hear the sordid tale of troubles. Yet, even with a willing ear, Liv couldn't bring herself to relive the last few days. Each time she opened her mouth to speak, her throat tightened and her lip quivered. All she was able to blurt out was the most painful detail – Findlay had turned her out and sent her Dr. Knox.

Janet's brow set, and she took a deep breath in preparation of some grand declaration, but before a single word could come, the man in the corner rounded the bar, coming to stand beside them.

"Janny. Are ye comin? I'm expected back, ye ken?"

She groaned, rolling her eyes at the man, but she turned back to Liv and rubbed her shoulder. "Love, d'ye mind? I've got somethin that needs tendin, then I'll be back. Can ye sit here til I'm done?"

The man shifted anxiously beside them, eyeing Janet in a strangely familiar way – in a way she'd once seen Findlay look at her. The recognition broke her heart anew and she turned in her stool toward the bar. "Aye. Go ahead. I've no place in the world to go, anyway!"

Janet leaned into her. "It'll just be a minute. Lad can't last to save his life."

Then she kissed Liv on the cheek and disappeared out of the pub.

Liv glanced up at the bartender with a glare as loud as having called his name. He moved toward her, leaning on the bar to listen.

"Give me a glass of somethin. I don't care what."

Bartender stared at her a moment, then he nodded and turned back to the bottles.

"Oi, Martin. Put it on my tab, will ya?"

Liv turned to protest, but the friendly faced man just smiled. "I insist. Ya seem ta be havin a rather unfortunate evenin. Least I can do to cheer up a sweet girl such as yersel," he said, lifting his own glass as hers arrived. She looked down at the frothy liquid and took a deep breath. Then she tipped her glass to Will and they both drank deeply.

The streets were growing quieter now as the wee hours of the evening crept into early morning. She clung desperately to her carpet bag, willing it to keep her upright as she followed Will up the road.

"You're certain I'm no troubling ye?" She asked, stumbling over the word *certain* as though an anchor was dragging behind it.

"Course I am, love. We've plenty room."

Rather than allow Liv to wait alone for Janet's return, her friendly companion offered not only banter, but to buy her drinks as the time wore on. He told stories of his home in Ulster, asked after her own home in Inverness, confessing to having visited more than once. Though she knew not any of the places he mentioned having visited, she enjoyed listening to him speak of it. By his account, Inverness was a far more exciting place than she remembered. Though, her corner of Inverness had no beauty.

She'd had enough to drink after an hour of his generosity that she confessed to running away from home, fleeing an angry mother to answer a job advert.

When Janet didn't return after an hour, William was too concerned to leave her in the public house alone. He offered her a room for the night, free of charge. It took several minutes of cajoling to convince her. Several minutes, and the sight of the bartender settling up to close for the night.

"I do mean to pay ye. I've *some* money. Isn't much, but I've some!" She said.

Will just smiled back at her. "Ah, it's no trouble, dearie. I'm not the kind of lad ta leave a poor girl out on her own at night. You've a place ta stay the night. And the morrow as well, if ya need."

Even with his sideburns and stern brow, a smile lit up his eyes, betraying dimples just barely visible in his cheeks.

She smiled at her new friend, letting him steady her as they reached the corner to his close. She glanced up at the archway, but couldn't make sense of the name.

"I promise, I'll be no trouble. And – oh! I'm a maid! If ye like, I might work for my bed -" She stifled a burp, covering her mouth as she swayed in the alleyway. "- pardon me! I mean to say, I might work for my bed, but in the mornin. No now."

Will chuckled, turning to unlock a door just off the alleyway. "Mind yersel. I believe Mr. and Mrs. Hare will be sleepin."

She nodded, pressing a finger to her lips in solidarity with a shushing sound. Then she entered the small entryway to William's lodging house, giggling softly to herself.

"Wait. Who're Mr. and Mrs. Hare?"

"My partner and his wife – oh, saints preserve us!"

She'd turned to watch him close the door and leaned a bit too far to the right, almost toppling into the small reception room. William lunged forward, bracing her by the shoulders and leading her to the settee.

He helped her sit down and crouched before her, inspecting her face. "I'm afraid you're drunk, lassie."

She scoffed. "No, sir. You're sadly mistaken. I'm no drunk. I'm *very* drunk."

William laughed, patting her on the shoulder. "Enjoy the whisky do ya?"

"Aye. Keeps the ghosts away."

"At least sometin does." William stopped, searching her face a moment with some unspoken sadness. Then he shook his head. "Here, let me take your bag, will ya?"

She released her hold on the carpet bag and slumped back. She feared if William didn't show her to a room soon, she might fall asleep right there on the settee.

"Ya sit tight, I'll shoot upstairs and have a look round – see which room is open. Be right down."

Liv nodded gratefully, letting her head lean back on the settee as she watched him run up the stairs, taking the steps two or three at a time.

The room was lit only by a nearby fireplace and a small oil lamp, both burning very low in the late hour.

She fought to bring her head upright, feeling the woozy disjointed sway of the alcohol and wanting nothing more than to lie her head back again and shut her eyes. She didn't dare lie down on the settee, but with each passing moment that William was upstairs, she found the pull of sleep harder to resist. She turned her head to watch what little flame there was left in the fireplace, listening to the crackle and hiss, as her head grew heavy.

Deliverance!

She startled, searching for the source of the voice. The space was dark now, and she felt the weight of the whole world somehow bearing down on her, holding her still.

Deliverance! No!

She tried to open her mouth to call back, but her jaw was locked shut, her lips pressed together with such force that she couldn't so much as hum. She shook in place, unable to turn her head or breathe. Something was wrong! She could feel someone there, feel a dozen someones there, all of them screaming her name, all of them wailing for her attention. She struggled to shut them out, but she could no more still them than she could move.

"Get off her ye fucks! She's no like that!"

DELIVERANCE!

Liv opened her eyes then and saw a severe man, his face hovering just inches from her own, his knees pinned to either side of her. She tried to flail at him, make him move away, but he was too heavy for her to budge. In the instant she realized where she was, her body began to shake. She turned then, breathing deeply, as though she'd run for miles in her sleep. The man was pushed aside and Janet's concerned face was there, searching her own.

"Did they touch ye, love? Did they hurt, ye?"

"What? No, they didn't -" Liv turned to search the room for her companion, William. Another familiar face surged from the darkness before her, coming to stare into her eyes. Liv recoiled, screaming as the eyes kept their focus on her face and moved closer. She recognized those eyes, dark brown and furious, but the gentle face that once framed them was gone now, replaced by blood and bone. Where Mary's sly smile had once been, there was now bared teeth and exposed muscle, her skin cut away to the bone.

"No! Don't touch me!"

She turned away from the face to find another, this one unfamiliar, but equally horrific, equally desperate to be seen. She scrambled away from the figures, their naked bodies open and raw, betraying the workings of muscle and tissue, the way Jamie's body had on Dr. Knox's dissection table. She shut her eyes tight, willing herself awake from this horrific dream.

"What did ye do to her?!" Janet screamed, but Liv couldn't find her in the chaos of the room. Everywhere she looked there was another face, or what was left of it, glowering at her from all corners. Liv kicked at Margaret, approaching from over the couch, her body naked and her belly open.

"We didn't do a bloody thing, woman!"

"Make it stop!" Liv cried, toppling off the settee to the hardwood floor.

"What is that bloody ruckus down there, you lot!?"

The woman's voice was distant, drawing the two men to the stairs.

"For feck's sake, get that mad bitch out of here!" One of the men bellowed, his voice new and darker.

Liv felt arms on her shoulders, moving her from the floor. She fought against the touch, slapping and clawing in every direction to stop the sudden onslaught of bloodied faces, the touch of their fingers nothing more than bones.

I can't breathe. I can't breathe!

"They're cut to pieces! Don't let em touch me!" She screamed.

"What'd she say?!" One of the men hollered, but Liv was on her feet, being dragged across the room. Blue light filled the space as the front door of the lodging house opened, betraying the light of early dawn. A moment later, Liv was being dragged down the small close, her voice echoing off the stone walls and into the main street.

"Livvy, come now! What were ye thinkin goin with them? Christ! Calm down!"

Liv could hear Janet's voice, but when she turned toward it, all she saw was Mary's dark, angry eyes, half her face cut away. Liv smashed her hand into it, shoving the face away.

"Jaysus girl!"

With that, she felt arms tighten around her shoulders, pinning them to her sides as Janet pulled Liv's hand from her face. "I'm tryin to bloody help, ye. Will ye stop, now?"

The city street appeared before her, but each person walking past, each sound she tried to identify all led to the same sight, the same horrific vision of torn flesh and rage filled eyes. Liv began to keen loudly, suddenly remembering her father. For the first time in her lifetime, she didn't blame him for leaving her.

"Deliverance! Stand up, lass!"

"I can't! Leave me!" She cried, clamping her hands

over her face to drown out the sight. Still, she could feel them. That same heavy presence that haunted her at night, it was there now - all around her, even in the busy early morning bustle of carts and workmen making their way to the canal or the Grassmarket.

Where's my bairn? Why did he take her from me?

"What bairn? What's this now? Come on lass, people are lookin!" Janet hissed, moving Liv across the street, holding her by the shoulders as Liv writhed against being touched. She closed her eyes, but even out of sight, they tortured her, letting her feel the burning sting of her skin being cut. She felt the searing pain streak across her belly, clutching at herself as she screamed.

"Please god! Kill me! Make it stop!" She cried. Janet grabbed her roughly, straightening her, and slapped her face so hard everything disappeared for an instant. She could see Janet's face - her true face - and the lines or worry etched on her brow.

"Calm down, lass. They'll take ye to Bedlam if ye don't stop. Come on! I'll take ye home! Where is Dr. Knox?"

Liv almost collapsed into Janet's arms, sobbing.

I should be home. My mother doesn't know where I am. I should go home.

Janet shushed her, then grabbed Liv around the shoulders, marching her down the cobblestone streets toward Cowgate. Liv didn't dare look up from her feet for fear of what might come from all corners. She didn't feel their touch now, but still she could hear them, hissing and screaming her name over and over. She pressed her palm to her sore cheek, praying the visions would not return.

Janet dragged her down the roads, shushing the

constant mutterings that poured from her lips. She felt raw and naked, waiting for attack, knowing she had no way to fight it. They made their way up a long slope and turned the corner.

"There ye bloody are! What are ye playin at, girl?"

Liv startled, squirming in Janet's arms as she tried to move away from Dr. Knox.

"Are ye this Dr. Knox? She isn't well. I'm takin her to Dr. Lennox."

Dr. Knox grabbed hold of Liv's face, forcing her to meet his gaze.

She screamed again, an indecipherable string of words without language. She could hear Dr. Knox and Janet arguing, feel their hands on her, moving her. She fought against them both, kicking and screaming wildly, as though she might still this vision with sound.

Ye wannae get your filthy hands on me, ye cunt?

Both Janet and Dr. Knox gasped.

"Don't ye speak to me like -"

Morde Meum Globes, ye fucker. Fucker. Fucker. Fucker. Fucker!

Dr. Knox startled, his eyes growing wide before he took hold of her face. "I should slap the mouth off ye."

Liv shook hard against her captors, fighting to loose their hold. She could hear them scolding and yelling at her, but none of their words made sense. There was a distant clang of a bell, and somewhere in the chaos, a familiar voice.

"Deliverance, sweet child! Bring her in! He's in the theater."

The smell struck her first, betraying the familiar space, then the yellow colors of the parlor, but these were no longer her reality. There was a strange veil hanging over things. The glaring eyes that followed just inches from her face, always impossibly close, smelling of metal and death – that was her new world, the one from which she feared no escape.

She felt hard stone beneath her hip as her captors dropped her on the stairs.

"Careful!" She heard a familiar male voice say. Then there were more hands on her, more concerned voices calling her name beneath the screams of the ones who wanted her to suffer.

"Deliverance, girl! Take control. Tell them to go away!"

Tell my mother! She'll worry! She'll be so worried!

Liv began to sob openly, screaming in her grief. She felt anguish, as though torn from a loving mother's arms. She recognized Fionnula's voice calling to her, but she could not find her anymore. There was only the dead, and Liv was sure they wanted to take her with them.

"How long has she been like this?" Findlay asked from somewhere in the room.

"Since I found her."

"Bring her over. Deliverance. Look at me. Can ye hear me?"

Deliverance? The voices croaked, taunting her from all sides. *She's no here!*

"Come now, get on with it!" Dr. Knox shouted.

Where is my bairn? Why'd ye take her from me?

"What?"

"Your bloody procedure! Calm her down!"

Fucker. Fucker. Fucker! Ye like to cut us up, don't ye, Rabbie?

"What is she sayin?"

Tell em! Tell em how your cock gets hard when you're cutting into us! When your slicing into the place your wife won't let ye touch anymore! Ye fuck! Fucker!

"Deliverance!" Fionnula called from somewhere, but Liv couldn't call back.

"Lennox! Bloody do something! I'll no have her speak to me like that."

I can't breathe! My mother will wonder where I am!

"It's no her!" Fionnula said.

Liv buckled on the table, flailing against the sudden appearance of an old man, leaning over her there, the skin that was left on his body now saggy and tired. She felt the world give way beneath her as she rolled off the metal table, caught just as her legs slammed into the ground. She kicked out again, screaming at the faces that taunted her. She felt arms around her, a familiar scent that once soothed her. Now it only taunted her.

Findlay was there somewhere.

"Well, are ye gonna get on with it?"

"Don't ye dare!" Fionnula hollered.

The voices seemed to bleed together, Fionnula's protest melting into Dr. Knox's demands. Finally, she felt a sudden coolness on her kegs.

"Fine then! If a simpleton like ye can do it."

Hands moved up the inside of her thighs and she fell back onto the floor as Findlay moved from beneath her. Her head landed against the stone just as Dr. Knox cried out.

"Ye bastard! Ye dare to lay a hand on me?"

"Don't ye ever fuckin touch her!" Findlay bellowed.

Liv lay there quiet, the pain in her head throbbing as she stared up at the wooden beams of the ceiling high overhead. The pain seemed to silence the voices.

She could see all their faces around her, but they'd stopped screaming. They simply stood over her, watching her as her vision began to grow dark. Liv tried to take a breath. No air came. Liv fought against the pounding in her head to make sense of the room, to make sense of the arguing voices around her as she clutched at the collar of her dress. She opened her mouth, fighting to inhale, but no air would come.

"Deliverance? My beloved?" Findlay called, his face appearing over her.

"Beloved?" Dr. Knox asked, mockingly.

Janet's shrill voice echoed through the room. "She's turnin blue!"

The bloody figures faded away, leaving her to stare up from the floor of the empty operating theater, as Findlay lifted her from the floor.

"Deliverance!" He cried.

She scratched at her collar, feeling her nails dig into her skin as she choked for air that wouldn't come. Findlay wrapped his arms around her middle, moving her as though she were the lightest thing, and he leaned her over the metal table. Findlay took hold of the back of her dress and tore it open, leaving the skin of her back to grow cold. The collar fell away from her throat, but still there was no air. She shifted on the table, unable to hold her own weight.

The table vibrated beneath her as someone slammed a hand into the metal surface. She forced her eyes open and found Fionnula's face just inches from her own, her hand pressed onto the open case of sharp tools Findlay kept. She dragged her hand over the knives, purposefully slicing her hand open. "That's enough!

Fionnula's hand moved swiftly, her thumb pressing

into Liv's forehead with enough force to shove her face back. Findlay grabbed hold of Liv, scolding Fionnula as she hissed words of binding and fury. Findlay pushed Fionnula's hand away just as Liv's lungs drew breath. She gasped for air, the blurred shadows at the corner of her vision fading fast.

"A madwoman and witch? Ye keep a grand household, Lennox," Dr. Knox said, his voice dripping with disdain.

Findlay wrapped his arms around her, holding her against him as she growled through desperate inhales. "Deliverance. My sweet Deliverance. Breathe for me, sweetheart," Findlay said, coaxing gently in her ear. "That's right, deep breaths."

Liv felt the warmth of his body against her back, the solid hold of his arms around her middle. He was cradling her against him, his body bent around her as though shielding her from the world.

"Is this why you'll no perform your own medical practice? Because she's clearly no maid to ye!"

Liv couldn't focus on Dr. Knox, her vision still blurred from near suffocation. Findlay loosened his hold on her, but did not let her go.

When she finally focused on the older man, he was holding his knuckles to his face, fighting to still a bloody lip. "She's *my* maid now. My property. If ye won't do what's necessary, I'll have to deliver her to Bedlam."

Findlay moved her to lean on the table again, straightening the open fabric of her dress. There was a loaded pause as Findlay's hand ran down her bare back.

He took a breath behind her. "Did ye beat this woman, Robert?"

There was a second's pause, and Dr. Knox straightened to his full height. "I did, indeed! She was stealin my property, and I felt it was necessary. Ye failed to properly disclose her tendencies."

When Findlay spoke, it was so quiet and dark, Liv was surprised anyone else heard him. She was almost equally surprised that his words didn't set the room on fire. "Get out of my house."

"And what of the wasted trouble? Her food and clothing? What of my household?"

Findlay moved with such speed that Dr. Knox lunged backward toward the stairs to get away from him. "Leave this house now, or you'll take more than just a bloody lip wit ye."

Dr. Knox backed up the operating theater stairs, darting his eyes from each of the three women in the room, then back to Findlay. Findlay stood at the bottom of the stairs, as though waiting for an invitation to go after the man.

Dr. Knox turned, stomping his way up, bellowing at Findlay. "Ye know your career is dead, don't ye? No one'll ever take ye seriously in the field. You're a disgrace! And don't dare think to attend another of my exhibitions. Your invitation is revoked." He stopped at the door of the theater.

With that, the doctor disappeared into the parlor, followed swiftly by Fionnula, her hand clutched around a bloody handkerchief as she hastened to show the man out. Liv leaned over the metal table, unable to move as she fought to keep the world still beneath her feet. How long before the visitors returned? How long before they tried again – and succeeded?

Her throat burned from spewing the vitriol of

voices that were not her own.

"Thank ye, Janet. For bringin her home."

Janet leaned over the table to squeeze Liv's hand. "Of course, Doctor. I'm glad she had ye."

The two continued their conversation, Findlay interrogating her for information about Liv's fit as he touched his hand to Liv's bare back, caressing the still sore marks.

"Ye may no wannae know," she said, frowning. Yet Liv wanted to hear her answer. She'd no recollection of the events of that morning – just the memory of dreams that became more – more than anyone should have to bear.

Janet swallowed. "She was bein done by a couple Irish lads."

"What…"

The word came in such a way to shake the stones beneath their feet.

Janet held her breath a moment, clearly afraid to continue. "She went home with one of them Irish lads – the ones with the lodgin houses. They're always offerin it up to the lesser fortunates and the people with nowhere else to go. He saw our Livvy there in a state and took her home – was the same lad Mary ran off with."

"Mary?" Findlay asked, his voice still soft, but carrying far more than his words betrayed.

"Aye. And our Livvy went with him, ye ken? When Marty – the bartender - told me who she left with, I ran straight away! I don't trust the lot of em, there. Strange folk. And – I dunno. I know they says Mary just had her heart broken and ran off home, but I just – I can't help but think the lad did worse than just break her heart. Then, this morning, I found the bastards – *both of em* – with her in the parlor. One of em on top of her!"

Findlay came up behind Liv again, and she could feel his body close to her, humming with a violent energy.

"She said they didn't hurt her, but it didn't look right, what I saw."

He moved closer still. "What were ye thinkin, lass?" He asked, his voice so soft she barely heard him.

His hands moved up the length of her arms, turning her gently to face him. He helped her up onto the table, taking her face in his hands to inspect her. She found herself glancing around the room, constantly waiting for one of the bloody visions to return. Findlay looked into her eyes one at a time, then stood to his full height, wiping the blood on her forehead with his sleeve, before kissing her there.

"Thank ye, Janet. I think I'll put her to bed. Will I be able to find ye? If I need ye?"

"Course! Livvy knows. White Dog is always a good start. I'll leave ye to it."

Liv felt Janet keeping constant vigil on her as the three of them made their way up the stairs. Then Janet parted their company, heading out the door as Findlay led Liv up the stairs.

CHAPTER FIFTEEN

He towered over her, leaning down to kiss her temple.

"I'll have Fionnula bring us up some tea, aye? Then I'll stay with ye while ye sleep."

Findlay stood to his full height and hovered there a moment, watching her with a furrowed brow. Then he slipped out the door, leaving her to the cool and familiar air of her room.

She closed her eyes, listening to the household around her. Findlay returned a moment later, pulling the small chair from the corner to sit by her bed. Liv inhaled sharply, her eyes fixed on the corner where the chair had been.

Findlay noticed her expression, taking her hand as he sat down beside her. "Come now, beloved. You're alright."

She didn't respond. She couldn't take her eyes away from the corner of the room. She stared, unwavering into Margaret's familiar gaze. The woman stood in the corner as she so often did, her navy blue dress bloody at its middle, her face pale and unfeeling. This image did not inspire the same horror as last she'd seen poor Margaret, but Liv feared that if she broke the spell of this stare, this vision would become something far worse – something bloody and raw, something that wanted to hurt her.

"Deliverance, sweetheart? What is it, love? What

d'ye -"

Findlay turned toward the corner of the room and froze, squeezing Liv's hand in his. The two of them sat there a moment, a loaded silence between them. She squeezed him back, pulling his hand closer to her face. Please God, make her go away.

"Ye finally see her then, d'ye?"

They both startled towards the door. Fionnula stood in the doorway, a full tea tray in her arms. Liv glanced back toward the corner and found Margaret gone. Findlay swallowed audibly, rising to allow Fionnula to set the tea tray on the bedside table.

He reached for the older woman's hand as she straightened. "Let me have a look, Fionn. That's a nasty cut there -"

"Leave it," she said, pulling her hand from his. "I've had far worse. It'll mend."

Fionnula took Findlay's seat, settling beside the bed to tend to Liv, running her uninjured hand over Liv's damp hair. The touch felt soothing, despite the lingering panic in her chest.

"They'll no bother ye further today, love. I've made sure of that."

Liv reached up to her forehead, a lingering stickiness to betray the place where Fionnula anointed Liv with her own blood.

"What did ye do?"

Fionnula just smiled. "Ah, nothing they wouldn't hang me for in darker times. Still – twas necessary. You've yet to learn how to send them away yourself."

Findlay scoffed, pacing toward the door.

Fionnula turned on him. "Don't ye huff at me, ye wee scunner! Ye know well what you've just seen. Bout bloody time ye opened your eyes to it!"

Findlay opened his mouth to speak, but stopped, glancing toward the corner of the room. He leaned into the doorjamb. "Your bum's out the windae, old woman."

"Don't ye 'old woman' me. You're no too old to take a lashin."

Findlay muttered to himself, exclaiming that she'd never given a lashing in her life, but his steam was lost, like that of a scolded young boy. He stood there in silence, averting his eyes as Fionnula poured Liv a cup of tea.

"This'll help ye sleep. They've made themselves clear now, but they'll no touch ye while I'm here."

Liv sat up just enough to sip her tea, feeling the hot liquid pour down her gullet, filling her belly. "How do ye know that?"

Fionnula smiled. "Because I've enough sense to tell them to leave and mean it, lass. You'll do best to learn the same."

Findlay grumbled, glaring at Fionnula when she shot him a look. "You'll deny it still, will ye?"

"I deny nothing."

"Then tell me ye didn't see her. Say it now, and own the lie."

He glared at her a moment, mouth open, but still silent. He glanced toward the corner of the room again. "God damn it, Fionn. I'm a man of science."

"Oh aye, always, and a right twit. Ye know well magic is no more than science they've yet to prove. You've quite a ways to go wit your 'science.'"

"Nonsense," he muttered softly.

"And what are ye thinkin havin her sleep up here? I already told ye, it's no place for a girl of her gifts."

He glanced around, searching for the energy to

maintain his feigned anger. He took a deep breath, ready to ascent.

"Though I'll no have her in your room. Unless you've hand-fasted the maiden, it wouldn't be proper."

Liv nearly choked on her tea, but Findlay shot her a scandalized look, his reddening face betraying him. "I'll no have ye -"

"Ah, come now. I was away a month. Are ye tellin me that weren't long enough for the two of ye to get together?"

Findlay was aghast. Liv was too weary to respond. She sipped at her tea and closed her eyes.

"Fionnula," he said, but no argument or lie followed. He ran his hand over his face, visibly deflating. "She will sleep in my room tonight. I'll take the guest quarters. Room will be freezin."

"It isn't proper for a young woman and a young man to sleep on the same -"

"I don't care whether it's proper or no," he said.

Fionnula turned back to Liv, her expression serene, her fight ended. She shot Liv a look, clearly fighting the smirk that pulled at the corners of her mouth.

"Well, I'll leave ye then. Ye help her downstairs. She'll be asleep soon enough."

Fionnula took her leave. Findlay sat with Liv while she finished her tea, then made good on his word, nearly carrying her down the stairs to his bedroom. He settled her into the bed, shushing her when a sound or the sight of something from the corner of her eye startled her, drawing her heart to racing again in wait of returning visions.

Once she was settled under the covers, Findlay went to the fire, crouching down to stoke the flames.

He stood with his back to her, the fire casting his shadow across the ceiling as her eyes grew heavy. She watched the shape of him, losing herself in the warmth of his bed.

"Findlay?"

"Aye, beloved?"

Liv swallowed, fighting sleep enough to form the words. "Did ye see her?"

Findlay leaned against the mantelpiece, his rolled up shirt sleeve catching on the rough wood. He paused, watching the fire. "I don't know what I saw."

The words filtered through, but Liv couldn't respond, the full hold of sleep settling in.

"Takin a lass to your chamber with no intention of marriage is -"

Findlay groaned. "I didn't say I have no intention – bollocks! D'ye think this might no be the time. That such a conversation is for Deliverance and I to have when -"

"And you'll be marryin down. You'll no rise in society with a maid for a wife."

"Ah sod off. I've never cared for such rub -"

Findlay and Fionnula were arguing in the study downstairs when Liv finally woke and was strong enough to leave the warmth of Findlay's room. The light outside betrayed a morning, though she'd spent a full two or three days recovering. Her body still ached, and her throat burned at even the thought of speech, but she was upright and shuffling out into the upstairs landing, her bare feet near silent on the floorboards.

"I know well you've no worry of that rubbish, but

will ye be willing to live with the consequences. Ye travel in higher circles than ye realize at times, lad."

"I've no concern for the opinions of others. And I haven't even asked her, woman. Will ye leave me be?"

"Will ye ask her? I've seen the way ye looked at her since she came intae this house. You're thirty years old, son. If no now, then when?"

Findlay grumbled something to himself. "When the poor girl is well, perhaps?"

Liv croaked on her words, forcing them out through her ragged throat. "Excuse me," she said, bowing her head as she made her way down the stairs. She felt a pounding in her head like someone slammed her in a doorjamb, and she longed for more of Fionnula's tea. Though it might not still the pain, it might certainly put her back to sleep.

"Ah, Deliverance, dear. You're awake. How d'ye feel?" He asked, moving across the room to greet her. She squinted up at him, pained by the simple act of turning her head. He noticed, taking her face in his hands. "We'll go slow then, aye? How is your throat?"

She shook her head. "No good."

"I can imagine."

"Here we are!" Fionnula exclaimed softly, returning to the study with a tray of tea. Liv felt strange in that space, still wearing only her shift, her dress nowhere to be found when she woke. She was wrapped in a shawl and clad in her bare feet, yet Fionnula and Findlay both treated her as though she'd appeared dressed like a queen.

"I couldn't find my clothes. I'm sorry -"

"Shh, now. Ye needn't worry. I'll run down the shops and fetch up something this afternoon. Just ye settle in and have some tea. Soothe that poor throat of yers."

Fionnula fluffed the pillows on the settee and helped Liv to sit down, then turned for the stairs. Findlay sat across from her, fixing his own tea as Liv turned to watch Fionnula climb the stairs. Her neck ached against the movement.

Findlay's tea cup clinked against his saucer a bit louder than it should, and Liv turned to look at him. He was staring at her with a troubled expression.

"What's the matter?"

Findlay surged from his seat, coming to kneel before her. He reached for her face, touching his thumbs against the sides of her nose. He pressed down hard, and she flinched.

"Love, will ye come here a moment?" He asked.

Findlay stood, and Liv let him lead her into the parlor, bringing her to the brightest window in the room. He stood her before him, pressing his thumbs into her nose again until she swatted at his hands. He stared down at her, his brow furrowed. "Will ye look up for me?"

She did as he asked. There was a strange tension under her jaw enough to make her wince as her head fell back. He took hold of her jaw, stooping low to look under her chin. Again he pressed his thumbs there, and she cringed, pulling from him. This spot was even more tender than her nose.

"No more, please."

"It hurts?"

She nodded.

He loosened his hold on her face, but didn't let go. His eyes moved over her, inspecting every inch as though he'd never seen her before. He touched his fingers beneath her chin. "D'ye know where ye got these bruises, love? Did Dr. Knox do this?"

She stared up at him, a confused set to her brow. He gestured to her chin and her nose, the two places she'd found sore to the touch. She touched her fingers to the bridge of her nose. "No. What bruises?"

He stared at her, silent.

There was a bustle from the upstairs hallway as Fionnula barreled down the stairs. She made a jovially startled sound at finding the study empty.

"Fionn, will ye fetch somethin for our Deliverance to wear. I think we have an errand that needs attention."

Fionnula assured him she would do it immediately, and disappeared down the hallway toward the front door. A few moments of nonsensical fretting and singing to herself, and Fionnula was gone.

Findlay still stood with Liv by the window, watching her face as though he feared she might disappear if he looked away.

Fionnula's light hearted mood carried out into the street as the sound of her calling her hellos on the street faded in the distance.

Findlay touched her face again, his thumb crossing over the sore spot along her nose. His face changed, pulling at his brow in sudden and overwhelming sadness.

"Forgive me?" He said, and his voice wavered.

Liv startled at the anguish betrayed in his voice. She took hold of his shirt sleeves, frowning up at him as her throat grew tight. "There is nothing to forgive."

Yet, his expression changed, his eyes welling over as he stared at her face. Then he bent to her, kissing her so forcefully that she feared he might break her. She clung to him as he kissed her again and again, pulling her into his arms to hold her. He whispered into her ear, his breath still wavering with some anguish she couldn't explain. "I'll never put ye in harm's way again. Never. Never."

He squeezed her to him so tightly, her body cracked in his arms.

CHAPTER SIXTEEN

Findlay's arm was wrapped around her shoulders for the entire walk down to Canongate. She had let Fionnula dress her in the new blue and white floral gown with more than a little trepidation. This wasn't the dress of a maid. Yet, it was in no way Liv's manner to rebuff a kindness, especially from an employer. She still felt very odd marching down the lanes with Findlay at her side, his tailcoat and hat drawing friendly gestures of greeting from those passing. They seemed to offer their tipped hat to her as much as to him. Fionnula, who walked just a step or two behind them, they ignored completely.

"Is this the place, then?" Findlay asked as they reached the White Dog.

Liv nodded, letting Findlay hold the door open for her to enter. The pub was quieter this early evening. Findlay crossed to the bar, leaning in to make inquiries of the dark mustached fellow.

When Findlay returned to them, he shook his head in mild frustration. "Our William isn't here, it seems. Nor our Janet. I'm sorry, love. D'ye think ye can find your way there from here?"

Findlay searched Liv's face with the same gentle concern he'd shown her all morning. She ducked her head from him, wishing to shield her face from view beneath the brim of her hat. Despite her oblivion to bruises when he'd asked, she'd dressed before a mirror, catching sight of the horrible yellow and purple marks that now peppered her nose and under her chin. He touched her chin gently, turning her up to face him.

"Aye, I think I know the way," she said.

He smiled down at her, leading her out of the pub. "Come on, beautiful."

They marched back out into the cold, Fionnula wrapping her shawl around Liv's shoulders as she led them up the hill toward the old castle. Despite the blustery day and people's hurried gaits, when they passed through Grassmarket, many tipped their hats to her as they passed, including many stall vendors who knew her face.

She stood in the familiar surroundings, remembering the unfamiliar sounds of Grassmarket in the late evening, William pointing out what he considered the most dangerous pub in town as they passed that night. Liv stood by a moment, waving in returned greeting to the butcher.

Liv looked around a moment, then turned toward West Port, letting her companions wrap their arms around her shoulders in a stance of protective support. Findlay let her lead them along, Liv glancing down every alley and side street for clues that might trigger a memory of the blurred evening three nights past. There was the sound of Grassmarket behind them, a couple voices calling their wares out to passersby before packing up for the night, and then some other strange commotion closer still. Liv moved slowly now, keeping her eyes to the side streets as they came to another close. She glanced up at the words overhead just as a middle aged woman came barreling down the alleyway with her husband.

Findlay grabbed Liv's shoulders, pulling her aside just as the couple rushed past. The woman turned on them, hissing low as she searched their faces. He eyes were dark with excitement, and her voice shook as she spoke. "Don't go down there. Stay away. They're murderers! Get as far from here as ye can!"

"Goodness!" Fionnula exclaimed, pulling Liv closer to her. Findlay stepped out into the alleyway, staring down the dark passage before ducking back to them, leaning in as though to share some conspiracy. "Fionn, take her home, lock the door."

"Findlay, my boy. Don't get yourself in trouble, lad."

Liv reached for him, clutching at his coat to pull him away from the alley.

He took her hand, squeezing it in his. "It's alright, I'll be safe. Just get ye home, alright? Do as I ask. Please."

With that, Findlay disappeared down the alley, his dark coat making him one with the shadows.

Dread settled into her bones as Fionnula dragged her down through Cowgate toward Surgeon's Square. What was Findlay going to do? What was that woman screaming about? Fionnula muttered gentle assurances with each question Liv posed, but despite her dismissive and calm demeanor, she held a death grip on Liv's shoulders, moving her with such determination that Liv could barely keep up.

When they reached the house, Fionnula did exactly as she was told, locking the door behind them. She made quick work of hanging her shawl on a hook and rushing into the kitchen, calling jovial promises of hot tea. Liv didn't call back. She stood still there, staring down the hallway into the parlor – to the woman that stood at the parlor window, watching the street outside.

"Are ye peckish, love? Would ye like a bit of early stew. It looks ready, if ye like."

Liv didn't respond. Instead, she moved down the hallway toward the parlor, watching the figure by the window, her stomach clenching with each step she took. Liv came to stand in the parlor doorway, listening to the familiar clanging of kettles and pots, Fionnula doing her best to pretend this was any other evening.

Liv watched Margaret's back and stepped into the parlor. She swallowed, forcing the whisper from her tightened throat. "Don't let him be harmed," Liv said. It was as much a prayer as a request.

The woman by the window turned her head, slowly glancing over her shoulder in Liv's direction.

"Well now, doesn't this smell lovely?" Fionnula proclaimed, barreling into the parlor with a tray of bowls and tea cups. "Come on, then. Come into the dining room, love, and we'll have a nice meal."

Fionnula disappeared through the study, but Liv didn't move. She watched the specter, willing her to betray her secrets and somehow promise Findlay was safe.

"Deliverance, sweetheart. She'll no hurt ye. Come on, now."

Liv turned to find Fionnula standing in the study doorway, holding her hand out for Liv to take it. "Can ye see her too?"

Fionnula came into the room to stand beside Liv, watching the window with a look of mild curiosity. "I can't, no. No now, anyway."

"Then how did ye know she's there?"

Fionnula stroked Liv's hair, pulling at a long curl and letting it spring back into place. "The same way I know the sun's up in the morning before I open my eyes, or that there's rain comin without a cloud in the sky. Ye notice them once, and you'll never forget the way it feels when they're near."

Fionnula took Liv's hand, trying to coax her out of the room.

"Why do they torment me? What have I done to them to make them so angry -"

The troubling thoughts brought a tremble to her voice. Fionnula took hold of her, pulling her into her chest to soothe her.

"You've done no wrong, love. They don't mean ye harm. I know it felt as though they did, but ye just misunderstood them."

"Misunderstood? They nearly killed me!"

"Shh, sh. As it were. To them, harmin ye wasn't the point, I don't believe. They simply wanted to be heard. Wanted to be seen."

Liv's lower lip curled. "Ye don't know what I saw. They were all cut up and bloody – all in pieces, they were. It was horrible."

Fionnula squeezed her tightly, shushing her still as though she held a small child in her arms. "Aye, I believe ye."

They stood there in the quiet of the room, and when Liv finally turned back toward the window, Margaret was gone.

"I just don't know what I've done."

Fionnula smiled. "Ye showed them ye could hear. They spoke in the only manner they knew how."

After another moment's pause, Liv let Fionnula take her hand and lead her out of the room.

The window glowed even in the late evening. Despite being assured by Fionnula that all was well – that Findlay could see to himself - Liv could no more settle than she could breathe underwater. She fidgeted the evening away, waiting for a sound to betray his return home, to hear the bell clang when he found the door still locked. Yet as the tall clock in the study chimed seven times, Liv found herself called as though by some voice to her former bedroom, and to the window where she'd seen the crying woman so many times.

Liv stood there with tears in her own eyes, staring out into the street below for any sign of the man of the house, returning alive and unharmed. Many moments passed, but there was no sign of the tall auburn haired man.

The clock chimed again to announce the half hour, and Liv began to search for the will to return downstairs. A strange grating sound rumbled in the distance outside; some tired old cart making its way through the cobblestone streets, perhaps. She turned away from the window just as a voice hissed in foul language on the street outside.

She returned to the window, scanning the scene below. There was nothing to be seen, the rooftops and eaves blocked view of half the street.

Liv spun for the door, pattering down the stairs in bare feet until she stood at the parlor window, peeking through the curtains to the street outside. There was a man and woman there, fighting to round a corner off of Surgeon's Square with a massive tea chest between them. Liv pressed her forehead to the window, waiting for the man to speak again, for her to be sure.

Yet, the pair disappeared with their burden down the alley.

Liv stood there silent, her heart racing. The Irish tinge of the voice was enough to light a strange fire of recognition. Yet, she'd wanted to be sure. If William was here, if he left West Port and came all the way to Surgeon's Square, then where was Findlay? Oh God, where was Findlay?

She ran down the hallway, wrapping her shawl around her shoulders as she unlocked the front door. Then, in bare feet she scurried down the alley to the main road, crossing it in silence. The street was empty, every respectable creature already home and having their tea. The alley beside 10 Surgeon Square was empty now, and Liv rounded the corner, tip toeing further in to see where they might have gone. The Anatomy School towered overhead, its dark windows void of light to betray anyone's presence. There would be no classes at this hour, no late studies to complete in the dark. Yet, as she came around the corner of the building, she startled, lunging back behind the building. The large black door to the Anatomy School was open.

Liv peeked around the corner, her breathing sharp and fast. She snuck across the alley way and pulled the door aside. It opened with an echoing creak. She thanked the lord that the hallway inside was empty.

Liv slipped inside the school, grateful to feel the warmth of hardwood floors under her nearly frozen bare feet. She moved down the hallway, listening intently to every sound. There were no voices, no footsteps, just the constant loaded silence of a massive space. She came to a hallway that ran down the center of the building and remembered where she was. Dr. Knox's dissection room was at the end of the hall to the left. She took a deep breath, remembering the horror of her last visit to this place, but she moved. She had to know if it was him – if it was William. And if it was, what on earth was in that tea chest?

She stopped for a moment, suddenly unable to breathe as a thought struck her.

Damn it, Livvy! He's a bloody giant! The man wouldn't fit in a grain barrel, let alone a tea chest. Be still! She thought.

Liv rushed down the hall, coming to stand just outside the dissection theater. The door was left ajar by mere inches. She let her fingers graze it just enough to hold it still as she peered into the massive room within. There were soft sounds, grunts and exhales, betraying a presence. She fought to focus her eyes to the flicker of candlelight within. Three dark shapes hovered within, the woman and two men in suits now struggling with the chest down near the dissection table. The tea chest moved in a cumbersome way, as though unbalanced somehow.

"There now. That'll do. Your lucky ye caught me. I was just on my way out. Here, follow me," the unfamiliar man said, leading the Irishman and his female companion up the stairs toward her. Liv spun on her heel, running further down the hall and around another corner. She waited, listening as the three of them made their way down the hall and up a flight of stairs. She waited, listening to their footsteps through the ceiling above.

Liv took a deep breath and ran back down the hall to the dissection room, slipping through the still open door to descend the stairs inside. The air of the room betrayed memory of troubling smells, the sweetness and acrid sting of blood and death. She loped down the stairs, her heart pounding so fast she could feel her chest vibrating with the force of it. Liv ran across the cold stone floor to the tea chest, and without a pause, tugged the latch free and opened the cover. She cried out, her voice echoing across the massive space as the dead eyes of an old woman stared up at her from within the chest. She stumbled backward, bracing against the dissection table, only to yank her hands away, shuddering at the thought of all the horrific deeds that had been done on that table. She turned back to the tea chest, stepping forward just enough to latch her pinky on the chest cover and shut it again. Despite the horror of what lay within that chest, Liv took a deep breath of foul air, grateful not to find Findlay within it.

Damn it, then where are you Findlay?

Deliverance.

She turned toward the stairs, startled by the strange voice. The same sallow faced woman stood before her, blocking her way toward the theater stairs. Liv whimpered in fear, terrified to see a new face. Would she bring with her an army? Would this vision take her breath away as they had before?

Liv turned for the stairs, ready to run past the vision, willing herself brave.

Eyes appeared inches from her face, moving closer at impossible speed. She flailed wildly, backing away.

"I believe you're mistaken, sir."

The voice came from the doorway above, footsteps betraying the return of the Irish couple and their companion down the hall.

She stumbled back from the stairs, her ankles slamming into the chest. She lost her balance, falling backward toward the stone floor.

A rough shape gripped her upper arm, yanking her backward and completely off her feet. Liv stifled a cry just as a massive hand clamped down over her mouth, dragging her back into darkness. She held her breath, wriggling against her captor as he pulled her into a closet, his scent filling the small, dark space. She froze.

"Be still, beloved. I have ye."

Her body went slack in an overwhelming relief.

"I tell ya, I heard someone down here, like!" William said, the door to the dissection room bursting open loud enough to clang against the wall.

There was a pause, some muttering between the two men as Findlay's chest rose and fell behind her.

"See now. Not much to steal in an Anatomy School. Unless you're a body snatcher, ae?" The second man laughed softly at his own joke. He was the only one. Liv listened to them descending the theater stairs.

"Right, then. Here ye are?"

"I thought it would be more," the female said.

"I'll have another eight pound for ye in a couple days."

William made an exasperated sound. "What's this now?"

The unfamiliar man made a soft humming sound of confusion. "I'm simply relaying what Dr. Knox told me. Another eight in a couple days' time.

A female voice spoke sternly as the Irishman muttered foul language just loud enough to be heard through the door.

"Pay him no mind, sir. We're much appreciative. Ya have a good night, then."

Findlay's breathing began to slow as they listened to the couple's footsteps retreating. A moment later, Findlay loosed his hand on Liv's mouth and dropped to his knees, pressing his face to the door to watch through the keyhole. As Liv stared down at the tiny golden point of light on Findlay's face, she swelled with gratitude to the point of tears.

He was alright.

Suddenly, the light across Findlay's face went dark, and a new set of footsteps made their way up the theater stairs. The theater door shut with a loud echo across the expanse of the theater, as though a thousand doors had all slammed at once. Findlay stood up, his body filling the space around her. She pressed her hand to his chest, wanting only to feel the solid shape of him. He wasn't like her visitors. He was real.

"Come on, now."

Findlay opened the door to the closet and took her hand, leading her through the theater to the stairs. She stopped, pulling from him.

"What's wrong?"

"There's a body. There's a woman - in the chest."

He frowned. "I know that."

"Are we just going to leave her, then?"

He took her hand, pulling her toward the stairs again. This time she didn't protest. "There's no we can do for her now. Come on, love. We need to get out before the door's locked."

Findlay stopped in the hallway, listening to the sounds of Knox's assistant in an upstairs office, then rushed her down the hall toward the back door. They were out into the alleyway seconds later, the stone faces of surrounding buildings growing black with the late evening.

Findlay barreled through his own front door, pulling Liv inside with more force than was needed. He ducked into the hallway, his hair a mess and his eyes dark with purpose as he sloughed off his coat. Liv felt the fabric brush against her skin, frigidly cold from the wet November air.

"Where've ye been then, lad? Ye had us worried sick!" Fionnula scolded him, but Findlay didn't speak, surging past them both to disappear into his operating theater. Fionnula chased after him, demanding to know what he'd done and where he'd been. Liv could hear them railing at each other in the bowels of the theater, but it took all her will to simply stay upright. Her hands began to shake at her side as she turned toward the study.

Fionnula's tone was high. "Are ye certain?"

"I saw it with my own eyes! Aye, I'm certain!"

"Then ye must tell someone! Damn it, lad!"

Findlay barked at Fionnula to be still as he bounded back up the operating theater steps. "He's my colleague! My mentor! Shall I simply turn him over without at least giving him chance to explain? Christ, just let me think a moment, woman!"

"Chance to explain, or chance to cover it -"

"To cover it -?" He entered the parlor, and stopped, turning to watch Liv as she stared off into the study.

He reached the top of the stairs and stopped, finding Liv in a near catatonic state. He rushed over to her, sending Fionnula for tea. "Come now, love. You're alright. Come and sit for me."

Liv let him lead her to the settee, slumping down

gently as he knelt before her. Fionnula returned quickly with a warm cup, patting her hand. "Ach, she's so cold, Findlay. Get her upstairs where it's warm."

"No," Liv said, but the sound was barely audible. She had to tell someone. She had to do something for that poor woman – the poor old woman who lay cramped and bent in the depths of a tea chest, her body growing cold in a locked classroom just across the way.

He knelt there before her, rubbing her hands in his to warm them, watching her with affection and concern. Liv stared at him, fighting to form the words.

"Here, lass. Drink," he said.

Liv took a sip, the liquid hot enough to burn, then she searched Findlay's face. Why wasn't he running out the door? Why wasn't he screaming from the rooftops for justice? Go, she thought. Do something!

Fionnula offered up Liv's own thoughts in word. "Findlay. Ye must say somethin – to someone, anyone."

"What am I to say, Fionn? I can't say for sure what I saw. And what if he doesn't know? It'll ruin him."

Fionnula glared at him. "He seemed quite content to see ye ruined when he was here just a few days past."

The two of them fell silent a moment as Findlay mulled this over. Liv watched his face, listened to the sound of his knees cracking as he rose to his full height, pacing across the room.

"I owe him so much. No matter what he might think of me, I wouldn't be here if it weren't for him."

Fionnula rolled her eyes. "Ye'd be anywhere ye like.

You're a brilliant man, with or without Dr. Knox."

Findlay grunted softly, dismissing Fionnula's praise. "Please, give me a moment, damn it!"

Fionnula set her jaw and returned her attention to Liv, holding the cup to her lips for her to drink. Liv pushed the cup aside with a gentle hand, leaning forward in her seat.

You knew.

Findlay turned to face Liv, his expression troubled. Fionnula sat down beside Liv, searching her face.

"What did he *know*, child?"

Liv heard words coming from somewhere, as though mulling them over in her mind, but just as those times before, her companions reacted as though she'd spoken – spoken someone else's words.

Yet Findlay didn't need her to say more. He pressed his palm over his eyes, and whispered softly to himself.

Finally, he looked at her and frowned. Then he left the room without a word.

Fionnula took a deep breath. "Ach, child. You've a deathly chill. Why don't ye go upstairs now, climb intae bed? I'll bring the tea up to ye."

Liv met Fionnula's gaze and nodded, letting the older woman help her to her feet. Fionnula bustled off into the kitchen, leaving Liv to make her way upstairs.

She felt a shudder run through her, reminiscent of the ones she sometimes felt when making her waters. Liv turned to face the study door. Margaret was there in a dark corner of the room, watching her in silence.

She stood still a moment, the sound of footsteps betraying Findlay coming up the stairs behind her. He stopped in the theater doorway.

"Deliverance? Are ye alright?"

He glanced between her and the dark places that drew her eyes. He leaned toward her, his voice soft. "She's there, isn't she?"

Liv took a slow breath, then nodded. The room took on the silence of a church, the two of them staring into the darkness; staring at a face only Liv could see.

Fionnula appeared in the kitchen doorway, startled to find them both there.

After a moment, Findlay turned to Fionnula, sending her to get her shawl as the blue light of the window betrayed the very last of daylight. She did as she was asked, disappearing through the kitchen toward her quarters.

Findlay came back to Liv's shoulder, his hand grazing the lower curve of her back.

"I lied to ye, beloved."

Liv could not turn her eyes from the specter's stern gaze. "When?"

He took a deep breath, staring into the study beside her, his tone a low whisper, as though he feared their unseen company might hear.

"When I recognized the lass on the table – that afternoon those months ago -"

"It was Mary."

He inhaled, sharply. "Aye. I lied because I didn't want ye to be troubled. I didn't want ye to put stock in your nightmares."

The two of them stood silent for a long moment.

Then, as he set his eyes on the corner of the room, he stepped past Liv, clutching his fists at his sides. "Margaret?"

The room hummed suddenly, vibrating with

something unseen and powerful.

Findlay flinched. He'd felt it, too. "Margaret, if you're there," he paused. "You're right. I did know. I didn't want to believe it, but – I knew something was wrong."

The space felt smaller, shrinking around them as Findlay reached out to the thing he couldn't see. "I'm going to make it right, Margaret. I swear to ye."

Liv watched as the phantom turned toward Findlay. He took a step back, as though he could feel her eyes upon him. The ghost's expression softened just so.

Fionnula entered from the front hall. "I'm dressed then. What am I to do?" She asked, wrapping her shawl around her shoulders.

Findlay turned and handed her a piece of paper. "Take this to the police, Fionn. And don't give a name."

"Don't give my name? Well, what if they ask -"

But Findlay was gone, the violent hum of his energy fading in his absence. Fionnula shot Liv a worried look and glanced down at the piece of paper in her hands. She frowned, taking a deep breath, then shrugged into her shawl and tied her hat to the top of her head. A moment later, she was out the front door, wrapped up against the cold of the first of November.

Liv turned back to the familiar face of Margaret. The vision seemed to ripple like the surface of a pond after a stone has been thrown. Then a moment later, she sifted through the wall of the study like sand blown in the breeze.

For the first time in the nine months she'd spent in Findlay's household, Liv felt truly alone.

CHAPTER SEVENTEEN

Edinburgh was coiled like a snake.

The streets were filled to bursting, people bustling forward with the drive of a herd of agitated cattle. Liv clung to Findlay's arm, letting him lead her down the closes and small side roads that would take them up the Royal Mile, trying his best to keep them away from the main crowd. Yet, there was no use. The closer they came to the center of the frothing city, the harder it was to move.

People lined the streets in all directions, teeming and frothing at the mouth for a glimpse of the murderer William Burke and the scaffolding where they would end his life.

"I hope they tie a good twenty six knots! Then we'll see his head pop right off, aye?"

"Wouldn't that be a bloody show!"

Findlay pulled Liv closer as they passed the two very drunk men – falling down drunk, and it wasn't even nine in the morning. Liv turned her face down, letting the brim of her hat shield her face from the rain as Findlay held her to him. Still, there was little even the giant Findlay Lennox could do to shield her from the crowd itself.

The city stank with an unholy purpose. People had come from all over Scotland to see this man swing, and the unwashed masses had pressed into the city center, some as early as days before the execution to get a good view of the event. The streets smelled of piss and filth, mixed with the body odor and breath of thousands of people, all pressed into each other, all surging in the same direction. It was nearly stifling.

"Watch it, oi!" A woman hollered as Findlay pressed between her and her companion. She turned on them, ready to spit venom, only to find herself eye level with Findlay's chest. She didn't say anything further.

Liv hopped up onto her toes to see over some of the heads. People were crammed into every space, every corner – even the windows of the buildings surrounding them teemed with faces, both young and old, craning to see the spectacle outside. She scanned the windows overhead. Janet worked three days straight without a break to make enough money to buy a spot in one of those windows. She was adamant she watch Mary's murderer hang from the best seat in the house.

Liv straightened, catching a glimpse of the scaffolding up ahead. Her stomach turned.

Edinburgh had practically caught fire in the weeks since William Burke and William Hare's arrests. The papers sold out everyday, leaving her to hear the details of the trial from Findlay or Findlay's colleagues. That is, when Findlay spoke to anyone. Now thousands of hungry spectators all teemed in the streets, striving to get closer to the scaffolding.

"Ye know that scoundrel William Hare turned King's evidence, aye? Bastard's gonnae walk the streets like you and I, he is!"

Liv glanced back at this man, her eyes wide. She'd

heard Hare testified against Burke, the round-faced and friendly Irishman from the pub, but this part of the news; that a known murderer – the man whose face she'd woken up to, glowering over her on the settee of Hare's lodging house, pinning her there while Burke apparently clamped his fingers over her nose and mouth, suffocating her – the man Janet threatened to beat with her bare hands when she found Liv there beneath him - this glowering coward of a man would walk away, as though innocent as a newborn bairn.

Liv curled into Findlay's arms. He seemed to notice the gesture, and held her tighter. Yet, despite this gentle embrace, Findlay was wound tight. He pushed them forward, excusing himself with polite words, but moving those around them with the hand's of a bouncer outside a public house.

"Oi, comin through. Pardon!" He hollered as the crowd grew thick and loud. With each few steps they took, Liv could see the frame of the scaffold, looming there over the crowd like a sickness.

Findlay turned on a man who complained at the notion of having a giant like Findlay blocking his view. Liv startled at the fury Findlay's expression betrayed. He wasn't himself this morning.

He hadn't been since that night in Surgeon's Square – since he'd tipped the police to Dr. Knox's dissection rooms, and to the body of the elderly woman they now knew as Mrs. Docherty.

Suddenly, the crowd surged, pushing from behind them with the force of a tidal wave. Liv fought to keep upright, Findlay taking hold of her as the voices cresendoed all around them. Liv turned to watch the scaffolding.

They were bringing William out.

Surly voices hollered from all sides, booing and hissing as the masses teemed around them. Liv's heart was racing. She felt tiny and lost, fighting to keep a hold on Findlay's jacket.

"You're alright, love. I've got ye," he said, his arm clamped tightly around her waist.

"Bring the bastard out! String 'im up!" A woman cried from somewhere nearby, echoed by others. A man pushed beside Liv, his young son's foot kicking her as the man passed with his five year old happily settled on his shoulders.

Liv turned to Findlay, her stomach clenching and churning. She'd wanted to come, wanted to see the man hang, but now that she stood amongst the masses of the city, tens of thousands deep, she felt wrong. The energy was so oppressive and angry, she felt as though a million ants were scurrying over her skin.

"I don't want to be here," she said, straining to be heard.

Findlay's attention was elsewhere, watching the scaffolding up ahead. "What's that?"

Figures appeared at the stairs of the scaffolding and the crowd broke. People shoved against one another with such force that Liv lost her hold on Findlay's coat. She turned for him, but the man with the child on his shoulders appeared, blocking Findlay from view. Liv was shoved forward, further into the crowd, fighting to keep her footing. She couldn't fall now, she'd be trampled under foot. Despite not knowing anyone around her, she reached for the nearest woman, desperate for something to hold her upright.

Liv's hand went straight through her.

Liv dropped to the cobblestones, her hands landing in puddles of rain and all manner of filth. She looked up at the woman, but the figure was gone.

Dear god. Not again, she thought.

The spector may have gone, but in her place, looming over Liv, was an oblivious man whose leather boot appeared, crushing Liv's fingers beneath his heel. She screamed in pain, pulling her fingers free and shoving her hands upward to hold off the weight of those around her. But the crowd pushed forward again, causing another woman and her husband to topple over Liv as well.

The three of them fought together on the filthy ground to stand, but something was happening on the scaffolding, and people were desperate to catch a glimpse.

The crowd seemed to gasp in unison.

"There he is, the bloody bastard!" Someone hissed nearby.

The people around them shoved in, their feet trampling every limb beneath their feet. Liv screamed to be noticed with the couple now trapped underfoot with her. No one seemed to notice or care as their feet stomped down on her ankles and fingers.

Suddenly, hands took hold of her shoulders, and Liv was on her feet, stern blue eyes inspecting her face for damage. "There ye are! I'm so sorry I lost ye."

"She's here."

Liv turned to be sure the trampled couple were upright as well, but Findlay kept his eyes trained on her. "What do ye mean? Who's here?"

Liv looked up into Findlay's face. "Ye know well who I mean."

Findlay frowned, then took Liv by the shoulders and shoved forward, a new passon fueling his efforts. They passed dozens, then hundreds, Findlay's size and demeanor stilling any protests that might have been offered had their cause been a foot shorter. Liv let him press her forward, her stomach growing tighter and tighter as the scaffolding loomed overhead. There was a figure atop the structure, surrounded by official looking men. She recognized the tall man, thinner now, the familiar smile he always offered her now gone.

William Burke took his place on the scaffolding as objects flew from within the crowd; rocks or rotten vegetables. The air was crisp and cold, and the rain came and went in torrential fits. Yet William stood clad in little more than a loose shirt and tired trousers, shabby from long wear in prison.

Findlay stopped pushing, pinning her back to his chest to be sure he wouldn't lose hold of her again. Liv watched as William Burke dropped to his knees on the scaffolding and began to pray.

"Oh, he won't hear ye now, ye bastard!" Someone yelled from over her shoulder.

Liv turned toward the angry man, his teeth blackened from rot. Yet it wasn't the furious face that startled her.

Behind the man, stock still and seemingly unnoticed by all around her, was Margaret. She stared up at the scaffolding with an emotionless expression, unmoved by the surging crowd. Liv swallowed, turning away from the image. Yet another figure caught her eye, the face mirroring Margaret's eerily still nature. Liv recognized this face, instantly – James Wilton. His face was changed now. No one would imagine this stoic creature daft – that is, if anyone else could see him.

Liv scanned the crowd, knowing before she began that she would find their faces, familiar and not, floating among the masses unaffected, still in a storm of people as they waited for this man to join them.

"Ye alright, love?" Findlay asked just as Liv spotted the old woman from the dissection room – the woman they'd found bent and cramped inside a tea chest at Dr. Knox's Anatomy School.

Liv nodded, slowly, her heart racing. "Aye, I'm fine."

On the scaffolding above, William Burke stood slowly, turning to shake the hands of the officials around him. Liv felt the presence instantly.

She turned to find Mary standing just beside her, her image solid despite the crowd that teemed in and around her. Liv searched her old friend's face, frowning. Mary didn't turn to meet her gaze, but kept her eyes fixed on the scaffolding above, just like all the other dead.

The crowd began to froth and boil, throwing her off balance as Findlay stood solid behind her, holding her there as she cradled her sore fingers in her hand.

William Burke turned to face the crowd as the executioner stepped forward with the hood to place over William's face. Burke scanned over the crowd, his face calm for a man about to meet his end. Liv watched as his eyes drew toward her. She startled, unnerved to see that face again, the dark eyes fixed in her direction.

William's eyes widened. Yet, it wasn't her face he'd spotted. It wasn't her face that stilled him there. Liv turned to watch Mary again.

William could see her, too.

The hood was over his head a second later, hiding the man's expression from view. The executioner pulled the noose over the man's head and stepped away from the prisoner. Then, as the crowd surged forward, hollering, and demanding a show, William gave a slight gesture with his hand, and dropped through the scaffolding with a sickening crack, leaving his lifeless form to dangle and sway at the end of the rope.

The crowd exploded around them, cheering the morbid sight with the passion of a child opening gifts at Christmas. Findlay held onto her with both arms, clutching her to him as the celebration surged around them. There was no celebration to be had in Liv's heart. Yet when she turned to find Mary, the stoic and waiting faces were gone, as though they'd never been there at all. Liv exhaled in relief.

She knew she would not see them again.

A few curious folks pressed closer to see the body swinging there, but Findlay seemed satisfied, turning Liv away from the sight to push back through the crowd.

Though leaving was easier, she felt weighted somehow. The crowd pushed past them, working hard to get closer to the scaffolding, but Findlay was on a mission. He had to return to Surgeon's Square. Preparations needed to be made for what was to come the following day.

William Burke was to be publicly dissected by Dr. Munro and his attending surgeons. Dr. Findlay Lennox was one of those surgeons.

Movement grew easier as they approached Surgeon's Square, the crowds thinning out the further away they went. Still, there were onlookers hovering around the college, the morbidly curious hoping to catch a glimpse of Burke's corpse as they brought him in for dissection.

Findlay marched Liv all the way to their front door before he finally released his hold on her. She glanced up to him, her brow furrowed. He didn't meet her gaze.

"Well, are ye satisfied then? Disgusting spectacle," Fionnula said as soon as they'd entered the house. "I'll never understand the curiosity of such an event. I understand ye wantin to see it, Deliverance, dear, but the rest of em? Bunch of sick bastards, if ye ask me."

Findlay didn't speak, but instead disappeared into his operating theater as Liv made her way into the kitchen.

Liv watched him go, frowning.

"Ah, don't worry about him, lass. He's just a bit out of sorts, is all. Goodness, what happened here?"

Fionnula grabbed up her apron, snatching Liv's hands up to inspect them. Liv looked down and saw red spattered across the white fabric. Her fingers were bleeding. Though her fingers hurt, she'd almost forgotten her injury – or the filth that caked her fingers.

"Come now. Let's have a wash and get ye bandaged up."

The operating theater door opened with a loud bang, and Findlay's footsteps stomped down the hall outside the kitchen. A moment later, he was out the front door without a word.

Liv frowned, but she didn't speak.

"Hey now. No frownin over that, love. He's in a state, but it'll pass."

Liv watched Fionnula's bent fingers work as she cleaned and bandaged Liv's hands.

The rain came and went throughout the day, the sound of it almost drowning out the agitated voices of the city outside. The cart that carried Burke's body came sometime in the mid-morning, bringing with it a good crowd. Findlay did not return for the rest of the day, leaving Liv to spend her hours reading, or sitting with Fionnula in the kitchen, watching helplessly as the woman worked. Liv was no longer allowed to take part in household chores much of the time, and certainly not with injured hands.

When dusk finally came, Liv made her way upstairs curling up under the blankets of her warm bed, standing by helplessly as Fionnula tended her fire for her.

The weight on the end of the bed woke her, and Liv stirred under the mass of blankets. The rain was still pattering against the window, but the fire was low now, its glow almost failing to light Findlay's face when she turned to find him sitting there in silence.

She thought of the last time he'd come to sit on her bed like this, of the passionate events that unfolded thereafter. She held her breath, sitting up to face him. He hadn't touched her like that since the night before sending her to Knox. She longed for it in every hour of the day.

"I'm sorry to wake ye," he said, staring down at the floor.

Liv shook her head. "It's fine. I'm glad ye did. Is everything in order for the mornin?"

"Aye."

Findlay rose and crossed to the fire, taking up the poker to stoke the flames. Liv watched him in silence, waiting for him to speak. He stood over the mantle, watching the flames.

"Are ye unwell, Findlay?" She finally asked, watching his slouched shoulders.

He glanced back at her. "No, no unwell."

She knew this was false, but she did not press.

Findlay stared at the fire for quite some time before he finally returned to the bed. He sat down and reached for her hand. Liv let him take her bandaged fingers, holding them gingerly.

"I've so little to offer ye, Deliverance."

Her eyes went wide, and she straightened."What do ye mean?"

He frowned, staring at her hands. "Dr. Knox wasn't wrong. I've no great discovery to share with the world anymore, nothing remarkable about me. This is as simple a practice as any doctor could keep."

"Is that no a worthwhile life, then?"

He exhaled. "I'll be makin housecalls and deliverin babies my entire life."

Liv smiled fighting with her sore hand to squeeze his. "Why are ye tellin me this? What worth is my opinion of ye?"

"Your opinion is everything, Deliverance."

She took a breath, holding it as she watched the flames flicker across his face. "Why?"

Findlay finally turned to meet her gaze. "Because I want to marry ye, love."

Liv's throat clamped shut, instantly and she nearly choked on the emotion. She'd slept in this guest bed, aching to help with chores, to make herself of worth as she lived under Findlay's roof, ate his food, fearing everyday he would send her away again. Yet as he sat there in the dark of that room, she saw tears welling at the corners of his eyes, searching her face for answer as her mind reeled.

Her lips curled as she began to cry, but she swallowed it down as best she could. "You do?"

"Aye. I can't stand ye bein so close, but not bein able to feel ye near me. I want ye in my bed. I want ye in my arms. I can't sleep another night without ye. I just can't."

Liv moved across the bed, wrapping her arms around his shoulders as he collected her into his arms.

"Are ye sure it's me ye want? I've no to offer ye? Fionnula's right, ye could marry some high stature girl _"

He touched a finger to her lips, stilling her words. "You're the one I want, Deliverance. No one else."

She fought to keep herself steady, to not burst into wailing tears in his arms.

He remained stoic there, despite the tears that spilled over, rolling down his cheeks. "Will ye let me hold ye tonight? While ye sleep?"

Her heart swelled. Dear god, there was nothing she wanted more.

Liv touched her fingers to Findlay's red curls and nodded. Then she pulled him by the hand toward the warmth of her bed. Findlay climbed under the blankets, still fully clothed and cool from the air outside, and curled his long body around her. Then Liv fell back to sleep in his arms.

CHAPTER EIGHTEEN

Liv woke with a start, waiting for her eyes to focus on the room around her. Her dreams no longer carried angry faces or visitors in the corners of the room. Still, sometimes she woke gasping for breath, William Hare's face burned into memory, hovering over her as she fought to breathe. The thought that he roamed the world free seemed to trouble her, no matter how many weeks passed.

The dreams had slowed in the months since the arrests, since she and Findlay began sharing a bed as husband and wife to be. Still she felt her stomach turn at any mention of the West Port murders. Findlay often took to her when he heard word of Burke or the one known as Hare, holding Liv to him as though he feared she might blow away. Though he intended it as an act of affection, it only worked to remind her of a strange guilt she felt – the guilt of having lived.

She took a deep breath, willing away the memory of the man's face.

The fire was low now, the room cooler in the early hours of the morning. Yet, warming the bed around her, cindering away as he did when he slept, was Findlay.

He jostled beside her, rolling over to lay a hand across her chest. "Havin a bad dream?"

He hadn't opened his eyes, and Liv wondered if he was attempting to soothe her in his sleep again. She touched her hand to his forearm, squeezing it against her.

"No, just didn't remember where I was for a moment."

He smiled, his eyes still closed, pressing his nose to her temple as he shimmied his hips closer to her. She could feel him pressing against her thigh, hard as he often was in the morning. Liv had grown accustomed to sleeping beside a giant, the bed often taken up by his long limbs wrapping around her as she slept. She'd never felt so safe and so warm at night as she did when she slept beside this man.

She turned onto her side, pressing her backside against him as she wriggled into every nook and cranny of him. He groaned, pressing himself against her ass. "Mmm, ye know well how to wake a man."

He began grinding against her softly, still half asleep. Liv reached her arm back around him, letting her nails scratch his bare backside.

"Well, that's it," he said and he was on her an instant later, tearing her shift up to give himself access. She opened her legs to him, laughing.

Findlay made his way downstairs to the theater shortly after breakfast. He still took a good number of patients, but none from Bedlam anymore. Despite the growing respect he'd earned for his 'groundbreaking' procedure, Findlay hadn't performed it on a single woman since the day Dr. Knox brought Liv to Findlay for treatment.

"I can't do to a woman what he asked me to do to ye. It's no right. I see that now," he'd said when Liv asked. Despite his aversion to the procedure, he still took her to his theater some nights, playing doctor as he had when she first arrived, ignoring the fact that they were now handfasted – that she was now his fiancé.

Liv left him to his work for an afternoon stroll, still unable to sit still in a household she'd once helped run. Reading books and writing letters to no one in particular would drive her mad, and Fionnula threatened to cane her every time she offered help around the kitchen.

"A lady of the house doesn't get her hands dirty!" She'd scold.

Liv had learned from a young age that this wasn't true. Still, she allowed Fionnula her territory. She knew full well she could get her hands dirty again once she was officially Mrs. Lennox. When she was Mrs. Lennox, no one could stop her from chopping her own parsnips.

When Liv tired of her book, she headed down into the Grassmarket to peruse the shops, demanding Fionnula let her run the day's errands herself.

The city was quieter now, finally settling in the wake of the West Port murders. She was happy to see it, despite the frigid February air.

Even a month after the execution, the rumblings of conversation always veered toward the West Port murders.

Sixteen people, the confession said, all suffocated or strangled – or worse. Many speculated that more still fell victim, and even young children shared gruesome stories when Liv passed them in the market, singing little nursery rhymes to commemorate the trial. Still, no one would ever know. Mr. and Mrs. Hare were long gone, as was the woman Burke called his wife, all of them chased out of town by murderous mobs.

Liv was grateful to find Findlay returning to his former self since their engagement. He took his tea with her and Fionnula most nights, and she loved waking in the morning to find him snoring softly beside her, reaching down to squeeze her ass when she half roused him in the middle of the night. His mood had changed with late January - his mood had changed with the execution and dissection of William Burke.

"It's a nasty business, that!" Fionnula said everyday when Findlay returned from the dissection.

"Nothing would give me more pleasure than to witness this man's disemboweling, I assure ye. A rather appropriate dessert after having watched the scoundrel hang."

The hanging drew tens of thousands. The dissection would have as well had the Anatomy School had the room. The dissection was so popular an event, those lined up to see the horror came to near riot in the streets of Surgeon's Square, calming only when the school arranged for each person to tour through the theater, catching a glimpse as Dr. Munro pulled the man apart like a carnival attraction. Findlay rushed home during the near riots to calm his soon to be wife. Then he returned to the school, determined to witness every moment of William Burke's undoing.

Liv stopped in to visit the butcher, a man she now knew to be named Kevin, and purchased a nice bit of

Haggis for their tea that evening. She was growing accustomed to the friendly gestures, their demeanor different now that she dressed in the clothes of a lady, rather than a maid. They were pleased to see her change in position; glad to see something like them had found a comfortable life for herself. She was pleased to know they cared.

"Livvy! You're mad to be out in this!"

Liv turned to see Janet rushing up from Cowgate, her shoulders hunched into her coat and shawl.

"It's too cold for a donder, ye! What're ye thinkin?" Janet demanded, scooping her arm into Liv's and squeezing her close. Liv returned the gesture, watching Janet's face for sign of trouble. In the days after Burke and Hare's arrests, Janet fell was forced to identify Mary's clothing at the police station. Discovering that she'd left her friend to die weighed so heavy on Janet's mind, that Liv feared she might hurt herself once or twice. Janet had changed much like Findlay after the arrests and trial, even taking to the streets with an angry mob when Burke's partner, Helen, was released from prison and seen walking through Old Town on her way to buy a bottle of whiskey.

"That wee trollop, whore, half-wife of a murderin bastard," she'd said as tears streamed down her pale face on the parlor settee. "Why's she walkin the streets, then? Why's she no hangin with 'im?"

Janet harbored an ache that Liv knew better than she'd have liked – the same 'guilt of having lived.' Yet, Janet's was worse. Janet blamed herself for leaving Mary to murderers. No amount of cajoling to pull that regret from Janet's heart.

Janet's face was red, but it looked to be from cold,

rather than tears this time. She walked as far as Surgeon's Square with Liv, but no further, still unwilling to come within view of the Anatomy School. Liv didn't blame her. She often found herself staring out the parlor window, watching the school across the way with stern eyes.

Dr. Knox still taught his classes there; still cut people apart, teaching hundreds upon hundreds of students, despite many crying foul of his being free. It was rumored Dr. Knox now moved about the city with a pistol and a dirk always at hand, so accustomed was he to death threats and angry mobs.

Good, Liv thought when she heard this bit of news.

"Serves him right," Janet had said before spitting on the cobblestones in a silent curse.

The last stretch of road was quiet, offering up little more than a bitter wind to welcome her home. Fionnula greeted her at the door, praising the haggis, sight unseen.

"Will ye look at that? A lovely choice. That'll do nicely! Our Findlay's in the study, love. I believe a letter's come for ye."

Liv furrowed her brow, confused at the notion that someone would have reason to write to her. She hung up her coat and shawl, making her way down the hallway to find him. She stilled in the doorway, feeling a strange hum to the space – a sensation she hadn't felt in months. The study was empty, betraying no sign of her fiancé.

"Findlay?" She called, glancing into the dining room and the back hallway. There was no sign of him. She called down into the operating theater, but again it offered only the echo of her voice.

She was beginning to grow concerned and hurried

back into the study and up the stairs. Findlay was sitting on their bed, his back to the door.

"Findlay, love. Are ye no well?"

He turned his head down, nodding to himself. Liv rounded the bed to be closer to him. He sat there, holding a letter in his hands.

She sat down beside him, and he held the piece of paper out to her.

"Forgive me for keeping this from ye," he said.

Liv took the piece of paper. She saw the signature and holding her breath, began to read.

Dear Dr. Lennox,

It is with great distaste that I sit to pen this reply to your neither expected, nor pleasing letter. It has been many months since we have heard from Deliverance, and it is much to my surprise to hear she is not only residing in Edinburgh, but with intention to marry. I must confess to you, Dr. Lennox, that despite your most assured skill and education, it would have been much more pleasing news to hear that Deliverance was intended to wed a man closer to her own station. I cannot imagine you've the pedigree nor the means to offer her a livelihood such as the one she has been accustomed, but as you assure me she has already accepted your proposal, I have little choice but to consent. I am sure my disapproval would be of little concern to the child, and her absence has already done irreparable damage to the family name. As much as it saddens me to admit, given her afflictions I imagine a man of more noble birth would find her troubling, to say the least. Perhaps a marriage to someone in the medical field is a blessing in disguise.

God willing.

As is written in her father's will, you will be accommodated with a sum of 10,000 pound upon marriage, and given the lack of male Baird heirs, the property and estate in Inverness will then fall to you upon my death. Given my rather good health, I would not expect that any time soon, if indeed you marry her in the aims of collecting her inheritance, which I cannot help but assume.

Please do tell Deliverance of my distaste, and inform her that she is making a grievous mistake.

Yours kindly,
Lady Amelia Morag Dewitt Baird, etc.

They sat there in silence, Liv staring down at the letter penned in her mother's familiar, graceful hand.

"You wrote her?"

He sighed. "I did. Long while ago. Finally came to believe she'd no respond at all. That's why I took so long to propose."

Liv stared down at the paper, breathless. Was he angry? Did he feel betrayed by her withholding the station of her birth? She'd never known joy in that life. A massive home without love was no better than a spacious mausoleum. Still, her father was no simple man, despite his madness.

"Your father was a Lord?" Findlay asked finally, not looking up from his hands.

Liv took a deep breath, turning the letter over to brace for whatever anger Findlay may feel at her having withheld this from him. When she finally spoke, it was hardly a whisper. "Aye."

Findlay swallowed, audibly. He glanced over at the letter and shook his head. "But ye said ye'd tended a household. Ye seemed to know the work well enough."

"My mother treated me as a servant from the time I was thirteen. I wasn't lyin to ye, I'm sorry I didn't tell ye everything. I didn't think ye'd hire me if -"

"You've been washing my chamber pot, Deliverance. Christ, I feel like a fool."

Liv reached for him, clutching the fabric of his sleeve. He did not pull away. She took his acceptance as invitation and moved closer to him, wrapping a leg across his lap to draw close. "I was the daughter of a Lord and I was the daughter of a monster. I abandoned that life, and I've no interest in returnin to it. I'd feel far wealthier cleaning your chamber pots the rest of my life than as the lady of that house."

He cringed, his fingers fiddling over something in his hands. Liv pulled him closer, glancing at the strange coin purse he held. She kissed his cheek. "Why did ye write her?"

He snorted in a half laugh. "To ask her blessin. I know you've no love for the woman, but with your Da gone, I thought it only proper."

"You're a greater gentleman than any nobleman I've yet met."

He muttered some salty language to himself, taking

the letter from her to stare at it again. Liv gestured to the small purse in his hand. "What have ye there?"

He glanced down at it, his mood somber still. He took a deep breath. "I'm almost afraid to tell ye."

"Why?"

He smiled to himself. "Well, Fionnula told me it was dark magic or some other rubbish. I've no belief in such a thing, of course."

Liv reached for his hand, but he pulled it out of her reach. "Ye might no want to touch it."

She furrowed her brow, watching him. "Findlay, please tell me."

He rose from the bed, setting the small coin purse on the bedside table before crossing to stand at the bedroom window. He stared out at the cold street below, flakes of snow flitting just outside the window. "Ye know I assisted in Burke's dissection, aye?"

"Of course."

He nodded. "Well, another physician – a bit younger than I – made away with something of the man when Munro wasn't payin any mind."

Liv picked up the leather purse, snapping open the top to look at the black satin interior. It was sturdy and clearly well made. Liv shut the purse and waited for Findlay to speak.

"The purse is bound in William Burke's skin."

Liv dropped the purse instantly, letting it fall to the floor at her feet.

Findlay turned at the sound of her gasp. "I'm no the only one. The lad had several things made. I've heard word there is a book on anatomy being bound in the very skin of his right hand."

Liv shook her head, moving across the bed to distance herself from the obscene thing, and perhaps even to distance herself from Findlay. His tone had taken on a strange darkness – an almost disinterested sense of the macabre, as though owning pieces of another human being was as commonplace as tea cakes.

"How can ye have such a thing? How can ye want such a thing?"

He glared down at the purse, snatching it up to inspect it yet again. He chuckled darkly to himself. "Ah, now. It's a wonder ye'd ask."

"Aye, I would ask!"

He opened the top, then shut it again, setting it on the table beside the bed. Then he turned his eyes to hers, staring her down. "I watched that man hang, and I thought it would be enough. Then I watched that man butchered, and I thought it would be enough. But it wasn't."

Liv moved away again. Findlay was almost beginning to frighten her.

"So when they offered to have this made, to give me somethin; a trinket to remind me that the murderer of my friends – the man who came near to takin the most important thing in the world to me – was dead, I accepted with a smile on my face and a bloody song in my heart."

Findlay rounded the corner of the bed, meeting her at the opposite side. He towered over her as she braced against him. He felt wild there, like something inside him had gone feral. He grabbed hold of her, pulling her toward him with purpose. "I cast ye out when ye needed me. I did that, and I let ye come into the hands of those men. I wake every bloody night in terror to think I nearly lost ye to em."

"Shh, but ye didn't -"

"And that bastard Knox! I sent ye to the man cutting them all up. Delivered ye to them! Ye think he didn't know? They say he didn't know those people were murdered. Greatest anatomist in the bloody world and they believed him when he said he'd no idea! Liar!"

Liv reached for Findlay, wanting to still this fury.

"And he's still free! I thought of ye bein taken to Dr. Knox, of my findin ye on one of his tables -"

Findlay's voice cracked, and he shook her as though the action might settle his grief.

"Findlay! Ye didn't know!"

"I deserve the reminder. I deserve to carry that slab of the man I wish I'd killed myself - with my bare fuckin hands."

Liv kissed him. It was sudden and panic fueled, but it was all she could think of to break him of this outraged spell. He startled at the sudden touch, then his grip on her tightened, and he pried her mouth open with his tongue, his intentions shifting instantly. He threw her back onto the bed, tearing his trousers open before lunging down over her. She recoiled, whimpering softly in trepidation. She'd known him too many times to count, but he'd never come to her like this – never with a fury in his eyes.

He grabbed her legs, yanking her toward him as he tore up her skirts. His eyes were red now, tears welling up and spilling over as he positioned himself over her and without warning, thrust inside her. Liv flinched against the pain of it, but wrapped her arms around him, holding him against her as he moved in her, his chest heaving with grief.

"I love ye, Findlay," she whispered, praying to soothe his heart. This drew only harsher cries as he thrust over and over, anguish in his voice. Finally he lifted his face to look at her, his expression contorted in a mix of grief and affection and pain.

"I'll never let anything happen to ye. I'll never let anyone hurt ye as long as I live," he said, his arms tightening around her. "I'm so sorry, my Deliverance."

She lifted her legs to lock them behind him, holding him against her as he took her. She'd never seen a man so overcome, and never loved anything so desperately. She could hear in his cries that he needed more than her body then. This was not a man taking his woman for pleasure. This was his healing, and she clutched him to her as she found her own eyes filling with tears. He held her tightly, his body moving against hers in the familiar way that brought her such release. She tightened her legs around him and let her body convulse as he moved.

"I love ye, Findlay. I'm here. I'm right here."

He grunted in rhythm, his thrusts doubling in power as he reached his own release and slumped down over her, his face buried in her shoulder.

She listened to his panting breaths, each one betraying words. "I need ye. I'm sorry. My love."

They lay there a long while, catching their breath. Finally, Findlay rolled off of her, frowning down at the rumpled state of her new dress. "I'm sorry. I didn't mean -"

She shushed him, caressing his cheek. "I've no complaints. Please, feel free to rumple my skirts any time of day."

He smiled, his eyes still red and wet. "Yes, M'Lady."

She laughed softly, watching him rise from the bed and wipe the tears from his eyes. Then he rounded the bed to the bedside table, taking up the purse and tucking it into his pocket. "I promise to keep it hidden from ye."

Liv sat up, straightening her now messy curls. She watched him tuck the purse into his pocket and took a deep breath. She was startled by the words before she said them. "I want it."

Findlay's eyebrows shot up as he looked down at her. He pulled the purse back from his pocket, staring down at it. "Are ye sure?"

Liv looked at the tiny purse, a perfect size to carry to the shops or to hide away some tiny treasure. She sat silent a moment. It was dark and morbid, this desire, but yet the thought of carrying that tiny effigy felt strangely satisfying. She nodded. "Aye. I'd like to have it."

Findlay squeezed it in his hand, gave it a little toss in the air, and then smiled. "Then have it ye shall."

He handed it to her, squeezing her hand in his. He glanced down at Lady Baird's letter where it lay on the floor, the giving a soft harrumph, he bent down to collect. "I'm contemplating letting Fionn read it, if you'll allow it?"

Liv nodded, watching as he straightened his suspenders and trousers. He leaned down to her, making Liv give his hair a quick fix before heading toward the bedroom door. The heady aroma of haggis and stew drifted in when he opened the door.

Findlay groaned in appreciation. "Och, are ye sure you're content to have haggis for the wedding."

She stood up from the bed, straightening her skirts. "Aye, anything ye like."

"Anythin I like. Says her Ladyship who's agreed to marry a doctor in a kirk outside Leith." He shook his head. "My mother would be beside herself if she were here to see this - Christ, just imagine what Fionnula will say. Findlay Lennox, marryin the daughter of a Lord…" He gave her an eyebrow waggle, and she was happy to see the humor despite his reddened eyes. "Will ye tell me about this estate she speaks of? When ye come down?"

Liv laughed at him, shaking her head. "Ye get downstairs. I'll be down shortly."

He nodded, lunging forward to steal one more kiss, then stopped just inches from her face. "You'll never leave my sight again, Deliverance."

Then with that, he was gone down the stairs, calling to Fionnula in the kitchen.

Liv stood there with the bedroom door open, giving her hair a quick fix before turning back toward the bed to collect the small coin purse. She stood by the bed in silence, ignoring that same quiet vibration she'd felt when she first came home. She wrapped her fingers around the morbid trinket and turned out into the hallway. The familiar heaviness seemed to ooze from the attic above. Liv had grown too accustomed to be afraid now. She took a deep breath, straightened, and then made her way up the stairs.

Her old bedroom door was open a crack, swaying as though the house itself was breathing. Liv pressed her palm to the door and pushed.

The figure stood by the empty cot, a pool of red at his feet, spreading out around him with each passing instant. The figure was tall and wide, and every piece of skin was removed from the whole of his shape. He stood dripping blood from every bend and every movement, the strange lines of muscle and bone peeking through in pink and white. Liv stared at the horror before her, her stomach growing tighter as she stepped further into the room. The mutilated face turned, betraying white and wide eyes in a featureless face. Liv stared at the ghost of William Burke, clutching the tiny piece of him in her hands – the very thing that had summoned him to her.

She swallowed, meeting his gaze, unwaveringly. "Get out of my house."

She spoke each word as though nailing them to the wall before him.

The muscles twitched in his face, the eyes moving over her. Then as she watched, the bloodied vision faded away, like mist on a windowpane. Liv took a deep breath, feeling the sudden lightness of the air.

"Sweet mother Mary! Deliverance Baird! Ye come down here this instant, ye! What is this I'm hearin? Good gracious! We've so much plannin. Ye can't be married in Leith, Findlay. It wouldn't do! Deliverance! Come down! Ye best no think I'll be treatin ye any different, even if ye are a Lady! My goodness!"

Liv closed her eyes and smiled. Then she turned and made her way down the stairs to receive Fionnula's feigned chagrin.

ABOUT THE AUTHOR

Michaela Wright has spent much of her adult life revolting against the fact that she wasn't born in Scotland. On the average day you can find her talking to one of her cats like Carol Channing, dancing around the kitchen while cooking the best steak you'll ever taste, and on occasion, wearing an AC/DC t-shirt and controlling the universe with her mind. She's also working diligently to prepare her daughter for world domination.

Michaela currently (give her time) lives in Northern Massachusetts.

Watch for the next title in
THE NAMESAKEN Series
by Michaela Wright.

HEARTLESS
(Coming in Early 2016)

Find Michaela online at:
www.michaelawrightauthor.com

81232711R00153

Made in the USA
Columbia, SC
26 November 2017